Serpent's Keep

David R. Beshears

Greybeard Publishing
Washington State

Greybeard Publishing
P.O. Box 480
McCleary, WA 98557-0480

ISBN 0-9773646-3-1

Serpent's Keep

Chapter One

Jacob Quigley reached down and picked up the travel bag. Ahead of him was a wooden double gate set into a rough stone wall ten feet high that enclosed the entire village. One side of the gate stood open and a guard watched the new arrival with casual interest. He saw a young man, probably in his early twenties, definitely from the outside.

Jake looked back behind him at the old, 40s era bus that was slowly disappearing down the dusty, narrow road winding its way through a landscape of grassy fields, twisted scrub oak and yellow and brown brush. The sound of the engine faded away, leaving behind an ominous silence.

As he neared the gate, he started to say something to the guard, but before he could open his mouth the man stepped calmly to one side and made way. Once through, Jake started down the main thoroughfare of Serpent's Keep.

The village lay comfortably in the Outland, isolated from the rest of the world and unaffected by external events. Its narrow cobblestone streets were quiet pedestrian thoroughfares where it was normal for citizens to stop and converse with one another, both of recent goings-on in the village and of adventures from long ago, in lands distant and mysterious. That is not to say that all of the citizens of Serpent's Keep could be trusted, neither in word nor deed, but all in all, the small village was a pleasant place in which to live. It was peaceful, filled with interesting characters, dark secrets, enduring mysteries, and the inevitable skeleton in the closet; a small community safely enclosed within its protective walls, hidden away warm and snug, deep in the Outland, and long ago forgotten by the real world.

Quigley Mansion sat alone, midway along one of the narrow side roads in the village. The estate took up most of the north side of the lane, surrounded on all sides by a high fence, making it accessible only through the tall, narrow front gate.

Jake looked in through the wrought-iron bars, dropping his travel bag at his feet. The house looked too small to be called a mansion, but he knew from his summer visits years before that it was one of the larger houses in the village. Still, just a child back then, to Jake it had been just a big old house, and the grounds had been just a big yard.

Across the street was the village plaza, a park of sorts that took up the entire south side of the road. Much of the plaza was surrounded by its own high wall. Directly across from the Quigley Estate was the north entrance to the plaza, an opening in the fence some forty feet wide. Through this opening, Jake could see several children playing in a large, grassy area. The plaza held a number of massive oak trees, some shrubs, a few benches and an occasional table. There were expanses of lawn, expanses of flagstone, and meandering cobblestone pathways.

Jake watched the children for a few moments before turning his attention again to the Quigley Estate gate. He reached into his jacket pocket and pulled out a large, ornate key. He inserted it into the lock, turned it, and pushed down on the latch handle. Picking up his bag, he pushed the gate open. It swung closed behind him as he started up the walk toward the house.

A large, dragon-shaped doorknocker hung in the center of the front door. Lifting and dropping it several times, it didn't sound nearly as impressive as it looked. Still, after a minute's wait, which gave Jake time to survey the grounds from the porch, the door opened and a tall, thin, graying gentleman stood looking down at him.

Mr. Griffin hadn't changed much over the years. Jake had last seen the man through the eyes of a twelve year old. He had been old then, and he was the same old now.

"Mr. Griffin?" Jake mumbled. Mr. Griffin twitched an eyebrow, but other than that, there was no movement. Jake cleared his throat. "Mr. Griffin, it's me... Jake. Jacob... Jacob Quigley."

"Good afternoon, sir." Despite his age, Mr. Griffin looked and sounded as alive, as fit, and as able as always.

Jake fumbled in his jacket pockets. He pulled out the gate key, continued searching, finally reached into the side pocket of his travel bag. He pulled out a folded and battered envelope. He held up the key and letter together. "I got the letter. I came as soon as I could."

Mr. Griffin took a step back into the foyer and made way for Jake. "You have been expected, Mr. Quigley," he said, without emotion. Mr. Griffin had always referred to him as *Master Jacob* when he was a child. He noted the change to *Mr. Quigley*. He wasn't sure what the change in status meant, but sensed that he had somehow lost something.

"Thanks," said Jake, stepping into the house. Once in the main hall, he set his bag down and took in the place. "Hasn't changed much, has it?"

"What would you have us change, Mr. Quigley?" The man's attitude hadn't changed, either. The patronizing, self-righteous—

"I don't know... new rug?" It was his turn now to raise an eyebrow. "A chair?"

Mr. Griffin was able to smirk without actually smirking. "I shall look into it," he said.

Jake let the matter drop. *The old fart...* Yet, in spite of the man's sanctimonious condescension, Jake liked him. His air of assurance and stability had always been a source of calm for Jake during his summer visits to Serpent's Keep. He was the essence of quiet strength, no matter what turmoil may be surrounding him. He was security.

Mr. Griffin was the house administrator for the Quigley Estate; as such, he was much more than just the butler. He had been with Uncle Tobias for as long as anyone could remember... at least fifty years. Jake couldn't imagine the one without the other.

Jake stood silent, Mr. Griffin patiently waiting behind him. He sensed an emptiness in the mansion. It looked the same, but it didn't feel the same.

There were two doors along the left wall of the main hall. One he remembered led to a sitting room, the other to Mr. Griffin's apartment. Straight ahead were the stairs to the second floor. To the left of the stairs there was a short hall and a door under the stairs that opened to a narrow stairwell that lead down to the basement. At the far end of the right wall was a wide arch that opened into the dining room.

It all seemed very still. The house too seemed to be patiently waiting on Jake.

"I was real sorry to hear about Tobias," he said at last.

"Your uncle shall be greatly missed, Mr. Quigley."

"Stop calling me that."

"Sir?" The question came from some place on Snob Hill.

"*Mr. Quigley.* Stop it." Jake stuffed his hands into his pockets. "Call me Jake."

Mr. Griffin's face visibly retracted. "I don't think so."

Jake's face slowly morphed into a slight grin, "All right. Jacob, then."

Mr. Griffin paused all activity, as if his entire being was sorting through a difficult problem. Once the mental processing was complete, he nodded imperceptibly. "Very well."

Jake noticed a young woman standing in the archway to the dining room. She might have been there for some time. Jake wasn't sure. She was still, unmoving.

"Who's that?" he asked. The woman was small and unassuming, probably eighteen or nineteen years old.

"That is Meara. She assists Mrs. Hodges on a part-time basis."

"Cleaning and like that?"

"She assists with the cleaning."

Jake nodded. Good ol' Mrs. Hodges. The housekeeper and cook for the estate. She had to be getting on in years.

"I guess Mrs. Hodges can use a hand around the place."

"Maintaining the estate is a considerable task, sir. If you require a meeting to review the Quigley concerns, I shall arrange it."

"Yeah," Jake grumbled. "Later."

"I shall arrange a time convenient to us both."

"Yeah," Jake said again. He watched as Meara moved back into the shadows.

"Meara," Mr. Griffin raised a hand in her direction. "Come here, girl."

Meara stiffened abruptly, then stepped cautiously into the main hall. Mr. Griffin waved impatiently at her. She took the last several steps quickly and stopped short.

"Sir?" she stood before Mr. Griffin.

"Meara, this is Mr. Quigley... the master of the estate." Mr. Griffin's statement held finality. It was now Meara's responsibility to respond. Meara turned to Jake.

"Mr. Quigley. Welcome, sir."

Jake glanced very briefly in Mr. Griffin's direction. With only a subtle change in Mr. Griffin's facial expression, he had made it quite clear that Jake was not to allow Meara to become familiar with "the Master of the Estate". There was to be no "call me Jake".

"Thank you, Meara," said Jake, and left it at that.

"You may return to your duties," said Mr. Griffin.

"Thank you, sir." Meara gave a slight curtsy, backed away, turned and left, disappearing back into the dining room and probably on into the kitchen.

"Shy, isn't she?" Jake asked, once she was gone.

"Meara is unaccustomed to strangers... Jacob." Mr. Griffin made the word 'Jacob' sound very much like 'Mr. Quigley'. "Your uncle hired her and asked that I find a position for her."

"You disapprove?"

"She would not have been my choice, were I looking to hire someone to assist Mrs. Hodges."

"Yet you kept her on, after..."

"Her work has proven satisfactory."

Jake was pretty sure that Mr. Griffin had felt then and felt now that it was his responsibility alone to manage the house and the staff. He was also pretty sure that Uncle Tobias had stayed out of Mr. Griffin's way, for the most part. He wondered what would have caused him to bring home a stray.

"So, does she live here?"

"I am the only member of the staff living on the estate." Mr. Griffin stated flatly, paused a moment, then took a step away from Jake and started toward the stairs. He gave only the slightest indication that Jake should follow.

Jake picked up his bag and followed.

Mr. Griffin spoke over his shoulder as they climbed the stairs to the second floor and started down the hall. "Mrs. Hodges prepared your uncle's meals at 8:00, 12:30, and at 6:00 in the evening."

"Yeah, well... I like 7:00, noon, and 5:00."

Mr. Griffin took the statement in stride. "I am certain that Mrs. Hodges can adapt." He opened a heavy door and held it open. Jake stepped through and walked into the room, tossed his bag on the bed.

"Where is Mrs. H?" Jake remembered a kindly woman, always fussing about, and frequently flustered by Jake's summer visits.

"She has gone to the marketplace. Purchasing vegetables, I believe."

"Tell her no cabbage." Jake mumbled, looking around the room. It was the room that he had stayed in as a child. "And no peas. I hate peas."

Mr. Griffin raised his level of snobbishness just a bit. "Perhaps you should prepare a list of your likes and dislikes."

"Maybe I'll do that."

Mr. Griffin stepped back into the hall and took hold of the doorknob.

"I'll leave it to you, then." He closed the door, leaving Jake alone in his room.

"Sure a lot smaller than the last time I was here..."

Chapter Two

Jake stepped out of his room and into the upstairs hallway. He glanced once at the staircase leading down to the first floor, but decided to wander around first, do a little exploring. He hadn't been in here in years, and now was as good a time as any to get reacquainted.

The master bedroom wasn't much larger than his old room, and the furniture wasn't all that different. There was a large bed, a desk, a dresser, and a few chairs. The only real difference was the private door that led to the one and only upstairs bathroom, which had its main door opening onto the hall.

Jake sat on the bed and looked carefully around the room; some nice paintings, a set of heavy drapes over the window, dark-paneled walls; an oval rug on the floor. The bed was firm but comfortable. The room was clean and comfortable.

He found nothing in the desk drawers but a few odds and ends, and the dresser had been emptied. Jake wondered what Mr. Griffin had done with Tobias' clothes.

He went back out into the hallway. The upstairs hall was in the shape of a large L. His old bedroom was at one end, with the upstairs bathroom and then the master bedroom along the north wall. At the other end was the library. Across from the master bedroom were the stairs leading down to the first floor. On either side of the staircase was a door.

Jake chose the door on the right. It led out to an open deck, enclosed on three sides and open to the west. He had spent many hours playing there as a child. Just as many hours were spent staring out across the village toward the Outland beyond the west wall.

People in the village spoke of how dangerous the Outland was, when they spoke of it at all. It was a strange land of dark forests and darker lakes, great cliffs and menacingly shadowy valleys and canyon-like ravines.

And yet there were hints of civilization in the Outland. There was a large farm to the north that supplied foodstuffs to the village. A day's hard march to west was a temple where a group of monks lived. And people spoke of a highway out there somewhere that seemed to start from nowhere and led nowhere.

And there was the narrow, single-lane, winding road that connected the outside world to the village. It wasn't visible from the deck, coming as it did from the south. It cut through the Outland like a thin, twisted wound, and was the only visible sign of the outside. Traveling this road, there was little to be seen on either side and there were no exits. The seldom-scheduled bus would bring the infrequent traveler from the outside world to the front gate of the village, and quickly retreat back to the real world. Jake had made that journey each year growing up, and to a small boy it had simply been part of the mystique of his uncle's home. Only now did he consider just how peculiar this place was, and now he would try to become a part of it. He turned away from his view of the west and went back inside.

The village was an island in the Outland, and the estate was an island in the village. The Quigley Mansion was old; perhaps as old as the village. It was well cared for, well kept, but its age showed. The furniture, the floors and carpet, the wood trim, the tapestries and paintings and drapes, all looked clean and cared for... and old. The very air had the smell of antiquity.

The mansion fit in well with the rest of Serpent's Keep. This was a world of no cars and of cobblestone thoroughfares, where everyone knew it was the twenty-first century but no one lived in the twenty-first century; where you could find oil lamps and electric light bulbs in the same room.

Jake walked past the head of the stairs and went on to the bend in the hall. There was only one door in this section of the hallway, located at the very end. It opened into the upstairs library.

Jake remembered his uncle Tobias spending quite a bit of time there, but had only been in the room a few times himself. It was high-ceilinged, with shelved walls and a cherry-wood desk and leather chair. Two high-back chairs sat in one corner beneath a single pole lamp. It wasn't a very large room, and all available space was filled with books. Jake read titles as he walked slowly past the shelves: 'Flora and Fauna of the Ancient Rainforest', 'Creatures of the Deep', 'Ancient Religions', 'The Science of Labyrinths', 'Spelunking', 'Desert Ecosystems', 'Survival in Extreme Environments', 'Holography', 'Cryptography and Pictographs', 'The Art of Symbolism', 'Beyond the Fourth Dimension'.

Uncle Tobias had very diverse interests.

"Mr. Quigley?"

Jake turned sharply, startled from his thoughts. Meara was standing near the door.

"Geez, Meara."

"I'm sorry, sir."

"No..., no it's all right. You just startled me." Jake waved a hand at the room around them. "Just doing a little exploring."

"Yes, sir."

"What is it, Meara?"

"Mrs. Hodges is back from the marketplace. She's quite eager to see you."

Mr. Griffin appeared suddenly behind Meara.

"That'll be all, Meara."

Meara turned quickly about, stepped past Mr. Griffin as he moved aside.

Mr. Griffin stepped fully in to the library. He gave the room a quick, cursory examination.

"Master Jacob... I thought perhaps now might be a good time to meet with Mrs. Hodges."

"That so?"

"You might want to discuss your meal schedule with her." Mr. Griffin raised a brow. "Perhaps you could present your list of likes and dislikes.

"Yeah, well..." *What's up with Mr. Griffin?* "Never got around to writing it."

Mr. Griffin stood in stoic silence. Jake grew increasingly uncomfortable and finally stepped away from the wall of books and started toward the door.

"Yes," said Jake. "Do let us attend to Mrs. Hodges." He stepped past Mr. Griffin and left the library.

Mr. Griffin examined the library more studiously, backed out and closed the door.

The kitchen was open and airy, and everything was overlarge. The cabinets reached all the way up to the high ceiling. The counters reached deep, and there was a large island of a countertop in the center of the room. The refrigerator and stove complimented each other, each being quite large and heavy duty.

The kitchen was very functional, and harkened to decades past.

Mrs. Hodges was putting away the last of the groceries. A two-wheeled, wire handcart stood next to the back door.

She turned when she heard Jake and Mr. Griffin enter the room.

"Master Jacob!" she beamed.

"Hey, Mrs. H," said Jacob, smiling broadly. She had grown older, but she was definitely Mrs. Hodges.

"The place hasn't been the same without your visits."

"Is that bad or good?" They hugged, and Jake felt that she was genuinely glad to see him.

"A lot quieter, that's for certain."

Jake heard Mr. Griffin emit a slight *harrumph* from his position by the door. He ignored him.

"I'll try to keep the rough-housing down to a minimum."

"Oh, don't you dare."

"That's very kind of you."

"Not at all. The house is in need of a young man's voice." There was melancholy in Mrs. Hodges' smile.

Mr. Griffin, still standing near the door, took the quiet moment to speak up. "Mrs. Hodges. Young Mr. Quigley has some concerns regarding food selections and meal times."

"No cabbage," Mrs. Hodges said with a mock scowl.

"And no peas," Jake added.

"I have not forgotten," she said. She went to a bin set into the far wall and pulled out half a dozen potatoes. There was work to be done, company in her kitchen or no.

Mr. Griffin gave another almost silent *harrumph*. "And he wishes the meal times adjusted."

Mrs. Hodges set the potatoes in the sink, turned on the water, and began scrubbing them. "Meals in this house are served at 8:00, 12:30 and 6:00," she said flatly.

"Why?" asked Jake, just as flatly.

"Because that's when the meals will be ready."

"But what if I want them at 7:00, 12:00 and 5:00?"

"Why?"

"Because that's when *I'll* be ready." Jake watched as Mrs. Hodges continued to scrub the potatoes clean. He could feel Mr. Griffin watching them both, no doubt relying on Mrs. Hodges to knock Jake down a peg or two. He must have been frustrated at the love-fest going on just a few moments earlier.

"7:00 is too early," said Mrs. Hodges at last.

"Lots of people eat breakfast a lot earlier than that."

"Your body's not ready for food at 7:00," she said firmly. "But 12:00 and 5:00 will do."

Jake turned away and started out of the kitchen. He nodded a silent good-bye to Mr. Griffin and spoke over his shoulder to Mrs. Hodges. "Love you, Mrs. H."

"I love you too, sweetie."

His old bed was comfortable enough, but with all that had happened throughout the day, Jake hadn't been able to sleep. He had lain staring up at the ceiling, listening to the faint sounds the old house made late at night. The ancient roof timbers creaked against a strong wind blowing in across the sleeping village from the Outland to the north, the large handmade nails that held the walls together shifted about and complained noisily; a loose shutter in a downstairs window fought against its latch. Shadows came and went, sliding from wall to ceiling and down again as the half moon outside moved in and out amongst dark clouds and moonlight shone in through the large window.

So Jake found himself standing out on the open deck in the early hours before dawn, looking out over the village. The sky was still dark and filled with stars.

Gas lamps were evenly spaced along the main thoroughfare and several cross-streets, but most of the illumination came from the bright, full moon.

The village was very quiet in the early morning. The sun hadn't been up long, and the streets were mostly empty. Jake walked down the center of the main thoroughfare, a wide cobblestone avenue lined with single-story, well-worn stone buildings set side by side, with heavy wooden doors and small, square windows. There were a few people out and about, and each one looked curiously at Jake as he passed. He had been a child when he had last walked these streets, and would be a stranger now to most who saw him.

He didn't go straight to the sheriff's office, but instead decided to wander about some first. He found the bank, the general store, the café; at the far end of the main thoroughfare was the wide entrance to the market place.

He reached the sheriff's office, but it was closed. According to the sign, Sheriff Smith wouldn't be in for another hour. Jake supposed that if there was an emergency, most would know where the sheriff lived.

He stood on the step and looked up and down the road. A woman was pulling a small, two-wheeled cart into the market plaza. The booths inside would be opening up soon. Produce, clothing, household supplies, hunting equipment, and just about anything else a person would want, was available in the marketplace.

Jake decided to have breakfast at the café. He could guess what Mrs. Hodges would have to say when he got back to the estate, after she had made and then cleared away breakfast, but he wasn't ready to head back without seeing the sheriff, and he might be able to pick up some information at the café. Besides, if he was going to be living here, he would need to get to know the folks.

The inside of the little restaurant was quiet, and Jake could tell that it hadn't been open for more than a few minutes. Looking about from just inside the door, he saw that all the heavy wooden tables were empty. A woman was moving efficiently from one to the next, setting out salt & pepper shaker sets and napkin holders. She slowed imperceptibly as he came in, glancing at him warily out of the corner of her eye. She looked to be about Jake's age.

He walked over to the nearest table and sat down. The waitress finished setting out the table sets and moved behind the counter. She looked once at a man who appeared at the kitchen 'food up' counter as she reached for the coffee decanter and a cup. The man nodded silently at the waitress and gazed unblinking at Jake.

"You're new here," said the waitress as she reached the table. Not a question; a point of observation.

"I've been gone a while." Jake watched as the waitress poured a cup of coffee and set it on the table in front of him.

"Yeah?" she asked cautiously.

"Jake. Jake Quigley."

The waitress looked somewhat taken aback. She looked quickly at the man watching from the kitchen, then back at Jake. "You're—"

"Tobias is my uncle."

She smiled faintly. "Yeah. Yeah, I remember you. It *has* been a while. You used to come visiting summers. You were just a kid."

"I grew up," Jake said calmly. He took a sip from his coffee. It was hot and very strong.

"I used to see you around," said the waitress. "I'm Sparta Vesper."

"Of course," said Jake. He remembered the name. How could he not remember that name? He didn't remember the face. "You've changed some."

"I grew up," she said, then nodded in the direction of the kitchen. "That's Wallace. He didn't. What can he do for you?"

"Scrambled eggs?"

"Coming up," said Sparta, starting back to the counter.

"Call me Jake," he said, calling after her.

"Call me Sparta," she called over her shoulder.

Jake sat back with his coffee and took another look around the café. It was definitely something out of the past—the distant past—which fit in well with the rest of Serpent's Keep. It was a bizarre mix of different periods from the past, with only the occasional glimpse of the present.

A dusty ray of sun shone through the one window, creating a bright square of light on the reddish-brown wooden floor. The surface was incredibly smooth from decades of cleaning, sweeping, scrubbing, polishing, and tens of thousands of footsteps.

Jake's breakfast came after a few minutes, and he ate quietly, thinking on what little he had already seen this morning, and how much more there must yet be to discover. First up, though, was to talk with the sheriff and find out what had happened to his uncle.

He had finished his eggs and was on a third cup of coffee when the door opened and a man came ambling in. The man was startled by Jake's presence, and faltered slightly as he entered, but managed to gently close the door behind him. He stared at Jake as he did so, then crossed the room and sat at the table set against the far wall. Sparta followed after him with a cup in one hand and the pot of coffee in the other.

The man mumbled at her as she filled his cup. He turned his head slightly at her response, giving Jake another few seconds look before focusing on his coffee. Sparta grinned at Jake as she turned away from the man's table.

"Regular for Mr. Dante," she called out to Wallace.

"Dante regular, coming up," he called back.

Mr. Dante sipped from his cup and carefully set it down on the table in front of him. He turned it slightly, so that the handle was just so, then looked up at Jake.

"So, you are Tobias Quigley's nephew, then."

"That's me," said Jake. "Jacob Quigley."

"Ah," the man nodded. "I am Cosmo Dante, Mr. Quigley. I run the bank here in Serpent's Keep."

"Nice to meet you, Mr. Dante."

"You should drop by the bank, at your convenience. I will personally assist you with the transition of the estate." Mr. Dante adjusts the position of his cup. "You will need to be able to draw on the account, allow or deny others access, and so forth."

"Others?"

"Griffin and Hodges," said Mr. Dante. "Griffin currently has free access, and the Hodges woman can charge to the account."

"I see."

Dante lifted his cup to his mouth and took a sip, slowly set it down again, adjusted its position on the table. "Mr. Quigley was trusting of those whom he deemed had earned that trust. An honorable man. I believe a good man."

"I thank you for your kind words, Mr. Dante."

"Few in the village would have any but kind words in regards to Tobias Quigley." Mr. Dante turned at the sight of Sparta coming from around the counter, his breakfast in hand. He smiled broadly, spoke as he carefully watched Sparta approach. "Excellent food, excellent service, eh, Mr. Quigley?"

Jake raised his cup in answer.

Al Smith had been the sheriff of Serpent's Keep for almost twenty years. He was well respected, and was probably the most trusted person in the village. He had a smile and a considerate word for everyone each and every time he saw them.

Jake came up on Sheriff Smith as the big man opened the front door to his office.

"Good morning," said the Sheriff, seeing Jake approach. "You must be Mr. Quigley, recently arrived from the real world."

"That would be me." Jake held out his hand and the sheriff took it. The man had a solid handshake without overdoing it.

"Nephew of our own Tobias Quigley," the sheriff said approvingly. "Come on in."

Jake followed Sheriff Smith into the office. It was a small room with a desk, a filing cabinet and a couple of chairs. Jake assumed the second door in the room led to the back room where there would be cells, maybe a bathroom and a storage closet.

"Have a seat, Mr. Quigley." The sheriff walked around the desk and sat down.

"Call me Jake."

"Okay, Jake." The sheriff leaned back and the old chair squealed loudly. He smiled and pointed in Jake's direction. "I remember you. It's been a while."

"A long while."

"Don't know that I would have recognized you, but I got word of your arrival." He sat up and put his elbows on his desk. The chair squealed again, but the sheriff apparently didn't notice. "What can I do for you?"

"I was wondering about my uncle's disappearance."

"What about it?"

"I'd like to know what happened... What were the circumstances? And how did a disappearance become a death certificate so quickly?"

"Well, as for what happened," Sheriff Smith wrinkled his brow, "your uncle was on another of his Outland excursions, last known position somewhere near the Temple. We know that he stopped there. And that's it. He was never seen again. As for the circumstances, he had been on this particular trip for only three days when last seen; he had left the village with two weeks worth of food, and he had been gone for just over three weeks when Mr. Griffin notified me of Tobias Quigley's failure to return."

"Had this ever happened before?"

"Tobias being reported missing? No. Griffin did inform me that Tobias would sometimes return later than planned, but not so late as to cause any serious concern."

"Do many people go missing in the Outland?"

"Enough to keep the village population stable," he said dully.

"Oh."

"Yes, sir." The sheriff stood and walked to a small, square table set in the far corner of the room. There was a fairly new coffee maker on the table. He put in a fresh filter, pulled the lid off a can of ground coffee and scooped in three heaping spoonfuls. Jake watched in silence. The sheriff picked up the decanter and went to the second door. When he opened it, Jake could see a row of bars running down one side. Sheriff Smith disappeared around the door, returned half a minute later with the decanter filled with water. He spoke as he poured the water into the back of the coffee maker.

"I found no sign of your uncle. Not a clue. I had no idea where he had gone, or where he had been headed. The only bit of luck I had was in coming across three monks from the Temple. They were on the main west trail, heading this way. They told me that your uncle had spent the night at the temple several weeks earlier, and had left the next day."

"I thought they didn't let strangers stay at the temple."

"They don't. Tobias Quigley wasn't a stranger."

"I mean anyone other than the monks."

"Tobias Quigley held more than a few special privileges in the Outland. A few here in the village, for that matter." Sheriff Smith returned to his chair and plopped down heavily. The chair gave out another painful screech. "Anyway, that's where the trail started and that's where it ended. There's been nothing since. If anybody had come across anything out there, they'd have brought it to me. Assuming they survived the encounter."

"Then what do you think might have happened to him?"

The sheriff looked at Jake for several long seconds. Jake assumed that he was trying to think of a friendly way to tell this uppity outsider from the real world that he had just spent ten minutes telling him that he didn't know what happened to Tobias Quigley, so why the hell are you asking me what happened to Tobias Quigley?

"There are a thousand ways to die in the Outland, Mr. Quigley. Nine hundred of them are going to leave no sign. Your uncle was probably the greatest Outland explorer that ever lived. So let's say, for the sake of this discussion, that he's not likely to succumb to most of those nine hundred...say eighty percent of 'em. He's going to see those coming, or at least he's going to know what to do. That still leaves... what? Almost two hundred of that nine hundred?"

Jake let out a surrendering groan. "Hundred and eighty."

Sheriff Smith gave Jake a consoling look. "I'm sorry, young man. I really am. Tobias Quigley was a friend, and an important and well-liked member of this community. If anything, absolutely anything, comes up, I'll be on it; in a big way. You can count on it."

Jake nodded slowly and stood up. The sheriff stood and held his hand out across the desk. Jake took it. "Thank you, Sheriff."

"Anytime, Jake."

Jake was all the way to the door. "Sheriff..."

"Yeah," the sheriff said, sitting back in his chair.

"You never told me how a death certificate was issued so quickly."

The sheriff smiled openly. "This isn't the outside, Mr. Quigley. We have our own way of doing things. The death certificate was issued because the circumstances surrounding your uncle's disappearance warranted a death certificate."

Jake stood at the door, hand on the knob. He thought about the finality of that statement. If his uncle wasn't dead, then he would have come back. Since he didn't come back...

"Thanks again," he said.

The sheriff watched as Jake left the office.

Chapter Three

Jake came into the kitchen just as Mrs. Hodges was coming in from the pantry. The smell of breakfast still hung in the air.

"Sorry about missing breakfast, Mrs. H."

"Quite all right, Master Jacob." It didn't sound quite all right.

"I had some business to take care of," said Jake, hoping to sound *masterly*. He didn't pull it off very well.

"As I said—"

"Quite all right... yeah." Jake leaned his hip against the island counter. He watched as she went about putting things in order. He knew that she would soon be leaving the kitchen and starting in on the upstairs cleaning. "Mrs. H., what do you know about Meara?"

"Don't you be getting involved with the little Missy, Master Jacob."

"No, no, nothing like that," Jake said quickly. "What do you know of her family?"

Mrs. Hodges kept at her work, but she looked to be ordering her thoughts. "Her mama runs a booth in the market, trinkets and such. Her daddy disappeared in the Outland a couple of years ago."

"What did he do?"

"Hunter."

"Did he do any scouting?"

"Couldn't say. He certainly knew the Outland well enough."

Jake nodded slowly. "Did my uncle ever hire him?"

"Possible I suppose, but Master Tobias knew the Outland as well as anyone in Serpent's Keep. I don't know that he'd need a hunter or a scout."

"Mmm," Jake nodded. "A couple of years ago? Is that when Meara came to work here?"

"I reckon the Master brought her in to help out the child's family. Putting in a few hours a day here helps set the girl's head right, and the few dollars she makes supplements what her mama brings in."

Jake nodded again.

With her morning work in the kitchen finished, Mrs. Hodges turned and faced Jake. "I'll have to be getting upstairs, Master Jacob. Will that be all?"

Jake returned Mrs. Hodges stare, frowned slightly. "Thank you, Mrs. H."

Mrs. Hodges started out of the kitchen.

"Sir," she said crisply.

"Sorry again about missing breakfast," he called after. Once she had gone, he pushed himself away from the counter and walked slowly over to the small kitchen table. A bowl of fruit sat in the middle of the table. He pulled the small bowl near him and grinned. Mixed in amongst the apples and pears was a pomegranate. She knew how much he loved pomegranates.

Jake was sitting in one of the high-back chairs in the library. The pole lamp beside him shone yellow light, putting Jake within a faint glow. The library, and the house in which in resided, had an air about it of the heavy quiet of a warm afternoon.

Jake stared off into the distance. He looked over at the door, closed now. He looked over at the book resting on the desk. He glanced over at the wall of books that he had been looking at when Meara and Mr. Griffin had drawn him away the last time he had been in the library.

He stood slowly then, walked over the desk and looked down at the book. As before, the title read "The Science of Labyrinths".

He rested a hand on the book, looked again at the wall of books to his right.

Jake stepped to the shelves and glanced again at some of the titles: "Flora and Fauna of the Ancient Rainforest", "Creatures of the Deep", "Ancient Religions", "Spelunking", "Desert Ecosystems", "Survival in Extreme Environments", "Holography", "Cryptography and Pictographs", "The Art of Symbolism", "Beyond the Fourth Dimension."

He pulled out a book. The title was "The Theory of the Parallel Universe." Casually flipping through the pages, he found references to trans-universe relationships, physics diversity theory and parallel universe interfacing. The volume, he noted, had opened at a passage discussing the intermediate plane thought to exist between all parallel universes.

Jake closed the book and put it back on the shelf, noting its location. He thought he might be looking at that one again someday.

He saw a large book with the title "Creatures in Myth", the lettering plain and the words faded. The volume itself wasn't much different than any other, less conspicuous even than the last. Still, something told Jake that this one was special. Looking at it sitting there on the shelf, it just...felt... different, though he couldn't say why. Maybe Uncle Tobias had said something about it years ago and the title had burrowed its way into the back of his mind.

He reached up and pulled at the book. Its position on the shelf was awkward and the book didn't want to come free. He realized then that it was stuck on something.

Not stuck...attached to something.

He heard a catch release. The sound had come from behind the shelves. Looking to his left and right, Jake didn't see anything. He took hold of one of the shelves with both hands and pulled.

Nothing.

He sidestepped to one side, to the next section of shelves, and pulled again. This time, he felt movement. Grasping one edge with his left hand, he pulled again and the shelf section opened out, hinged on the right side, the width of a narrow door.

Oh, boy..., thought Jake. *Just great... haunted house stuff. Uncle Tobias, you crazy old sneak...*

Jake had been quite serious about his search, but he hadn't really expected to find anything as exciting as a secret room. At most, some secret papers; maybe a stash of some ill-gotten riches. He had been looking for skeletons in the closet that Mr. Griffin seemed to have wanted to keep hidden.

It appeared now that Jake may have gotten far more than he had asked for.

Tobias Quigley had been the sort of uncle that any kid would have admired. Mysterious, secretive, always off and about on one adventure or another, none of which he was able to provide specific details about, yet from which he had drawn many a wild tale. When he had spoken to young Jake, the man's eyes had sparkled and his smile had been broad and genuine. He laughed and shouted and waved his arms over his head and spoke of grand quests and dangerous lands.

And then he would hide away for days on end, buried in books and charts and old parchment bearing old smells.

Jake had loved his Uncle Tobias more than anyone else on Earth. And Tobias Quigley had left Jake Quigley everything.

Everything...

Jake peered into the darkness behind the shelves. He could tell there was a cavernous space beyond, but nothing more. Taking one last look at the library behind him, Jake stepped through the bookshelf opening. He felt along the wall to his right, and then to his left. He found a switch and flipped it up. Three recessed ceiling lights lit up the room.

It was more of a hall than a room, about twelve feet wide and twenty feet long. Six statues stood on short pedestals, three along each side wall, set about five feet apart. They reached nearly as high as the very high ceiling.

Dragons...

Serpents...

Each was a unique species of dragon. One was winged. One was snakelike and clearly lived in the water. One was heavyset, well-muscled, and looked ready to breathe fire and destruction. One reminded Jake of an overly large desert lizard. One looked thin and agile, with delicate hands and fingers. One looked cerebral and protective.

On the face of each pedestal was an image of a geometric shape; oddly shaped polygons set in raised relief.

Jake walked cautiously down the center of the hall of statues and through an arched opening at the far end. He found another light switch on the wall just inside.

This room, running to Jake's left, wasn't much larger than the hallway that he had just come through, about twelve feet across and running less than twenty feet to his left, with the ceiling set at a much more familiar height of less than eight feet. The main difference between this room and the last, however, was that this room appeared to be very functional.

There was a large, heavy desk near the far end, facing the left wall. The only chair in the room was a large, leather chair behind the desk. A large, hand-drawn map hung on the wall behind the chair.

Jake approached the desk. The top was clear. The bottom left drawer was empty. There was a small, thin, leather-bound book in the top left drawer. He sat down and set the book on the desk in front of him. He opened it.

It looked to be a notebook of some sort, but only the first few pages had anything written on them. The first had a diagram containing a set of six geometric figures pulled together into a single, six-sided form. The individual polygons looked like those that he had seen on the serpent pedestals in the Hall of Statues.

The second page contained two short paragraphs:

It has been known for centuries that this time would come... the gathering together of the artifacts and restoration of the path. Each step is a dangerous one, but none so feared as that final footfall when the way is opened and I must step through to the other side.

The preparations are almost complete. It is difficult to awaken after having been asleep for so long... I dread what is to come.

The third page contained a darker passage:

The Rhetani must be prevented from recovering the artifact and opening the way. I am dismayed that this action, which I have anticipated for so long, for which I planned and yet hoped would never come, has arrived. More troublesome still are recent events that must be dealt with, and I grow increasingly concerned that the gathering and the restoration may fall to my nephew. Such was not to have been his fate, but I can find no other solution.

Jake closed the book and leaned back in the chair. He felt numb. This sounded major, in a very major way. What had his uncle gotten himself into?

What was going on?

He spun slowly around in the chair.

The statues, and the artifacts spoken of in the notebook, these were clearly related in some way. The geometric shapes...

The gathering of the artifacts...

Such was not to have been his fate...

That didn't sound good.

Jake sensed the presence of someone else in the room. Looking up, he saw Mr. Griffin standing just inside the room, one foot still in the Hall of Statues.

"Hey, Griff," he said calmly.

"Good evening, Master Jacob."

"Been expecting you."

"Sir?"

"You seemed anxious when you found me in the library before."

"Not at all, sir." Mr. Griffin walked toward Jake. Jake frowned and turned the chair so that he was again facing the desk.

"Whatever."

Mr. Griffin stepped nearer. He indicated the room, at the notebook in particular.

"Are you sure that you should be doing this?"

"Why try and hide all this, Griff?"

Mr. Griffin looked again at the notebook, glanced then around the room. He said nothing at first, finally stiffened his resolve. "Master Quigley was very secretive regarding his activities. Even with me. I accepted that there was a part of his life that I was not to be a part of."

Jake leaned back. "Yeah... and?"

"And... I do not know your uncle's wishes."

Jake straightened, startled. He smiled then, almost laughed.

"Poor ole' Griff." Jake looked long and thoughtfully at Mr. Griffin, closed his eyes a moment, then opened them and sat up straight, spoke as if quoting: "I bequeath to my nephew, Jacob Quigley, all that I own, all that I dream, and all that I am, in the hope that my life's quest will become his quest."

"Master Quigley's last will and testament."

"In its entirely. Exactly one sentence."

"Yes."

"I think he meant more than the furniture. Don't you?"

"I believe so."

"He quite clearly meant more than material wealth. And when he spoke of 'life's quest', I think he meant more than some spiritual or philosophical state of being. I think that it was something quite tangible."

Mr. Griffin appeared to think that one over. "I would suppose so, Master Jacob."

"Come on, Mr. Griffin. You were with my uncle since before the invention of fire. You may not have known exactly what he was up to, but you knew it was something heavy. And you knew about this room; and about that hall of statues, which I am for damn sure certain has some significance. And have a look at Tobias' choice of reading material: labyrinths, spelunking, holography, cryptography, extreme environments, parallel universes..."

"As I have said... Master Quigley chose not to include me in that part of his life."

"Yeah, yeah," Jake waved impatiently. "Get over it. You knew that this was going on. And I know that you are one smart old fart. Are you trying to tell me that when you read his will, you didn't make the connection between that reference to 'life's quest' and all of this?"

"I did make the connection," Mr. Griffin said flatly.

Jake leaned forward, spoke softly now. "Uncle Tobias has turned over to me some lifelong mission of his. He didn't make it obvious to an outside observer, but to you and to me, he made it clear."

It took a moment, but Mr. Griffin finally nodded in agreement. "Have you discovered what this... *quest*... might be?"

"Not exactly." Jake absently tapped a finger on the top of the desk. "On that, Tobias was extraordinarily cryptic." Jake glanced up at Mr. Griffin, "Quite the man of mystery... he never told you anything about it? Nothing at all?"

"No." Mr. Griffin paused and looked about them. "He never so much as spoke of this room. I never entered it, until now."

Jake grew thoughtful again. He placed a palm on the leather notebook. "Secret places, hidden accesses, mysterious journeys. It has something to do with gathering artifacts."

"Sir?"

Jake looked tired. "Nothing."

"Yes sir." Mr. Griffin managed to show some concern. "Why don't you come downstairs, Master Quigley. Hot tea would do you good."

Jake gave a tired grin. "You go on, Griff... I think I'm just going to sit here a while."

Mr. Griffin finally nodded and stepped back. "Very well, sir."

The command center was nearly dark. The overhead light had been turned off. The desk lamp was on, though, and it gave the top of the desk a dull shimmer, spread its glow across Jake.

His head rested on his folded arms. He had fallen asleep.

Something woke him...

He slowly lifted his head. He looked the top of the desk, then at the wall beyond.

He looked curiously then at the base of the wall. There was a very thin sliver of light where the wall met the floor. Pushing himself back from the desk, he stood and walked around the desk, never losing sight of the light.

Approaching the wall, he laid his palm against it, pushed at it, tapped at it. He gave the wall a light slap.

The wall had been designed in sections, flat panels separated by raised vertical strips. Jake began pulling and pushing at the strips, then pushed at the panel above the light.

Nothing...

He lifted his hand up to a horizontal strip a foot above his head. He pulled. He pushed.

Jake heard the clicking sound of a catch release.

He lowered his hand and used the flat palms of both hands to push.

The section panel opened.

The room beyond was barely six feet wide, twelve feet long. A tiny window was set in the far wall, allowing the colorful rays of the early morning sun to stream in.

A high counter ran down the left wall. A scattering of supplies were on the counter and on shelves set above the counter. There was a small backpack, a utility belt, canteen, an assortment of knives, a compass, several flashlights, batteries, handheld mining lamps, first aid supplies, wooden matches.

Jake looked closely at a box filled with small, sealed pouches. These turned out to be an assortment of dried fruit, trail mix, and jerky.

Hanging on a hook beside the door was a ring of keys. Lifting them from the hook, Jake was surprised at how heavy they were. In the morning light, he could see they were very ornate, but couldn't really make out the designs. He took them back to the desk and looked at them under the light of the desk lamp.

Six keys; stamped onto the face of each key was a geometric shape.

The polygons were the same as those he had seen in the notebook... and those on the face of the pedestals...

Jake looked in the direction of the Hall of Statues.

"Oh, dear uncle..." he whispered. *Secret places, secret rooms. Mysterious quests... what the heck are you all about?*

Jake absently weighed the keys in his hand, wandered in the direction of the archway. The hall was dark. Running a palm against the wall to one side of the archway, he found the companion to the switch on the far side of the room. Flipping the switch, the overhead light came on.

The six statues, three on either side of the room, towered over the aisle running down the center of the room.

Three dragons on the left, three dragons on the right.

Jake looked at the keys in his hand. He started down the center of the hallway. He looked at the geometric images set into the faces of each pedestal. As he passed each statue, he looked up at the face of each dragon. The winged dragon, the water serpent, each of the others in turn...

He stopped in front of the husky beast of fire and destruction. He found the key with same geometric pattern as the one on the pedestal, looked up into the face of the monster looming over him.

"What do you have for me, old boy?"

The creature stood silent, mocking. Looking closely at the polygon shape itself, Jake could see no place to insert the key.

"Won't talk, eh?" Jake studied then, inch by inch, every feature, looking for the keyhole where this key belonged. He knew that he was on the right track, but the intricate design work hid the keyhole, and whatever lay beyond, very well.

He studied the statue all the way to the base, and then studied the base. Finding nothing, he moved around to the side of the statue and began again. Moving then on to the back, he sensed that here was where he would find the home for the key. He studied the top of the pedestal first, the surface of which was made up of large whorls of carved stone.

And there it was. He knew that it was what he was looking for, even though to all appearances it was little more than a shadow. He inserted the key. It slid in cleanly. He turned the key and some hidden apparatus within gave out a solid, satisfying click.

One small section of the top of the base released and popped up just a little. The section was one foot square, with the key set in the center. Jake lifted up the lid and peered down inside.

In the small compartment was a leather scroll, rolled and bound loosely with a leather strap. He reached in and lifted it out. It was very smooth and very soft. With the scroll in hand, Jake lowered the lid and removed the key. He hurried back to the desk where he would have room to examine the scroll under the lamp.

Chapter Four

Jake walked slowly around the desk, eyes never leaving the scroll that now lay flat on the desktop. The words were clear and easy enough to read, but it seemed shrouded with inner meaning.

Seek a northerly path and find now the pylon within the stone. The one will point the way to where footfalls echo down empty streets and windows be but dark and lifeless eyes.

Northerly path. Well, that he got. He could do that. The north gate out of Serpent's Keep opened to a northerly path. That would get him going. As for the rest of it...

Pylon. Wasn't that some sort of support post? A tower?

Within the stone? Was he supposed to find a stone with a post sticking out of it? That didn't make any sense at all. That had to be wrong.

The one will point the way... That could mean anything. The one what? Would somebody be there to guide him? Would there literally be a "1" on this stone?

As for *empty streets* and *lifeless windows*, that sounded like an abandoned town. But Jake couldn't remember ever hearing of an abandoned town to the north; or in any direction, for that matter. It seemed, though, that if he found and traveled a certain path in the north, and found this stone with a pylon, that it would lead him to this... place. And once he got to this place, he would do... what?

Jake circled around the desk once more and sat down. He pulled the scroll around and read it again. He held his head in his hands. Slowly then, a thought crept into his mind.

Gateway... Couldn't a pylon be a gateway?

A gateway within a stone. That didn't make any more sense than a post in a stone. But perhaps, when taken with everything else... Jake stood up, grabbed up the scroll and went to wake Mr. Griffin. Jake needed a sounding board to bounce ideas off of.

Mr. Griffin, standing precisely in his full-length dressing gown and wiping sleepily at his eyes, stared down at the scroll laid out over the counter in the kitchen.

Jake was leaning over the counter, staring down at the scroll.

"I think that somewhere to the north I'm going to find a very special stone. A specific path will lead me to it."

"Yes sir."

"Hidden on or in this stone is the secret to a gateway. I think that's what this reference to a pylon means."

Jake watched Mr. Griffin nod silently.

"So," Jake continued, "If I can find this gateway, and go through it, I'll find a town or a village. It will probably be abandoned.

Jake looked uncertainly at Mr. Griffin, as if expecting the old man to break into hysterical laughter. Mr. Griffin, however, held his silence.

"I know..." Jake said defensively, "find a stone with a gate, somehow magically walk through this mystical stone... all pretty weird."

"Not at all, sir."

"Really?" Jake was surprised. "Sounds pretty weird to me."

"I believe you have surmised correctly," said Mr. Griffin. "But I have never heard of such a place."

"Yeah."

"Many questions remain."

"A few," Jake grumbled. "If I can find this stone, how exactly do I then find the secret that will lead me to this gate? It must be well camouflaged. Simple logic tells me that it wouldn't be out in the open for just anyone to find."

"The one will point the way," quoted Mr. Griffin.

"Yeah. So it says. I need to find out what that means."

"You may not be able to resolve that question without actually examining the stone."

"But will I recognize the stone without knowing what 'the one' reference means?"

"I cannot say."

Jake appeared to scrutinize the scroll, but was in fact looking far beyond. "If I find the stone, if I find the gateway, if I find the town... what then? What am I supposed to do when I get there?"

"I do not believe you have has yet discovered anything left behind by Master Quigley that would definitively answer that question."

Jake stared at Mr. Griffin in frustration. "Whatever it is that I'm supposed to do... why hasn't Uncle Tobias already done it? What was he doing when he disappeared?"

"The answer to that may very well have an impact on the task at hand."

"Doing *whatever it is I'm supposed to do* may require that I first accomplish whatever it was my uncle was attempting at the time that he vanished."

"He was last seen at the temple."

"So I should go there first..."

"They do not openly welcome strangers, Master Jacob."

"Maybe not, but you're right. That's where I need to go. And they're going to talk to me."

Now that Jake had a plan, or at least the beginnings of one, he was both excited and a bit anxious. Mr. Griffin had asked to go with him, but Jake had said no. As tempting as the offer was, he felt that Mr. Griffin would be more valuable at the mansion. He was certain there were more answers to be found in the secret rooms, in the pages of the books that filled the library shelves, in places as yet undiscovered.

So Jake spent the following day preparing for his journey. He filled the small backpack with some of the provisions and gear from the supply room, along with some extra clothes. He put the compass and some matches into a side pocket, and put the canteen and knife onto the utility belt. He wasn't ready to live on jerky and trail mix alone, so he asked Mrs. Hodges to make up a couple of lunches and some hardboiled eggs. His plan was to only be gone a few days. He knew the trip out to the temple wasn't that far, and he would most likely want to come back to Serpent's Keep before going out again in search of this abandoned town alluded to in the dragon scroll.

Back in the Command Center, he studied the large, handmade map of the Outland that was mounted on the wall. As he had noted before, it was a bit light on details. There were the known landmarks: the river, the Great Cliff. The Farm to the north was represented, and of course the Temple to the west. The major trails were displayed, and a handful of the lesser.

Jake thought it best to keep the original map safe at the mansion. He found paper and pen in the desk drawer and set about to make a smaller version of the map. Once he was finished, he stuffed the copy into the side pocket of the backpack and went downstairs to see if dinner was ready. He would be leaving first thing in the morning.

Meara was waiting for him at the foot of the stairs, dressed in night clothes.

"Master Jacob," Meara nodded nervously.

"Is everything all right?" Jake reached the last step and stopped.

"Yes, sir," Meara started quickly, and then paused.

"You sure?"

"Master Jacob... You should not be going into the Outland alone. Begging your pardon, sir."

"I can find my way, Meara." Jake stepped around Meara and started across the room. "I'll be fine."

She started after him. "Let me guide you, sir."

That stopped Jake short. He turned and looked carefully at the girl, trying to decide whether or not she was joking. She was not.

"You know the Outland?"

"Very well."

"Your father?"

"I went with him many times," she gave a sharp nod. "He was a hunter and a guide."

"So I understand," said Jake. "Did he ever serve as guide for my uncle?"

"Master Tobias needed no guide."

"So I've been told, but—"

"He did sometimes seek my father's counsel."

"Did they ever go into the Outland together? Not as master and guide, but as collaborators?"

"Yes."

"When your father disappeared?"

"Yes." Meara stood silent, offering no more. Jake chose to ask no more, at least not for the moment. He suspected that it was all tied together somehow; Meara's father, Uncle Tobias, the temple, the quest, the statues and what they represented; whatever Tobias was after when he disappeared.

Meara was young, certainly not yet twenty, but there was little doubt that she had more experience in the Outland than Jake. Perhaps she could keep him alive long enough for him to reach the temple and ask his questions.

"To the temple and back," he said. "No more."

"Yes, sir," she said excitedly.

"Your job is to keep me from making a fool of myself out there. Keep me out of trouble and keep me from getting lost."

"I can do that."

"Yeah, well, that may not be as easy as it sounds." Jake leaned close. "No heroics, Meara. I mean it. You're not my bodyguard."

"Yes, sir. No, sir."

Jake turned away again and started in the direction of the dining room. "We leave before first light. Get your gear together. I'll bring mine down later and you can look it over, make sure I haven't forgotten anything."

Meara was already turning about and rushing toward the back of the house. Jake had a sneaking suspicion that she was already packed.

Mr. Griffin watched Jake and Meara from the front door. He was quite distressed and had let Jake know of his concern all through the prior evening and again in the morning. The very thought of taking Meara along on the trip, no matter that it was only to the temple and back, was quite ill conceived. If Jake felt it absolutely necessary, then he should allow Mr. Griffin to accompany them.

Jake would have liked the additional company. But more than the fact that there were tasks at the mansion that needed doing, Jake, for right or for wrong, was concerned about Mr. Griffin's age. Griff had been an old man for as long as Jake had known him. He was probably the oldest man Jake had ever known. He seemed in good shape and was to all appearances a healthy man. But he was still an *old man*, and Jake had no way of knowing what to expect out there.

Jake said none of this to Mr. Griffin. He felt guilty enough just having such thoughts; he could never voice them aloud. He just told him that he needed Griff at the mansion, and that was that.

Jake could feel Mr. Griffin's cold eyes watching him now as he stepped through the estate's front gate, Meara following after. He looked up then, gate held half open. "Three days, Mr. Griffin," he called up to the dark figure on the porch. "After four, notify the sheriff. You have the route we'll take."

"Very well, sir."

Jake closed the gate and followed after Meara, who was already half a dozen paces down the walk.

"Good luck, Master Jacob," said Mr. Griffin, though by now Jake and Meara were already out of sight.

◊ ◊ ◊

The morning air was damp and slate-gray. There was a slight breeze blowing down the main thoroughfare, cold and sharp against the face. Jake was glad when they turned onto a narrow side road and out of the wind.

The sun wouldn't be up for another half hour, and they saw no one until they reached the West Gate. All citizens of Serpent's Keep had to do their time standing watch at the gates, and the poor soul at the West Gate this morning thought at first that his relief had finally arrived.

"Where you been?" he asked. "You're late."

"Not really, no," said Jake. He and Meara stopped two strides from the heavy wooden gate. The young man on watch remained in the three-walled four-by-four shed that served as the watch post.

"Hey, Frankie," said Meara.

"Meara?"

"We're heading out."

Frankie stared blankly at her, not quite sure if he had actually heard her speak.

"So we'll be needing you to open the gate," said Jake.

"You're going out?'

"That's the plan," said Jake.

"Yeah... okay." Frankie moved in between Jake and the gate, reached down and lifted the heavy timber that served to lock the gate. All the while he gave Jake a careful study, not quite sure what to make of this stranger heading into the Outland with Meara.

It took all his strength to half-carry, half-drag the timber to one side and out of the way. That done, he stepped back in front of the gate and pushed down on the large, strong latch and leaned back, pulling at the heavy door with all that he had.

Jake stepped quietly through the opening as soon as there was room. Meara followed after, calling back over her shoulder, "Thank you, Frankie."

The main west trail out of Serpent's Keep was eight feet wide and cut straight into a thick forest of scrub alder and tangles of underbrush, with an occasional lone evergreen standing stark and solitary. A fog hung overhead, hiding the treetops, occasionally drifting down to the forest floor and floating smokily across the trail.

They traveled in silence for several minutes, with the only sounds disturbing the predawn quiet being the rustling of fallen leaves stirring in the breeze and the scurrying of small animals.

They reached a fork in the trail where both directions appeared to be well traveled, both narrowing only slightly from the path they were on.

As Meara watched Jake pull out the map he had made, she pointed first to the left fork, "We need to go left," she said.

Jake nodded as he studied the map. He found the fork on the map, the path that each route took. As he folded the map and put it away, he glanced up at the glowing fog. Somewhere beyond that fog, the sun had risen.

"We should reach the temple by late afternoon," said Meara.

"Is the trail like this all the way?" he asked. Up to now, the trail had been clear and open.

"It narrows just up ahead, but the route between the Keep and the temple is the most used in the Outland, other than the farm road."

From his research, Jake knew the farm road was the route running between the village and the farm to the north.

They started forward again, Jake leading the way down the left fork. It narrowed beyond the first bend, closing in on either side until it was only four to five feet wide. The vegetation began to change as well, becoming darker and thicker; much more evergreen, and more heavy moss, more moisture hanging in the air, more dew hanging on the leaves of the underbrush.

A thousand yards further and there was another split in the trail. Meara told him to continue left. He went left without pause. Over the next few hours they came up on several more side trails, and at each one his guide pointed the way without much thought. She definitely knew her way around this part of the Outland.

They stopped at a wide spot in the trail about midday, the sun high overhead and doing its best to burn through the last of the low clouds, and set about to have lunch.

The clearing looked like it was frequently used for midday breaks; a fallen tree that lay across the back of the clearing offered a place to sit, and appeared to have been worn by years of such use. A small circle of stones in the center of the clearing held the ashes of dozens of past cooking fires.

Jake studied the perimeter of the clearing as he climbed up onto the fallen tree and set his pack beside him. He could see numerous trails leading away from the clearing and into the woods. Each small path was lost quickly in the shadows of the forest.

"Some folks try to hunt out there," said Meara, who was studying Jake rather than their surroundings. "Most don't."

"The hunting's not good?"

"It is better to bring your supplies with you."

"Dangerous?"

"Can be," she said. "When you go out there to take care of business, don't go far and don't stay gone long."

"Got it," said Jake. He took a strip of dried meat and a chunk of cheese from his pack and used his knife to cut a piece from each. Meara did the same and they ate quietly for a few moments. "Your father taught you well," Jake said finally.

"He knew his way around, sir."

"He spent a lot of time out here?"

"He liked the Outland."

"And he passed that fondness along to you?"

"Not so much," said Meara. "I respect the Outland, but that's not the same thing."

Jake wondered if the reason that Meara didn't like the Outland was because she felt that it was responsible for her father's death. He wanted to ask, wanted to know if it might be related to Tobias, about whether or not it was Tobias' sense of duty and responsibility and guilt about her father's death that had led to her position in the household.

But in the end, he couldn't.

"Do you know if my uncle felt the same way about the Outland as your father?"

"I don't think so," said Meara. "He knew the Outland better than anyone, but I don't think it was so much that he liked it out here. I think he needed to be out here."

That's quite an assumption, thought Jake.

"He used to spend a lot time out here, but only in the last couple of years did it become... something more."

The temple was a sprawling structure, the original building lost and misshapen from numerous additions globbed onto it over the years. Three tall, narrow, cylindrical spires rose above the treetops. The thick walls were made of wood and stone and concrete and mortar. The main door, set into the center of a protruding forward wing, was made of dark, heavy wood and black metal straps.

Meara climbed the two steps and stopped, staring at the door. After a moment's pause, she lifted and dropped the large knocker set in the center of the door. It gave a solid, resounding thud. She lifted and dropped it a second time, then turned and looked down at Jake. "Let's see what we get," she said.

Jake nodded solemnly and the two of them waited. After a full two minutes, they heard the sound of a wooden cross bar being lifted, and the door smoothly glided open. A tall man in a heavy robe and hood stepped forward and stopped. Jake saw that the monk took in the surroundings before finally turning his attention to Meara.

"Yes?" he asked simply.

"Hello, John," said Meara.

She knows him, thought Jake.

"Meara," said John.

"Don't give me your monk posturing."

"What do you seek, Meara?"

"We seek to get inside."

"You know the tenets of the temple."

"And you know that I wouldn't be here if it wasn't important."

"That doesn't really matter."

"You let my uncle stay here," Jake blurted out. He kept to the foot of the steps. The monk looked down at him, then quickly back to Meara.

"What do you seek, Meara?" John asked again, choosing to ignore the stranger's outburst. Without further information, there was as yet no purpose in initiating a second conversation with Meara's companion.

"We seek knowledge," Meara droned.

"As do we all."

"Airs again."

"I need to find out what you know about Tobias Quigley," said Jake.

Meara saw a flash of interest pass across the monk's face. "Master Quigley was his uncle," she said.

John the monk turned his full attention to Jake for the first time, studying his features and his stance. "Tobias Quigley was a good man," he said. "His absence will be deeply felt."

"Can you help us?" Jake climbed the first step. He watched as John stiffened and then calmly took a step back into the doorway. He thought for a moment that the monk was going to close the door on them.

"I can promise you nothing," said John. He backed fully into the front hall and made way for Meara and Jake.

The front hall had a high ceiling, a floor of wide, wooden planks, and walls of square stone on which several torches flickered red and orange flame.

A low open archway opposite the front door was the only other access to the room. John closed the door behind them and led them through this and down a narrow, dimly lit passage. They passed several open doors, beyond which Jake occasionally saw a monk sitting at a table or working over a desk.

They followed John around several turns and down several side passages before coming finally into a library. The book-lined walls rose twenty feet on all sides, with several tall, very narrow windows set into the far wall. Gas lamps were placed in the center of each of four large tables. Two more lamps hung from the high, beamed ceiling.

John walked to the first table and signaled for them to be seated. "I shall return," he said, stepping away from the table just as Jake was sitting. The monk left by the door through which they had come, closing it behind him.

Jake stood and walked toward the nearest wall.

"They know you around here," Jake stated.

"All my life, sir."

Old leather-bound books lined the shelves. Jake walked along the wall to where the shelves were replaced with diamond-shaped cubbyholes. Sitting in these cubbyholes were dozens of leather tubes, each two to three inches in diameter. Sliding one out, and then several others, he found they ranged in length from about eighteen inches to as long as two feet or so. Painstakingly written on the side of each was a title, most of which he couldn't understand, as they were written in a language he wasn't familiar with.

He turned from the scrolls and was moving back toward the table just as the door opened and John returned. Another man, shorter and much older, was following him. At the sight of this second man, Meara hurriedly stood and bowed her head.

"Master Peter," she said.

Peter waved his hand for her to sit. "Always a pleasure to see you, my dear," he said pleasantly. He turned his sharp gaze to Jake. "I am told that you are nephew to Brother Tobias."

Meara spoke up quickly, not yet daring to sit, "This is Master Jacob Quigley, recently arrived in Serpent's Keep."

"Call me Jake," said Jake. He held out his hand. Peter looked at it curiously, as if completely perplexed as to what to do with it. He smiled finally and took Jake's hand. His grip was sure and strong.

"Brother Jacob," said Peter, as if correcting Jake.

"Okay," said Jake. "Should I call you Brother Peter?"

"That would be fine." He waved again for them to sit, then nodded curtly to John. The younger monk walked over to the wall of cubbyholes and searched through one section until he found the canister that he wanted. He returned to Peter and handed it to him.

Peter opened the tube and pulled out an old scroll, set it on the table in front of Jake and Meara. "I think you should look at this," he said, unrolling it. "It was the reason for Brother Tobias' last visit."

"He was looking at this?" asked Jake.

"And not for the first time," Peter nodded.

Jake hovered over the aging scroll. "You do know that I have no idea what it says..."

"It is an ancient script," said Peter. "Rarely used and unknown to most."

"But not unknown to you," said Jake matter-of-factly, looking at John, then at Peter. "...or to my uncle."

"That is correct," said Peter, resting a silencing hand on John's arm. He laughed lightly. "Your uncle called the script Old Scratch. He said that he much preferred the *entertaining vulgarity* of today's tongue."

Jake mumbled as he stared dazedly down at the scroll. "That certainly sounds like Tobias." He leaned back in his chair. "Why show me a scroll that you know I can't read?"

Peter held up a hand, raising a finger as if to indicate that Jake had struck upon the point.

Meara spoke up. "What does the scroll say, Master?"

"There are several ways to interpret the script, and so the exact meaning is dependent on that interpretation."

"Naturally," grumbled Jake. "How did Tobias interpret it?"

"He did not fully confide in me, Brother Jacob."

"But you do have an idea."

"I can extrapolate, make assumptions... based on his queries of me."

"And?"

Peter gave a long sigh, smiled distantly and leaned forward over the scroll.

"And the reason I wished to show it to you." he said, indicating the first section of text. "This passage refers to gates. And there is an inference to other existences. The *other existence* reference is rather ambiguous, but I interpret the phrase as *place not of here*." Peter paused and then pointed to the next section. "It then speaks of the necessity to protect all existence, and later the hiding or disguising of '*the ways*'."

"Does it say anything about how these ways are disguised, or how to recognize them?" Jake asked.

"I am sorry, no. And that didn't seem to be a concern of Brother Tobias."

Jake furrowed his brow. Peter took this as a sign to continue.

"Here it refers to an object, an artifact, used to make clear the way. This particular phrasing of *'the way'* is different than the others. The wording is slightly different, and the interpretation places a different level of importance on it." Peter looked up from the text. "Your uncle showed a repeated interest in this passage."

"Any idea why?"

Peter gave an apologetic expression. He then slid a finger down to another section of the writing.

"A later passage," he pointed to another section of text, "speaks of defense of all existence, and the *segmenting* of the artifact."

Now that is *interesting...*

"The final passage refers to the closing of the path to those who would bring about destruction." Peter straightened, eyes darting from the scroll to Jake and back again.

Meara whistled softly. "I don't know if your interpretation makes it any clearer than the original script."

"Some of it does," said Jake. It confirmed, in Jake's mind, his own interpretation of pylons as gateways. And then there was the segmenting of the artifact.

"I am glad," said Peter.

"What can you tell me of this artifact?"

"Only that it was of supreme importance in an earlier time," said Peter. He studied John the monk, then Meara, trying to decide how much to allow them to hear. He finally turned back to Jake. "There is another scroll, older perhaps than this one. It speaks of a Guardian. This Guardian is closely tied to the Artifact, and the scroll states that it was the Guardian who was responsible for the partitioning of the Artifact into individual segments."

"So if we could find out more of this Guardian—"

"But he must have died thousands of years ago," said Meara.

"The scroll states that the bond between Guardian and Artifact was eternal," said Peter. "And I believe it likely that Brother Tobias was somehow bound to both."

The guest cell to which Jake was shown was just large enough to hold a bunk, a small table and a chair. There was a narrow window set high in one wall. An oil lamp on the table emitted a dim, warm glow, creating soft shadows that danced across the stone walls.

Jake sat down on the bed, turned and lay back, stared up at the heavy-beamed ceiling. He tried to relax. He was exhausted, but there was too much going on in his head for him to sleep. He feared that sleep would be a long time coming, and they had a very early start in the morning.

Once they had finished up in the library, Peter had shown Jake and Meara to the dining hall, where they were given a plain but filling meal. None of the other monks spoke to them, but the two strangers were under constant, if discreet, observation. After dinner, they were allowed to clean up before retiring to their cells.

They were to remain in their rooms until morning bell, one hour before dawn. After the morning meal, they would be leaving the temple.

Chapter Five

Jake and Meara reached the west gate of the village two hours before sunset. They had stopped several times along way, and had taken a few side trips down paths that had looked interesting, despite Meara's restrained objections. Jake wanted to get a better feel for the lay of the land. He knew that he would soon be spending some time out here.

The gate looked larger and darker from the outside. There was a large, metal ring hanging on the wall beside it. Meara reached up and gave it a long pull; Jake heard the peal of a heavy bell beyond the door.

"Who is it?" asked someone from the other side of the gate.

"Master Jacob Quigley," said Meara.

Jake heard the wooden bar lock slide over and a few moments later the door opened.

"Welcome back, folks," said the young man on guard. He was not the same person that had let them out the day before. Their exit had no doubt been logged in somewhere, and their return had been anticipated.

Jake stopped at the intersection of the side road and the main street of the village. It was quiet, with only a few people out and about. He would have thought it would have been busier this time of day. He turned to his guide and companion. "Why don't you head on home, Meara?" he suggested, his voice as quiet as the village around them. "We can discuss the trip in the morning."

"Of course, sir," said Meara.

"And thanks. I appreciate all your help."

"Glad to, sir."

Was she more formal now that they were back in Serpent's Keep? He started to say something, but thought better of it. "Tomorrow, then," he said, and started across the street.

The street to Quigley Mansion was empty and still, though he could hear people in the plaza on his right, mostly the laughter of children some distance away. He had his key in hand when he reached the gate, and was quickly through and starting up the front walk when Mr. Griffin opened the front door.

"You waiting for me all this time?"

Griffin raised one brow, but otherwise was still as stone. "Simply good timing, Master Jacob."

Jake climbed the steps and started through the front door. He looked tired.

"Not worried about me?" he asked. He sounded as tired as he looked.

"Was your trip successful, sir?" Griffin asked, following him into the house.

"Made it back. That's something."

"Quite so, sir. An unexpected, but most welcome outcome."

Jake started doggedly up the stairs. He spoke without looking back at Mr. Griffin.

"Think I'll clean up." He needed to rest.

That evening after dinner, Jake returned upstairs and went out onto the deck that looked out to the west. It was just after sunset and the sky was splashed in orange and red and purple, sending colorful streaks of light across the treetops of the Outland. He sat in the large wooden lounge chair and watched as the colors shifted and stretched with the sinking of the sun. At one point a streak of light struck at what must have been one of the spires of the temple, some thirty miles away, creating an intense star of light in the heart of the Outland.

As dusk slowly crept up on the village, flickers of light shone as street lamps were lit and as light poured out through the small, square windows of the homes and shops throughout Serpent's Keep. Sounds seemed to carry further in the oncoming dusk, though they were strangely muffled, as if the oncoming night was throwing a heavy blanket over the land.

Jake let his mind wander in the calming backdrop of the village settling in for the evening. His thoughts were conflicted, however, and he found himself torn between what sometimes felt like two very different objectives. The first was to find his uncle, whether alive or dead; the second was to identify and pursue the task that his uncle had started and apparently expected his nephew to carry on and complete.

He knew where he wanted to focus all of his attention, but also felt an obligation to the quest that he had been given.

Was there a way to pursue both?

That had been easy enough to do up to this point. Seeking clues for the first was the same as seeking clues for the second. Now, however, he was afraid that was going to change.

Or was it? If he set out on the first stage of the quest, would he be following the path that his uncle had taken before him? Would he therefore, sooner or later, overtake his uncle, or at least find another clue as to his whereabouts and his fate?

What else was there to do?

He was still missing so much. He didn't know what he should be searching for or where to look for it.

Jake heard the sound of someone coming out onto the deck. There were only so many possibilities as to who it might be, and only one whom it was likely to be.

"Hey, Griff," he said, without turning.

"Master Jacob." Mr. Griffin stepped up beside him. He cast his gaze in the direction that Jake was looking. After so many decades, the old man knew every twist and turn and shadow of the village. Of the Outland beyond the wall, however, he knew almost nothing. It mattered little to him, though, beyond the interest that his former employer had held for it. "Mrs. Hodges asked that I see about you."

Jake didn't respond. After several moments, Mr. Griffin continued, still not looking at the young man. "Apparently, you didn't have much of an appetite." Mr. Griffin made every effort not to display any shared concern.

Again Jake said nothing. This time, Mr. Griffin patiently waited. For almost a minute, the two of them looked out at the scene laid before them.

"My uncle had an interest in parallel universes," Jake said at last. It was a casual comment, not intended to draw a response. "Alternate universes." A shrug. "The books in the library."

Mr. Griffin looked calmly to Jake, then again turned his attention to the village.

Jake continued. "Take that, and tie it to the reference in his notebook... the one where he said that '*a way would be opened*', and that he would have to step through to the other side."

Jake grew quiet again. After a few moments, Mr. Griffin looked side glance at him. He considered speaking, considered saying something, *anything*, but chose to remain silent. Eventually, Jake went on.

"I think Tobias found a way to travel between these... *alternate...* universes." Jake turned to look directly at Mr. Griffin. "There is a scroll at the temple that refers to *gates* and *other existences.*"

Mr. Griffin felt it was now appropriate to chime in with a thought of his own. "Our own serpent's scroll; its reference to the pylon in the stone."

"Yes." Jake nodded. "Have you noticed that each of the six dragons looks like it comes from a completely different environment? Six worlds, each residing in an alternate universe." Jake looked back out at the village, at the Outland beyond. The colors of the sunset were growing darker. "Numerous occurrences of the six polygons, and in the notebook... the joining together of these into a single geometric shape."

"The Artifact," said Mr. Griffin.

"The scroll at the Temple speaks of the segmenting of the Artifact."

"The individual polygons."

"Each polygon can be found on a serpent's pedestal in the Hall of Statues. Each serpent, and therefore each polygon, represents another world."

"And the gathering together..." Mr. Griffin said flatly.

"I have to go to each of these other worlds and find the artifact segments. I have to bring them back and somehow restore the Artifact to a single piece."

"Sir." Mr. Griffin spoke coolly. "For what purpose?"

"To open the way."

"Master Jacob... it sounds as though the way was closed so as to prevent something dreadful from happening."

"I know." Jake's tone grew self-questioning. "The notebook. *'The Rhetani must be prevented from recovering the artifact and opening the way'.* And the scroll in the temple spoke of hiding the way, closing the path against those who would cause destruction."

"And yet now you speak of opening the way."

Jake shook his head tiredly. "Tobias clearly wants me to restore the Artifact. I have no doubt of that."

"Tread carefully, Master Jacob." Mr. Griffin wasn't quite as certain.

Jake stuffed his hands into his pockets. He was beginning to feel the chill of the oncoming darkness, both real and metaphorical.

"I have to go north. I need to find this stone. I need to find the pylon, the *gateway,* that will lead me to this other world."

Chapter Six

Jake watched the odd little man cross the street and approach him. He had left the mansion to gather some supplies for his next trip out and was about half way to the marketplace.

"You're Quigley," the man stated. He took a final step and blocked Jake's path.

"Yeah," Jake said warily.

The man nodded and eyed Jake. "You went out to the temple."

"That something I should have checked on with you first?"

The man chuckled at that. "Not at all, not at all."

"Glad to hear it. Thought maybe I had violated some rule."

The man lost his smile. "I's curious, though. Wha'd you go there for? Why take the girl? It's dangerous out there."

"So, I *am* supposed to check in, then? Clear my reasons with you?"

"Just curious."

"And I'm busy."

"Not trying to stir up trouble," the man raised a hand defensively. "It's... it's dangerous out there."

"So you said."

"I's lost friends out there."

"Sorry to hear that," Jake made to go. The man managed to move without really appearing to move, continuing to block Jake's path. "I really do have to go," he told the man.

"I's almost killed out there."

"Good to see you made it back in one piece."

The man tapped his temple. "Not exactly one piece," he said softly.

"Well, alive then." Jake tried to step around the man again, but was blocked yet again. "If you don't mind," he said.

"There's bandits out there," the man said, more urgently now. "They'll take your stuff, and your life."

"Apparently, it's not all that safe here in the village."

"Worse yet, there's creatures. Creatures ya' won't find nowhere else."

Jake was pretty sure this guy was nuts, but that didn't mean he hadn't seen something out there. Still, he was afraid of encouraging him. "So I understand," he finally said.

"Creepy-crawly things, and wolves with brains; and flyin' things."

"Flying things?" he asked, despite his own good judgment.

"Why do ya—"

"On your way, Mason," came a voice from behind Jake. A moment later, Sheriff Smith stepped up beside him. "Don't you be bothering Mister Quigley."

"I twarn't botherin' nobody," Mason said defensively. "He oughtn't be takin' the youngin' into the Outland."

"That's not for you to decide," said the Sheriff.

"Still 'tain't right," he mumbled.

"Meara has spent half her life in the Outland, and you know it," said Sheriff Smith. "Now move on, before I drag you in for being a nuisance."

Mason started to say something, but the Sheriff's sharp look decided him against it. He turned aside and walked quickly into the street and away. Sheriff Smith watched the retreating figure until he was certain the man wasn't going to turn back and renew his harassment of the newcomer. He turned then to Jake.

"Mister Quigley. I see you've returned safely from your trip to the Temple."

"I imagine you knew I was back three minutes after I came through the West Gate."

"Not quite that fast," said the sheriff, scratching at the back of his neck, "But most likely before you reached home."

Jake pretty much assumed that was the way of things. There was little doubt the sheriff knew all the goings on, at least within the high, stone walls of the village.

"Listen," said Jake. "About Meara..."

"An excellent choice for a guide, Mister Quigley. Pay no attention to Mason."

"She insisted—and she seemed to know what she was talking about."

"She is her father's daughter."

"I made it absolutely clear she was not to put herself in harm's way."

Sheriff Smith held up a silencing hand. "Son, I consider myself a pretty good judge of character, and I don't believe you would knowingly put Meara Gyles in danger. And Meara is about as smart as they come when it comes to the Outland."

"Well, I—"

"I would say only this..." Sheriff Smith's tone grew just a tad ominous. "Her father had more Outland smarts than she did. He's gone. Your uncle Tobias had more Outland smarts than Meara and her father and everyone else in this village put together; and he's gone." He pointed in the direction that Mason had gone. "Whatever he told you about the dangers of the Outland, you can take that and double it."

"I'll do that," said Jake.

Sheriff Smith stepped away and started across the street. "Have a pleasant morning, Mister Quigley."

The marketplace was a large open square, a grassy plaza lined on all sides with three-walled booths that offered everything from clothes to vegetables to kitchenware to gardening tools. As a child, Jake had found it an interesting world within a world. Now, as he walked the rows of booths and looked in at the wares, he was certain that many of the faces that looked back at him were the very same faces from those years long past.

He stopped at a booth lined with pots and pans and ironware.

"Hello, Mrs. Numidia," he said. Mrs. Numidia hadn't changed at all. She looked exactly as she had years earlier, when Jake would run around the grassy plaza, taking in all the sights and sounds and people. He probably remembered her most because Mrs. Numidia was the wife of the blacksmith. A blacksmith was something special to a twelve year old boy.

"'morning to ya, Master Jake," she continued about her work, organizing her wares in preparation of the day, but her tone of voice was pleasant. "Thought I wouldn't recognize ya, eh?"

Jake smiled. "You heard I was in the village, and how many other strangers do you see?"

"Oh, I know ya anywhere, boy," she said, then quickly put on her sad face. "Sorry to hear 'bout Master Quigley."

"Me, too."

"So, what brings you to the market? Anything I can offer? I give ya' the welcome back special, I will." Her returning smile was genuine and yet just a little unsettling.

"Nothing just yet, Mrs. Numidia, but I'll keep that in mind." Jake started forward, on towards the next booth.

"Nice to have ya' back, just the same, Master Jake."

Jake passed by several more booths, stopping then at a booth selling a variety of leather clothing. After a bit of good-natured haggling, he bought a pair of hiking boots and two pairs of pants. His feet were still sore from his last trip out, and he could use footwear designed for the travels that he had in mind.

Jake stood at the bench in the supply room off the Command Center. He had brought back gear and supplies from the marketplace, some of which he had stowed away, some he had packed for his trip. To the gear he had packed, he added additional equipment from the supply room, most of which he had taken with him on his short jaunt to the temple. He was putting in more rations and there were the heavy-duty clothes he had purchased. He had found that his city clothes weren't going to hold up very well in the Outland, and he had no idea what to expect if he actually found a way through the gateway.

Mr. Griffin appeared in the doorway. He showed mild interest in the items on the counter, but remained silent.

Jake continued putting his supplies together. "Ya' know, I asked the guy selling knives where I could find something with a little more... you know... *oomph*... and he clammed up tight. I mean he turned to stone; just stood there."

"Such things are not available in the market," said Mr. Griffin.

"You don't say?" Jake said sarcastically.

"His response was to be expected, sir. The market in which such items are to be found is not publicly acknowledged."

"Items?"

"Implements of battle. Defensive and offensive."

Jake closed his pack and lifted it off the counter. "And you know where to acquire such... *items*?"

"I may have heard rumors, sir."

Jake slipped one arm through the shoulder strap. He walked out of the supply room and into the command center. "Why don't you see what you can find out? Maybe we'll do some shopping when I get back."

Jake reached the Hall of Statues and stopped. Before him hovered the six dragons, towering over him, threatening and mysterious. "I've a feeling I'm going to need some help from this unspoken of dark underbelly of Serpent's Keep."

"Yes, sir."

They made it as far as the bottom of the stairs before Meara confronted them. She looked as prepared to go as Jake.

"Not this time, Meara," said Jake.

"You must let me come with you."

"No," he said.

"You're going to need me, sir. More so than before."

"That's enough, girl," said Mr. Griffin. He was much more stern than Jake. Nonetheless, Meara wasn't quite ready to give up.

"Master Jacob, to go out there alone is just foolish."

"No more," said Mr. Griffin.

This time, Meara did give up. She bowed her head in silent acknowledgement and shuffled away. Jake watched her leave, then started toward the front door.

Chapter Seven

Jake walked north down the center of the village's main thoroughfare. Dawn was still an hour away, and the street lamps burned low, sending a golden glow across the thick fog that hung above the street and lay across the tops of the buildings on either side. Shadows crept out of the doorways and down the side streets. Jake saw no one until he reached the North Gate.

It was much the same as the West Gate; a heavy wooden door set into the city perimeter wall, a thick beam holding it closed against the Outland beyond. The woman on watch stepped out of the small guard station.

"Good morning, sir," she said. She didn't appear surprised to see him.

"Good morning," said Jake. He stopped and nodded at the gate. "I'd like to go out, please."

"You bet." The woman braced herself and slid the beam aside. She lifted the latch and pulled at the heavy door. Once opened, she stood to one side and made way for Jake.

"Good luck to you, Mister Quigley," she said as he passed her.

Beyond the gate, Jake stopped to take in the scene. Ahead was darkness, the forest pushing in towards the village perimeter wall. Behind him, the door creaked on its iron hinges as the guard pushed it closed. After a few moments, he shifted the pack on his back, adjusted the utility belt around his waist, and started forward.

It wasn't totally dark. Jake could see the trail winding its way through the Outland's north woods, a path of brown dirt with scruffy patches of grass and weed, with trees and brush creeping in from either side, reaching in from black shadows that moved and shape-shifted as he strode forward.

The darkness grew steadily grayer as the early morning approached dawn. By the time he reached the first fork in the trail, Jake could read the hand-drawn map that he pulled out of the side pocket of his backpack.

He had expected this fork, had been anticipating it and had begun to worry that he had somehow missed it. He looked to the map for verification and to remind himself of what to expect next. Satisfied that he was indeed where he thought he was, he refolded the map and continued ahead.

He knew that the left fork would continue north and in the direction of the farm that supplied much of the food for the village. The right fork, the path that he believed he had to take, struck out northeast into land largely unknown and only sparsely mapped.

The trail narrowed almost immediately, and the brightening sky was frequently hidden from view by high branches reaching across from one side of the path to the other. There were sounds in the woods; animals scurrying across the loamy forest floor and in the branches of the brush and the trees. Jake occasionally heard the movement of larger animals, but never saw them. Several times, he heard what sounded like animals fighting. Once he heard what he could only imagine to be the cries of an animal dying unpleasantly.

He stopped every couple of hours to rest, drink from his canteen, and snack on jerky or cheese. He studied the map, marked what he believed to be his path and his current location. Three times he came up on a fork in the trail when there was no indication of it on the map. Each time, after making note, he chose the path that kept him going in a northeasterly direction; always deeper into the unknown.

By early evening he was far from any mapped trail, and was marking the map with what he believed to be the path he was taking. At one point the trail withered away and ended, and he had to turn back and take another route. He wondered if his uncle had traveled these trails, and if he had, why he hadn't included them on the map.

Jake came into a small clearing and decided to stop for the night. It was a few hours until dark, and this would give him time to set up a decent camp, gather wood and make a fire, and cook a hot meal.

Taking heed of what Meara had said, his first trip off the path and into the woods was short and brief. Once personal business had been taken care of, he set about to gather the wood for the fire. He found that he was able to get all that he needed while staying within twenty feet or so of the clearing. Walking just beyond the perimeter of the clearing, within tossing distance, he quickly picked up and threw into the clearing all the wood that he would need.

Finally, with a small fire going, Jake settled in for the evening. He set a small pot of water on the fire and started it heating. As it warmed, he took a chunk of smoked meat, a potato and several raw vegetables from his supplies and cut them into pieces, letting them drop into the water. With the soup going, he sat back and took out his map. It would be some time before dinner was ready, and he thought he might as well put the time to use.

He felt warm and relaxed, his mind was calm and the campsite was peaceful in the glow of the firelight. The sun had set but the sky hadn't yet turned dark.

Jake stiffened suddenly at the sound of an animal sound that came from the shadows behind him. It was a low, guttural noise, as if coming from deep down in a large animal's barrel chest.

Without standing or turning, he reached down and pulled his knife free from its sheath. The throaty noise continued, and he could also hear the rustling of dried leaves and branches—whatever it was, it was coming towards him. He looked from side to side, carefully watching the perimeter of the clearing. He saw nothing; no other movement. He heard nothing but the sounds coming from behind him.

Jake jumped to his feet and turned sharply about, his knife held out in front of him.

A shift in the shadows just beyond the edge of the clearing; a movement between trees, behind a large bush. The guttural sound stopped. There was only the sound of snapping twigs, the rustling of dead leaves and pine needles.

A very large wolf stepped out of woods and into the clearing. Jake took a step back and crouched slightly, readying the knife.

Large wolf... lots of sharp teeth...

City boy... little knife... primary use: cutting up carrots...

"Oh, boy..." Jake mumbled, backed up another step. The wolf moved forward a step.

Jake had never seen a wolf close up before, but even so he thought this one looked somehow... different. It was bigger than he had seen on television, and broader, bulkier. It had a large head and its face was almost flat but for the snout, with its mouth full of teeth.

It paced smoothly to one side, always watching Jake. Jake kept the knife pointed at the animal.

Jake froze suddenly. Something was wrong; he could feel it.

He saw a shadow out of the corner of his eye. Turning his head slightly to the left, he saw that another wolf had come into the clearing—out of the woods that he had been certain were empty.

Turning his head slightly to the right then, he saw another wolf, just inside the clearing, watching him.

Jake turned back to the main wolf, the leader. He saw something in the face, in the eyes. The animal seemed to be saying something...

gotcha...

Jake gave an involuntary shiver. He knew the wolf hadn't actually spoken, but he knew that's what the animal was saying.

There was the hint of a grin on the wolf's face. The eyes sparkled.

Another sound then... from behind him.

Oh, man...

"Back off," came a woman's voice.

Meara?

"I don't think I can do that," said Jake. He did not look back, dared not take his eyes off the wolf.

"Not you, sir," said Meara. Then, to the animals that were preparing to move in on Jake, "You don't want to do this."

The lead wolf appeared as though he was rethinking the situation, looking past Jake at Meara standing somewhere behind him. The two wolves on either side looked to the lead wolf for guidance.

The wolf lost the hint of the grin, now wore a scowl. It looked directly at Jake again. The piercing eyes and dark expression seemed to say *we will finish this later*. It turned about sharply and leapt out of the clearing. His two companions turned about and disappeared into the shadows.

"What the heck was that about?" asked Jake. He turned around and faced Meara. "And what are you doing here?" He sheathed his knife.

"I'm sorry, sir," said Meara.

"That's it?"

"I couldn't let you come out alone."

"You couldn't *let me*? Isn't there some rule in Serpent's Keep about the staff having to do what the Master of the House says?"

"Yes sir." Meara lowered her gaze. "I suppose so."

"And what do you think Mr. Griffin is going to say when he finds out?"

"I couldn't say, sir."

"He'll probably ground us both." Jake looked back in the direction the lead wolf had taken away from the clearing. He looked again at Meara. "How'd you do that?"

"We have an understanding."

"An understanding..."

"Yes sir."

"You and the wolves. You have an understanding."

"Yes sir."

"How does that work, exactly?"

"They agree to leave me alone; I agree not to kill them."

"Pardon?"

Meara shrugged halfheartedly, embarrassed. She moved nearer the fire. "My father had a confrontation with them a long time ago. Since then, they know better."

"Some trick," said Jake. Sooner or later he was going to have to get a little more from her than that. He moved up beside Meara and sat beside the fire. Meara sat to one side.

"My father had no choice," she said. "So now..."

"Yeah. They know better."

Meara shrugged again. Jake would to let it go for now. He picked up several sticks from the pile beside him, absently fed the fire.

"They're smart... aren't they?" *Wolves with brains...*

"Yes."

"I mean, *really* smart."

"Yes."

Jake slowly nodded, looked out beyond the clearing. Seeing this, Meara looked into the woods, studied the shadows, listened to the sounds.

"I don't think they'll be back tonight," she said.

Jake decided to accept that. He looked questioningly at Meara. "And so now what am I supposed to do with you?"

"Sir?"

"Did you at least let someone know that you were coming out here?" he asked.

"My mother."

Jake nodded silently.

"And there's the gate records," she said.

"Great," Jake grumbled. "The sheriff knows by now. One more headache I have to deal with."

"Sheriff Smith looks beyond mere appearances, Master Jacob."

"I didn't mean—"

"I don't see the problem, sir."

"I'm responsible. If something was to happen, I couldn't forgive myself. And I don't think the folks back at the village would forgive me, either. I wouldn't blame them."

"How important is this quest?" she asked suddenly.

"Very."

"Serious enough that you are willing to risk your life," she stated flatly.

"But not yours."

"It's worth your life, but not the life of someone else?"

"That's not—"

"Will something bad happen if you fail?"

Jake doesn't answer. His expression said it all.

"So." Meara raised a brow. "Don't you think you should give yourself the best chance of succeeding?"

This is just great, he thought. "You're standing the late watch," he said at last.

Over the next several days, Jake and Meara mapped a large section of the northeastern Outland, carefully documenting each fork in the trail, recording the locations of major features, hazards and obstacles. They didn't see the wolf pack again, though Jake was certain that he heard them several times as they traveled, and once on the second night as they camped. Meara was certain it was something else, but could not or would not say what that something else might be.

It wasn't until midday of their first day together that Meara asked what they were looking for. Jake didn't have the slightest idea. He could only hope that he would recognize it when he saw it. He told Meara to keep her eyes open for anything just a little bit different, just a little bit out of place; anything that made her go 'hmmm'.

She seemed amused by this.

On the fourth evening they set up camp on a wide ledge overlooking a large ravine. It was hundreds of yards across, a thousand yards deep, and ran east to west as far as he could see. The sides of the ravine were steep and the floor was hidden beneath a canopy of dark trees and darker undergrowth.

Meara called it the Great Ravine.

Jake couldn't understand why a natural feature as significant as this wouldn't be on the map. Meara said that it was spoken of now and then, but no one she knew had ever seen it or knew where it was. Not her father, not anyone. Jake asked how that could be, and Meara simply shrugged, saying that it was really out of the way and there wasn't much to bring a body out this far.

"What do they say about it?" asked Jake.

"They say that it is a gash in the skin of the world; a wound that has never healed."

"Well, if they talk about it, then somebody has seen it, and if somebody's seen it, then why isn't something this big on a map?"

"Not everybody puts things on paper, sir."

Jake studied their surroundings. Wouldn't Tobias have documented it? And since he hadn't, did that mean that his uncle hadn't been here?

Maybe Tobias had intentionally left the ravine off the map. If so, why?

"Let's keep a sharp eye out," said Jake. "Just in case tourists around here get eaten."

The clearing was wide, allowing them to make camp well away from the trees and away from the edge of the ravine. They gathered firewood from the perimeter of the clearing, stepping warily into the shadows and returning quickly into the fading daylight. They took out three large bushes that lined the eastern edge of the clearing, opening up the perimeter there and making it more difficult for anything that might want to creep up on them in the night to do so without being seen.

They had a campfire going by dusk. Jake unpacked food supplies and together he and Meara heated up rations of meat and potatoes.

As they settled in around the fire and ate their dinner, Jake began to notice a change in the noises around them. The world was growing... quiet. The sounds of nature that he had become accustomed to over the previous days and no longer heard on a conscious level now slowly faded away.

Their absence had drawn his attention.

Putting another bite of potato into his mouth, he glanced over at Meara.

She had noticed it, too.

The world around them had gone silent.

Jake set down his plate and slowly rose to his feet. He studied the woods that encircled the clearing, but saw nothing, heard nothing. Looking up at the sky, he saw only one small wisp of cloud in the dusk of a darkening sky.

He looked again at Meara, now standing. She was looking in the direction of the ravine.

Oh, man... thought Jake. He sucked in a long, cool breath and slowly let it out. Not letting himself think anymore on it, he walked cautiously toward the edge. As he drew nearer, he began stretching forward, leaning forward, as if this somehow made it all safer. He could hear Meara beside him, saw her then out of the corner of his eye.

He stopped at the very edge of the ravine. Far below, the world was dark, with varying shades of black and gray, the treetops poking up from the darkest shadows.

And there was movement.

"Do you see that?" asked Jake, very quietly, very calmly.

"Yes sir," whispered Meara.

Shadows skimmed above the treetops. Large, black silhouettes, gliding silently, creating darker shadows that danced in the trees below them. At first, Jake saw only three of them, but as he watched, he saw another and another, until finally there was at least half a dozen.

From their position on the ledge high above, it was impossible to judge their size, and because of the distance and the shadowy darkness, it was impossible to discern what they were.

There's creepy-crawly things, and wolves with brains, and flyin' things...

"I don't think those are bats," said Jake.

"No, sir. Those ain't bats."

"So, what are they, then?"

"I couldn't say, sir."

Not out loud, anyway, he thought.

"Yeah," he said aloud. "Me neither."

Jake and Meara stood at the edge of the ravine until it was too dark to see, then returned to their fire and fed the dying embers until the flames were a foot and half high. They took turns on watch, as they had previous nights, but neither got much sleep. From what they could tell, the *flyin' things* never left the ravine... but something had scared nature into silence when the sun went down.

By morning, the world had returned to normal. They could hear the sounds of birds and small animals in the trees and brush beyond the perimeter of the clearing. Low clouds had come in before dawn, and the sky hung low and gray above them. Looking down into the ravine, the trees and floor were hidden from view beneath a thick blanket of fog. Jake saw nothing in the mist.

They decided to follow the ravine east. This would take them ever farther into uncharted territory and further away from

Serpent's Keep, whereas west would have taken them in the direction of the farm, though probably far north of it.

They were able to follow the edge of the ravine for most of the morning before the terrain finally forced them to move into the woods. Travel was difficult until, an hour after midday, they found an animal trail that wound through the thick undergrowth and eventually brought them again to the ravine's southern edge.

The fog had cleared away and they were able to see the thick forest that covered the floor of the ravine. It was much shallower here, only a third as deep as further up-ravine. Continuing east, the trail they followed moved steadily downhill, the ravine grew steadily shallower, the floor seeming to rise up to meet them. By late afternoon, Jake and Meara were at the mouth of the ravine.

Jake watched Meara cross a wide clearing and stop at the dark brush that crowded the mouth.

"Here," she said. She had found a narrow path into the ravine.

"Here, Meara," said Jake. He stood at a large stone standing in the center of the clearing. Other than a few scraggily weeds, there was nothing else in the clearing. "Have you ever seen anything like this?" The rock was five feet high, irregularly shaped, four feet wide at its widest. There were numerous flat surfaces. He cautiously laid hand on stone. It was cool to the touch.

"I believe that's granite, sir," said Meara.

"Yes it is," said Jake. "But that's not what I mean." He had seen exposed rock in weathered, eroded hillsides, and in the side of the ravine they had followed. But this was different. A lone rock, on level ground, the only object in the center of a clearing.

As if it had been put there.

Meara returned to his side. "Is this it? What you're lookin' for?"

"I think so... maybe."

"What do we do?"

"I don't know." Jake pulled his hand back and rubbed it on his shirt.

Somehow, I have to make this thing give up its secret.

Chapter Eight

Jake had no idea what to do. He had hoped that once he found the stone, he would then find some further clue. As yet, however, he had nothing.

Camp was established. Meara sat off to one side, having made herself comfortable where she could sit and watch Jake, while at the same time watch the dark, heavily wooded mouth of the ravine. Jake would sit and stare at the stone, stand and circle the stone, stare up at the sky high above the stone, and occasionally walked to the mouth of the ravine that opened to the clearing in which the stone rested.

Find now the pylon within the stone...

The one will point the way...

Some one or some thing...

Jake studied the variations in the surface of the stone, looking for images of a one, or one of something, but found nothing. He tried shining light on the stone from various angles, looking for shadows that could be interpreted as a one, but again found nothing.

With the setting of the sun came a whole new set of images, shadows created by the flickering flames of the campfire. Meara kept the fire burning big and bright, pushing back the darkness that crept in from all sides, the shadows that reached out from mouth of the ravine.

Jake appeared to ignore it all, focusing all his attention, all his frustrations, on the stone standing complacently in their midst, waiting in silence for someone to speak the correct incantation, press the right button, twist the right knob, dance the right dance...

He grew increasingly concerned that there was something left behind at the estate that he needed—something still hidden away or locked away, some final key that would open the stone.

He slept little. Meara looked on most of the night; she watched Jake, and she watched the shadows. She watched the mouth of the ravine. Strange sounds and strange smells came from in there. Animal sounds that were something other than animal sounds. Sounds of live things moving, flying, creepily and stealthily walking. Sounds from the throat that did not come from the throat of any animal that Meara had ever seen or ever heard; thoughtful, studious sighs...

Animal smells that Meara had never smelled before; musty, musky, peculiarly leathery and yet not leather...

Meara knew that *they* knew were out there, watching as she watched, waiting as she waited. *Observing...*

They never came out of the dark of the ravine. They chose not to... perhaps they knew what Master Jacob was trying to do and they wanted him to succeed.

Morning gray came slowly to the clearing. Another hour passed; sunlight crept across the clearing and up across the stone. It brought no revelation, revealed no secrets...

Jake held his hands out in frustration. "What do you want?" he demanded.

The stone was silent.

Jake saw the shadow of his hand move across the stone. Not for the first time, he was drawn to the different shapes and shadows on the rough surface. But there was nothing there. There was nothing there...

The answer is here...

Jake turned away from the stone and looked at Meara. He didn't know what to do. Meara shrugged a shoulder and shook her head. She stood then, slowly, looking behind Jake, looking in the direction of the mouth of the ravine.

Behind him... at the dark, menacing, shadowy mouth of the ravine. He felt a cold, terrifying chill. Behind him. Behind him... It took everything he had to turn around and face whatever it was that awaited him.

It was a serpent... a dragon... *something...*

It stood just inside the clearing, watching Jake, studying Jake. Without moving its head, it turned an eye to Meara, then returned its attention to Jake.

It stood twice as high as a human. Its hide was scaly, colored in multiple shades of green and brown. It had powerful hind legs, slightly smaller front legs that looked as though they could be used as arms and hands. Massive leathery folds were bundled up on its back. Wings?

Is this the shadow they had seen when looking down into the ravine?

A flying dragon?

It took a step then, startling Jake, who took a stumbling step backward. The creature paused a moment, then took a second step, and then glided smoothly to the stone. It climbed atop the stone and settled itself in as though it was some gigantic, massive bird making itself comfortable on its perch.

It turned its horned head and stared down at Jake with one gleaming yellow eye.

"Tobias..." it said. The sound came from somewhere deep inside the creature, pushing up through its throat and pushing out harsh and low.

Did the dragon think that he was Tobias, or was he asking for his uncle?

What do you say to a dragon?

"I'm Jake," he finally stammered.

"Tobias," the dragon stated again. It raised its head up and took in the entire clearing, stopping its visual sweep only briefly on Meara. She stood fast; did not run, but did not move any nearer.

"I'm sorry," said Jake. "Tobias isn't here."

The dragon turned its head sharply and stared down at Jake. "Where... Tobias?"

"I don't know."

The dragon leaned forward and studied Jake closely. Its breath was hot, pressing down and taking the air away. It sniffed noisily, drew a breath in through its long, hollow nostrils, suddenly raised its head up and back. It eyed Jake curiously. "Blood," it said.

*Geez, it wants to eat me...*Jake thought in a panic.

Meara took a step forward. "Yes," she said. ""Master Jacob is blood. Tobias and Master Jacob."

The dragon glanced at the small human at the far end of the clearing, then looked down again at Jake. "Tobias' blood," it stated firmly.

Jake stammered. "My uncle. Tobias... my uncle."

"Tobias," it said again, this time with some affection.

What does this creature have to do with my uncle? What does it want of my uncle?

Meara slowly approached, finally standing directly beside Jake. The dragon continued to watch them, shifting position slightly in order to make itself more comfortable. The stone that it sat upon looked to have been worn down from years, perhaps centuries, of serving as the dragon's perch.

The one will point the way...

Is this the one?

Meara whispered, "The one—"

"—will point the way..." Jake finished.

"The *one* is a dragon?"

The dragon was calm, breathing easily. It seemed somehow comforted by Jake's scent—Tobias' blood...

"Its claws," Meara whispered, nodding her head in the direction of the stone perch. Jake saw again how the stone had been worn down from years of service as the creature's roost. The three claws of each foot fit snugly into deep grooves in the rock.

Jake realized then what Meara was suggesting.

The one will point the way...

Jake looked carefully at each deadly claw.

Not the dragon... the claw.

One of the claws pointed to a blemish in the great stone; a dark recess no larger than the width of Jake's thumb, no deeper than the knuckle.

Jake stepped forward, afraid to look up and see what the serpent's reaction might be. He sensed nothing from the creature and continued toward the stone. He reached a hand out and without taking time to consider what might happen, pushed his thumb into the dark blemish, the dragon's claw not half an inch away.

The area around the stone grew warm, as if the rock was heated from a noonday sun. The clearing was bathed in a suffuse light, centered at the stone.

The great stone began to fade in the wash of bright light, the colors disappearing first, and then the shape itself; the dragon all the while maintaining its perch, unperturbed, now sitting atop a soupy cloud of bright whites and grays. Seconds passed, and the cloud began to coalesce, until finally a primitive stone archway, seven feet high and seven feet wide, stood where the great rock had once stood. A clear shimmer swirled within the opening. High atop the ancient gate sat the dragon.

"Enter the gateway, Blood of Tobias," it said.

Jake looked quickly over his shoulder at Meara. "You wait here," he said.

"No sir," she said sharply. "I'm coming with you."

"No you're not. I mean it. If I don't come back, I need you here. If I don't come back, you go for Griff." Jake didn't wait for her to respond. He turned back to the gateway, glanced briefly up at the dragon, then stepped determinedly into the arch.

Chapter Nine

A tiny point of bright light appeared in the center of his vision. At the very instant it appeared, it rushed at him, growing rapidly in size, until half a heartbeat later it was on him, over him, all around him, turning his world into white nothing. Another half heartbeat and the white turned dull gray.

Jake felt an odd sense of falling forward, though nothing in his surroundings, if it could be called surroundings, gave any indication of movement. He involuntarily held his hands out in front of him, and was taken aback when he realized that he had no hands, no arms, no body. He had the peculiar sensation of sucking in a panicked breath though he had no mouth, no chest, no lungs, and there was no air.

Two virtual heartbeats later, Jake saw another tiny point of bright light appear in the center of his virtual vision. As before, it rushed at him, pressed against him, pushed at him and over him. This gray in-between place turned white. Immediately after, there was a sudden explosion of color and Jake stumbled forward into a different world.

The sky overhead was clear blue, brushed with only a few wispy clouds floating high overhead. The sun looked liked the sun back home, felt warm on the face, felt comforting and reassuring. He could breathe the air, though it smelled a little different. It had a faint metallic taste.

Directly ahead was the main street of a small town—strangely still and quiet. He turned and looked behind him. A stone archway like the one he had just stepped through stood stoic and silent in the middle of an open field. As he watched, it shimmered and faded, the colors of the stone began to coalesce.

In place of the rustic archway stood a four-sided stone pylon, slate gray and smooth as glass.

Jake's gateway home was gone.

That... could be a problem, he thought, but then noticed a small design recessed in the center of one face of the pylon. Looking closely, he saw that it was the same polygon design as he had seen on the key for this gate; the same as one of the shapes used in the design of the complete artifact image.

He was pretty sure then that if he found the artifact piece, it would fit.

He turned about again, a bit more reassured, and started forward toward the town. He had no choice now. He had to find the artifact in order to get home.

Coming into the town, he saw that many of the buildings were boarded up, giving no indication of what may lay within. There was no movement but for a single curtain drawn out of an upper-floor window, left open and unboarded, fluttering in the light breeze.

There was a sharp bend in the main street where the road jogged right, and just around the corner Jake saw one lone automobile parked on the street. It was a four-door sedan, but not of any make or model that Jake had ever seen. It was boxy and nondescript, so dusty that he couldn't see in through the windows. The tires were low and the car now rested on the rims.

The entire town appeared empty... abandoned.

Directly ahead was a restaurant, fronted by two large windows with faded curtains drawn; not very inviting. To the left, the main street turned again and continued on for a good distance. Jake decided to walk around a bit and get the lay of the land before going into any of the buildings. He crossed the street and followed the road left, striding down the center of the thoroughfare.

Not far ahead was a side street. He could see a general store midway on the left. He made a mental note; there might be some supplies there. Continuing down main street, he passed more cross streets, a newspaper office, and a small hospital (more of a clinic, really). The road continued to wind around and he passed the city hall, and then a church.

Finally, the main street turned sharply and sharply again, and abruptly ended in a cul-de-sac. Turning about slowly in the center of the dead end, Jake found himself looking at an old wooden house. Small, narrow, single-storey, it appeared out of place in a commercial setting, however small-town this community might be.

Gotta' start someplace, he thought, and walked toward the home. He knocked on the front door and waited. When no one answered, he opened the unlocked door and entered the living room. There was a couch, a chair, and a couple of end tables. Dull light shone in through the window. A picture hanging above the couch depicted a dilapidated barn in a wilderness setting, with tall trees shadowing a swayback roof.

In the dining room was a wooden table with six chairs. Dust had collected on the smooth tabletop.

The appliances in the kitchen were fifty or sixty years out of date. The refrigerator, stove, toaster, all looked right out of the mid-twentieth century. Even the overhead light globe and small chrome-trim breakfast table looked late-fifties era. Jake reached over and opened the refrigerator—and found it empty. In the cupboards he found one can of carrots. He noticed the words on the label were in English.

Jake hated carrots, and put the can back on the shelf.

Leaving the kitchen, he turned into the narrow hall. There were four doors: two on the left, two on the right. The first one on the right was the bathroom. As with the kitchen, everything looked like it came out of an old nineteen fifties movie. The tub had claw feet and a shower curtain hung from a metal ring frame. The toilet tank was set high on the wall, with a long pull chain. Jake gave it a yank and was a bit surprised to find that it worked.

The other doors in the hall led to the bedrooms. Two had full-size beds, one had a twin. All had old-style furniture. The closets still contained clothes, different in style to anything Jake had seen before, but not too bizarre.

There was a small writing table beneath a curtained window in one of the bedrooms. In the drawer, beside a pad of paper and pencils, Jake found an old revolver. There were three bullets in the spindle. He decided to take this with him, and put it into his pack.

Across the street from the house was a small schoolhouse. Just as with the house, the front door was unlocked. Jake stepped into the main foyer and looked around. A bulletin board on the wall displayed several notices behind a glass face. One stated that all five classes were going to dismiss early on Friday so that the teachers could conference.

The notice was dated *May 12, 1959.*

Was time different here than it was back home?

Or... had the town been abandoned for half a century?

He reread the notice. *Five classes?*

To the right, just beyond the bulletin board, was the door to the front office. Just beyond this and straight ahead, the foyer opened to the main hall. Glancing into the hall and looking left, he saw a number of doors, each inset with fogged glass windows.

Jake turned back and went into the front office, deciding to check this out first. There were several desks behind a counter to right, and on the left an open door led to the principal's office. On the principal's desk was a daily desk calendar with Tuesday, May 12 sitting on top.

Did something happen on May 13?

He gave the room one last look before going back into the front office and on into the front foyer, then into the main hall. The linoleum floor had once been smooth and shiny but now was dull with a thin layer of dust. If he looked carefully enough, Jake could see the occasional tiny footprint of rodents.

Whatever had happened, at least something had survived.

The first door that Jake came to had a large black "1" stenciled in the center of the glass panel. Going into the classroom, he stood beside the teacher's desk and looked down the four rows of small student desks. Clearly this was a very early grade, probably first or second. The alphabet, displayed in a row high along one wall, reinforced his assumption. He was heartened to see all the familiar letters represented. With this and the other evidence he had found, it appeared to Jake that this world was very close to his own. If that were true, then any encounters he may have should be that much easier to deal with.

He walked down the center aisle to the back of the class. He had the eerie sensation that twenty ghostly young faces were looking up at him. The silence was like a loud ringing in his ears.

Running the length of the back wall was a waist-high set of shelves divided into twenty box-like compartments, each labeled with a student name. He noticed something odd in the spelling. There were a lot of w's and y's where there shouldn't be: Dwnn, Dowglys, Lwanne, Shywn.

Staring at the names, he recalled reading somewhere that there was an old dialect that used w and y as vowels. Welsh? He couldn't remember, but that sounded right, though these weren't Welsh names or spellings; he wondered, though, if there might be a Welsh influence. Was this alternate world somehow tied to Wales? That would be bizarre. Maybe this was a Welsh town in this alternate world.

What kind of a weird connection would that be?

He left the first classroom and stepped back into the hall. There was a water fountain directly across from him, and he went over to it and pushed down on the plunger. After a few seconds, water began gurgling out. He let it run for a full thirty seconds before bending over and taking a cautious sip.

He quickly decided to let it run a bit longer.

After another minute or so, he tried again. Not quite so bad this time; he assumed the lines had finally cleared and he was getting water from the source. He pulled his canteen free and opened it, took a deep swig, and then filled it from the fountain. This done, he continued his search of the classrooms.

The second class was much the same as the first, maybe a grade or two higher. He opened a few desks, looked in the teacher's desk, but nothing really caught his attention.

He found a slingshot in the teacher's desk of the third class, mixed in with other odds and ends that must have been confiscated from the students throughout the school year. A *wrist-rocket* if he remembered right, and he knew that it could do some serious harm to an enemy. It might come in handy if he ran out of bullets for the pistol.

The last two classrooms had full-size desks, but from the books and wall displays, Jake figured this school didn't go beyond sixth grade. Stepping into the student closet at the back of the last classroom in the hall, he found a closed umbrella leaning in the corner. It was tall, with a wooden handle and a metal tip. Jake picked it up on a whim and used it as a walking stick, stepped smartly out of the class and down the hall, tapping the tip on the linoleum.

Once again outside, he walked out into the cul-de-sac and began backtracking the way he had come. Reaching City Hall, he climbed the two steps and went inside.

On the wall behind the counter was a large sign that read: *Welcome to Rwndyll.*

"Rwndyll," said Jake. He tried several pronunciations, finally deciding to go with giving the 'w' a 'u' sound, right or wrong. He stepped around the counter and went into the back rooms. He found the office for the mayor, a conference room and a supply room. The supply room looked as though it had been ransacked; the shelves were bare but for a few empty boxes and some paper strewn about. He poked and pushed the litter about with the closed umbrella, then went back out to the main lobby. He had just gone into one of the side rooms off the lobby when he heard the front door open and the sound of footsteps.

Jake quickly pushed himself up against wall between the lobby and the office at the first sound, carefully pulled the pistol out of the side-pocket of his pack. The sound of muffled voices trailed away to the back rooms.

"He's here, I tell ya'," came as a harsh whisper. "I saw him."

Jake slid along the wall toward the door.

"And he had gear," said the same man.

"I saw it, too," said another. "New gear."

That doesn't sound hopeful, thought Jake. *I don't think I want to meet these guys.*

He peered through the open doorway. When he saw no one, he stepped out into the lobby and started hurriedly toward the front door.

"There he be," said someone, and then Jake heard the shuffling and scrambling of a dozen feet coming. He didn't turn to look behind him, but flung open the door and leapt over the steps of City Hall and down onto the street. He cut left and the left again, realizing too late that he was heading toward a dead end. Up ahead the road 'T'd. If he went left, he would be entering the cul-de-sac with the school. He would be trapped. Instead he cut right and was quickly confronted with a high stone wall. The road ended.

He noticed then a storm drain in the center of the road. The lid was a heavy metal lattice that allowed rain runoff to empty into it. Jake thought quickly, trying not to panic. He could hear loud voices and heavy footsteps. They were getting closer.

He knelt down and laced his fingers into the lattice and pulled.

It was stuck.

He thought of using the umbrella as a pry bar, but immediately dismissed that idea. It wasn't strong enough. He stood over the drain, one foot on either side. Reaching down, he pulled again, this time straight up. The lid lifted free and Jake hurriedly walked it forward and set it down. Without looking to see what he was getting into, he quickly scrambled down into the drain, reached out and pulled the lid over after him. He started down the narrow ladder, looking up only when he heard the thumping of rushing footsteps and loud, peculiarly jovial voices. Several faces were peering down at him through the grate.

"Hellooo there, rat."

Jake didn't respond. He continued down the ladder. Another half dozen rungs and he reached the bottom.

"Ya' not gonna' like it down there," the man taunted, to which the others laughed heartily. "You come on back up now, and you'z can walk away from this, pretty'z ya' please."

Okay... definitely not Welsh...

What little light that reached down from above showed Jake that the only direction open was south. He had to lower his head to step into the drain and moved forward in a crouch; he was immediately wrapped in darkness. He could hear the gang of marauders taunting him from above. *"Hey, come on back... hey, at least leave us the gear, dude..."*

Jake swung his pack around so that he could reach into it. Rummaging around, he found the hand lantern and pulled it out. It had a manual crank charger. He gave the handle six or seven good turns and flipped the large switch. The yellowish light didn't reach out too far, but it was enough to keep his panic at bay. He pulled the umbrella free of the pack's side strap and shifted his pack back into position. Holding the closed umbrella defensively out in front of him, he started forward again.

He hadn't gone more than a few yards when he came up on a junction; one line came in from the left, and the line he had been following continued straight ahead. He decided to continue forward.

The sounds of those on the street above slowly faded, and Jake finally found himself all alone. The world was only as large as the reach of the light from his lantern; not much more than five feet high (the height of the tunnel), and reaching not much more than six feet ahead. Each step he took pushed this tiny universe forward the same distance that it collapsed into darkness behind him. The only sounds were the echoing scrapings of his feet on the concrete floor, his own heavy breathing, and an eerie, hushed, wind-like white noise coming from the darkness ahead.

After a few minutes, Jake began to notice a very subtle change in these sounds. His footsteps, his breathing, even the white noise, all began taking on a deeper, more hollow timbre. Hardly noticeable at first, but with each step the shift in resonance become more distinct, more real.

And then Jake took a step and knew without a doubt that he had entered a chamber. The low ceiling overhead lifted away and he was able to stand up straight. The wall on his left continued ahead into the darkness, but the right wall was gone, was replaced with the deep black, a void that stretched away to some unseen ominous threat.

There was no telling how large the chamber might be.

There's something in here...

Jake was absolutely positive that he wasn't alone. He tried to quiet his breathing, to push away the white noise. The only sound left was the beating of his heart.

No—wait—there was something else...

Breathing...

How many? More than one... More than five...

There's something in here...

Jake took half a step back, uncertain as to what he should do. The beating of his heart grew louder, the pounding in his chest more powerful.

This must be what the marauders were talking about. *"Ya' not gonna' like it down there"*, they had said.

Well, I am definitely not liking it, he thought. *I am really, really not liking it.*

He continued to listen, studying the sounds, trying to sense changes, increasing threats.

Breathing... definitely breathing.

Should he go back? But did he want these things, whatever they were, coming up behind him in the tunnel?

Maybe he should face them here, whatever they were.

Jake cautiously inched back into the chamber. He held the lantern up with one hand, the closed umbrella with the other. He took another step, moved the lantern slowly from left to right, looking for some sign, looking for anything that wasn't floor. He kept close to the left wall, feeling some security at the presence of that solid slab of concrete close beside him.

Claws on floor...

Jake stopped. A very, very cold chill washed through him. He turned and pressed his back against the wall, jabbed the tip of the umbrella at the dark. He held the lantern up high. Nothing, nothing; there was nothing.

Claws on floor...

He could hear something moving out there in the dark. He waited, umbrella moving slowly left to right, right to left.

Shadows then, just outside the range of the lantern; dark grays in the black, shifting smoothly, gliding just beyond the light.

Flickers of bright white, shimmering sparkles, *reflections of the eyes...*

And then something stepped into the light.

It was just about knee-high, and looked like a gigantic rat.

No. Not a rat. A tiny dragon, but not a dragon.

What the...

Kind of a cross between a dragon and a rat...

A dragon rat? A rat dragon?

Jake felt a little woozy. He watched the thing squat down in the center of the circle of light provided by the lantern. It looked intently at Jake, pushed its two front legs out in front of it, each foot brandishing three dragon-like claws. Its skin had a brownish-green, serpent-like look to it. The nose had heavy nostrils, and two horns swept back from its head.

Dragon, and yet it had a very distinctive rat-look about it.

A second rat dragon came up beside the first, slowly squatted down beside its companion, never taking its shimmering eyes off Jake. A moment later a third came up on the other side of the first and sat back on its haunches. As it stared at Jake, it casually scratched its belly with one long, curved claw.

The shifting shadows behind them meant there were more out there.

"Hey," Jake said nervously. The first rat dragon cocked its head sideways, but otherwise there was no response. The one sitting up raised its scratching claw and studied it, as if it expected to find something, and then rested its paw on its round belly.

Jake took a slow, easy step to his left, attempting to continue his progress south. The three watched him, but made no overt moves. Encouraged then, Jake took another step and then another.

And bumped into the corner of the chamber.

If there was another way out of the chamber, it was on the other side of the room, through these three creatures and however many more waited in the dark.

"This is a dead end, isn't it?" Jake asked rhetorically. *This chamber has one way in and one way out.*

The middle rat dragon cocked its head again. The scratching rat dragon reached around behind with its scratching claw; Jake didn't want to think about where the claw was going or what it was scratching.

Jake started moving back the way he had come, keeping his back pressed firmly against the wall and his closed umbrella between himself and the creatures. He was within a few slide-steps of the exit out of the chamber when he saw a quickly shifting shadow move into his path. He stopped and warily moved the lantern to his right. He took another cautious step, and the circle of light pushed up and over a fourth rat dragon that was sitting up tall and staring him down.

Jake glanced back at the others. The one in the center had a curl to its lip and a sparkle in its eyes that gave Jake the unsettling impression that it was amused by the situation.

"Now, I just want to get out of here," said Jake, his voice quivering slightly. "No trouble, now."

The rat dragons didn't look as though they were inclined to step aside. Jake continued pointing his umbrella from one to the other. It didn't look particularly frightening or dangerous.

Jake had a thought. "Quigley," he said sharply. "My name is Quigley." He nodded jerkily. "Tobias was my uncle. Tobias. Uncle. Uh… blood! Him and me. Me and Tobias Quigley."

He really did half expect these ugly little creatures to move aside at the mention of the name. They, however, did not appear to be the least bit impressed.

Jake suddenly, and quite accidentally, pressed the button on the shaft of the umbrella and it quickly opened with a loud *whump*. The three rat dragons jumped backwards into the dark. The fourth creature, stationed at the exit to the chamber, scurried backwards into the tunnel. Jake, seeing his one and only opportunity, turned and ran towards the startled dragon, pushing the opened umbrella at it as he went. After a few steps he found himself falling, stumbling, jostling over the rat dragon. He, the rat dragon, the umbrella, the lantern, all enmeshed in a scrambling, flailing jumble. Jake frantically pushed himself forward, wanting only to get past the creature and escape down the tunnel. The rat dragon, for its part, was desperately thrashing about defensively, not sure what had happened or what was going on.

After several seconds of blind struggling, Jake found himself on his hands and knees with only concrete beneath him. He stumbled hurriedly to his feet and ran. He didn't know if the rat dragon, if any of the rat dragons, were following, and wasn't about to slow down to find out. The sphere of light created by his lantern bounced into and out of existence as his whirling arms sent the lantern behind him with each swinging stroke.

He almost missed the junction that he had passed earlier. Sliding to a stop, he quickly turned into the side tunnel and continued running. It wasn't until he had gone a hundred yards or so that he slowed down enough that he could take the time to listen out for anything that might be following him. Slowing his step, slowing his breathing, he tried to stretch his hearing out behind him, tried to pick up the sounds of claws on concrete.

For the moment, it seemed, he was alone.

He passed another junction, another line going south, decided to continue east just a bit further. Another few minutes, and the line that he was traveling turned sharply south. He was now paralleling the line that he had passed before.

Smaller drain lines, set into the walls about chest high, emptied into the tunnels every 30 or 40 yards. Jake could feel cool air coming in through these lines from the streets above, and was thankful for it. Without it, the air in the tunnels would quickly grow stagnate and stifling. As it was, he was feeling very claustrophobic, especially knowing there were things down here, in the dark, perhaps just beyond the range of his lantern.

The tunnel Jake was following made another sharp turn, this one back to the west. At the next junction, he took the south route. He wondered if he would be able to find his way out, should he have to return the way he came. With that in mind, he stopped long enough to map out in his mind the path he had taken, returning to the junction that, left would take him to the rat dragon nest, right would take him to the ladder leading up to the street.

He went on then, choosing routes that kept him going south whenever possible, choosing east if he felt he had traveled a considerable distance west, and west if he felt he had traveled too far to the east.

He estimated that he had traversed most of the distance back through under the town, and was now somewhere near the southern city limits, when he came into another chamber. By the deep echoes of his footsteps, Jake was pretty certain this room was larger than the last chamber he had been in.

"Oh, man..." he whispered. The sound of his hushed voice rolled away from him and rolled back, making him shiver. He listened, anticipating that creepy sound of dragon claws scraping across the floor, holding the lantern out as far he could reach. There was only darkness and the sound of his own breathing.

He stepped cautiously into the chamber, following the wall but always looking into the black void in the center of the room. After a few steps, he stopped.

Is something there?

There seemed to be a dark mass just beyond the sphere of light created by his lantern. He leaned forward, towards the center of the room. The mass took a more distinct form, but was still beyond the range of the lantern.

Straight lines, straight edges; not a creature.

Jake stepped away from the wall and slide-stepped into the center of the room.

It was a staircase of some kind. A concrete staircase set into the center of the chamber. He held the lantern up high and looked upward, up to where the stairs led. He could see nothing.

Taking a nervous breath, Jake held his umbrella out in front of him, pointing it up the staircase. Only then did he notice that the thin metal framework of the umbrella was bent and broken, the cloth canopy ripped to shreds, and the staff bent at a 30 degree angle. It had taken quite a beating back during his tumble with the rat dragon.

He tried to close the umbrella and shape it into some semblance of a stabbing weapon, and took the first step up the stairs. He was climbing into darkness.

After seven steps the open staircase transformed into an enclosed stairwell. Continuing upward, he knew that by now he had to be above ground and must be inside one of the buildings that he had passed when he first walked through the streets of town. Another dozen steps and he was standing on a small landing, enclosed on either side by concrete walls. Straight ahead was a large, heavy wooden door.

Jake tucked the umbrella under his arm and pushed down on the latch. Pushing the door open an inch, daylight streamed in. Peaking through the narrow opening, he saw blue sky above and beyond, and a wooden railing two steps beyond the door.

He turned off the flashlight and tucked it into an outside pocket of his backpack. He found the pistol, and with weapon in one hand, the umbrella in the other, he pushed the door fully open and stepped outside.

He found himself on a raised walkway, four feet across, with a wall behind him and a waist-high deck rail in front of him. From here he could see most of the town laid out in front of him. He could see the streets that he had taken traveling north, and he thought he recognized which rooftop belonged to city hall, and which belonged to the school.

Stepping to the rail, he looked down on an enclosed courtyard. It was a twenty-foot drop to dirt and weeds and stone. Looking off to his left, he saw a steep, narrow staircase leading from the walkway down to the ground. In the center of the courtyard, twenty yards or more from the staircase, stood a stone pedestal. Sitting atop the pedestal was a small box.

Jake slowly walked along the catwalk, towards the staircase, continuing to study the pedestal. As he reached the top of the stairs, he noticed a large, open archway set into the opposite wall. The wall was a good sixteen feet high, and the opening reached almost to the top. Jake could see eight or ten feet into the room beyond the archway; nothing moved.

There's probably something really, really bad in there.

He glanced again at the pedestal, at the box sitting on the pedestal.

That's it, he thought. *What else would it be? Where else would it be?*

Jake started down the narrow, rickety staircase, watching the opening in the wall on the other side of the courtyard. Reaching the bottom of the stairs, he started cautiously toward the pedestal. The enclosed area had a strange smell. *Fire and brimstone,* Jake mumbled to himself.

He was halfway to the pedestal when he heard the sound: the loud *whump* of large, beating, leathery wings. He looked up into the sky and saw a dragon pass overhead, swing around and come to rest on the top of the wall. It was a massive creature, with a large, broad chest and horned head. It gripped the lip of the wall with huge, deadly-looking claws.

It looked down at the puny human standing in the middle of its yard. After several seconds, during which it sized up the situation, it spread its wings, pushed off the wall and dropped down to the ground a dozen yards from Jake. It folded its wings, shifted its feet and turned its head slightly to better study the intruder.

Jake, the *intruder*, took one step back and waited. The dragon shook its head jerkily from side to side and took two dragon-sized steps forward. Jake stumbled backward and almost fell.

"No fear," said the dragon. "Blood."

Jake could barely speak. "Quigley. Yes."

"Blood," the dragon repeated. "Not me to fear here. Not *Rhetani* fear here."

Jake nodded, regained his footing and tried to stand straight.

The dragon cocked its head. It sniffed the air. "Tobias?" it asked. "Blood."

"Blood," Jake placed a hand on his chest. "Blood. Tobias. Uncle. Tobias, my blood."

"Blood," the dragon stated flatly.

"Yes," said Jake.

The dragon took another step forward. "*Hu*-man to fear here."

"Yes," said Jake. The dragon had to be talking about the marauders. "The bad humans."

The dragon snorted, as if thinking about the marauders left an unpleasant taste. "Bad," the dragon repeated back.

"And those little ones," said Jake. "Like you."

The dragon looked at him curiously, clearly trying to understand the human's words. It suddenly rolled its head back and let out a deep, bellowing howl. Jake fell backward, terrified, dropping to the ground and scrambling. The dragon continued howling, and Jake tried to aim the pistol and continue scooting away from the giant beast all at the same time. It took him a handful of seconds to realize that the dragon was laughing.

When the dragon finally looked down again at Jake, it tried to reassure the foolish human. "Chenling," it said. "Chenling. No fear chenling."

"Chenling," said Jake, as if he understood what the word meant and that knowing this would somehow make everything all right.

The dragon clearly saw through this and grew very thoughtful. After a few moments, it gave a slight snort. "Pets," it said.

"Pets?" Jake blurted.

The dragon gave him a studied look, trying to understand what the human's peculiar response might mean. Had it used the wrong word? No. It remembered quite clearly. Tobias Quigley had called them *pets*. They were pets. It leaned closer to the human of Tobias' blood. "Pets," it stated again.

Okay, thought Jake.

"No fear," said the dragon.

"I won't."

The dragon straightened up, leaned back and again grew thoughtful. "*Hu*-mans-bad hurt chenling."

"They're a nasty bunch, all right."

The dragon turned its head slowly to look over at the box on the pedestal. It let out a long, slow breath. The air in the courtyard grew warm and there was a strong, metallic smell; the same smell that Jake had noticed when he had first entered this Other World. The dragon looked sad. "Time take box?" it asked. Its voice was low and coarse.

"I think so," said Jake. *What did the dragon know about this?* He decided not to ask. The blood of Tobias Quigley should already know what it was all about.

"Take box," said the dragon. It turned then and walked in the direction of the archway. "Fear *hu*-mans-bad."

"I'll be careful," said Jake. He watched as the great dragon disappeared into its lair. Once he was alone again in the courtyard, he put away his pistol and walked over to the pedestal. The box was made of a dark wood and the lid lifted easily. The artifact piece was inside. It had the look of a small stone tablet, but was made of some metal or plastic unknown to Jake. It was smooth on front and back, cool to the touch. It was light, but he could tell that it was made to last. It was shaped like the image that he had seen on the pylon, and on the pedestal of the serpent statue in which he had found the scroll, and on the key that he had used to open the compartment. It was one piece of the full artifact that he had seen drawn in his uncle's notebook.

Jake pulled his backpack around and put the artifact inside.

Time to go home...

He looked around the courtyard. The only way out was back the way he had come. He went to the stairs and climbed them up to the catwalk. After walking up and down the walkway and deciding there was no safe way down, he returned to the door that would take him back into the storm drains. Before going in, though, he turned and looked back across the rooftops of the abandoned city. He found once again the likely location where he had first entered the drains. It was a long way back, and if he didn't find another way up, that's where he was going to have to go. He wondered if the band of marauders was still lurking nearby. Probably not; they no doubt figured the rat dragons had gotten him.

Assuming he made it all the way back, and assuming the marauders were gone, he would then have to travel the streets all the way back this way again.

Oh, man...

He opened the door and stepped back into the darkness.

Backtracking through the drains was easier than he thought, but it still took time. Along the way, he found several ladders leading up to grated drain lids, but discovered that none of them could be opened. He supposed this was intentional. One way in, one way out, with the only other access to the surface being the dragon's courtyard.

He made a few wrong turns, circled back around on his path a few times, backtracked several times, but eventually reached the original storm drain access that had brought him down. He climbed the ladder and listened for any activity on the street. When he heard none, Jake carefully lifted the lid and climbed back up onto the street.

The sky was already starting to gray, and if this world was anything like his world, that meant the sun was going down. Dusk was coming. He didn't want to get stuck here overnight. Besides, if he was gone too long, he knew that Meara would either try to come in after him or hurry back to Serpent's Keep for help. Either way, she would be putting her life in danger. Jake had to get back to the clearing.

If he had more time, he would have liked to go into the small hospital. He had to suppose the place had been ransacked more than once over the years, but he may have been able to find a few supplies that had somehow been missed by others. He resisted the urge and continued cautiously but rapidly through the streets of the abandoned city.

He had just passed the newspaper office when he heard voices coming from down one of the side streets. Quickly stepping back, Jake slipped into the front lobby of the small-town newspaper.

The main room had the front pages of editions from years past framed and set behind glass on the walls. Jake noticed that these too were in a dialect of English, if not his English. He glanced out the small front window for signs of danger before going behind the counter.

There were a few things tossed about, indicating that vandals had been through the place, but they hadn't really done too much damage. There were papers scattered about, cans tipped over; an old phone sat undisturbed on a desk. He couldn't help but pick it up and listen: no dial tone.

He found an old style printing press in the center of one of the back rooms. Beside it sat racks of type. Interesting, but he really had to get moving. He was about to step out of the room when he noticed there was paper still in the press.

Were they printing the latest edition when whatever happened, happened?

Jake leaned in over the page and read the article headings of what looked to be the front page.

The main headline stated "Mayoral Debate Tonight".

Nothing ominous there...

Other headings were just as ordinary. There was an article about city elections, a small blurb about conserving water, and one of their sports teams was doing very well this year.

The date of the unfinished edition was Wednesday, May 13, 1959.

The principal's calendar at the school: May 12, 1959.

What happened on the thirteenth?

Jake went back out to the front of the office and glanced out the window. The street appeared empty. He opened the door a few inches and listened. It was quiet. Before stepping outside, though, Jake decided to arm himself. He pulled out the pistol and made sure one of the three bullets was next in the spindle.

He wasn't taking any chances. He had the artifact piece, the way out of town was a few minutes away, and the gateway was a few minutes beyond that. He wasn't going to let a gang of thugs keep him from getting home. Not just for himself; this quest that Tobias Quigley had set him on was important.

He had to get home.

Jake had made it another couple of blocks when he again heard the sounds of men bantering amongst themselves, joking and laughing. This time, the voices came from behind him, and Jake quickly turned down the next side street and ran into the general store. He hurried past the one checkout counter and down an aisle of empty shelves. Reaching the back of the store, he turned and knelt on one knee, facing the front door of the store, pistol held ready.

Seconds passed. He could hear the voices growing louder as the group came nearer. From their tones, it didn't sound as though they suspected he was nearby. They were simply passing by.

When it was quiet again outside, Jake stood and returned to the front of the store. A bulletin board on the right wall had several notices pinned to it. There was a call to attend the Mayoral Debate for Tuesday evening.

Someone was giving away their beloved parakeet, including cage.

A stack of newspapers was on the wooden check out counter beside the old cash register. They were dated Tuesday, May 12th, 1959.

Jake didn't take the time to look through the rest of the general store. He didn't think there'd be much left, and he was within reach of the town's southern boundary. He slipped quietly out the door, turned right and hurried back to the main street. Within minutes, he was out of the city.

The pylon containing the gateway was still there, waiting to reveal its secret to one with the knowledge. Jake was certain he had that knowledge. He took the artifact from his pack and placed it into position in the pylon. It fit perfectly.

Nothing happened.

Jake removed the artifact and stepped back. *What am I missing?*

"I really need for you to open up," he said, growing concerned now.

Nothing.

Jake raised a hand to lay it on the pylon. He thought maybe it would recognize who he was. But instead of feeling the smooth, cool surface, his hand disappeared into the pylon. Startled, Jake quickly pulled back. He rubbed his fingers together and made sure that everything had come back intact. He smiled, then.

Some sort of *hologram* was hiding the stone archway—his gateway home.

A hologram that looked just like the original pylon... He knew that it had been a solid form earlier. He had laid a hand on it when it had changed from the stone archway to the pylon.

And it had been solid just a minute ago when he had placed the artifact into it.

So the artifact had opened the gate, as he had thought it would... it just didn't look any different.

Jake felt a sudden rush of anxiety—He had opened it... It was open... *right now* it was open. How long would it *stay* open?

He hurriedly tucked the artifact into his pack, raised his hands out in front of him and stepped into the pylon.

As before, he found himself in the in-between place. This time, he knew what to expect, and he watched for it. He saw the white speck of light appear, rush at him, and turn the world into white for a brief moment; he watched existence shift to dull gray. Again he had the sense of falling forward. Again he saw another tiny point of bright light appear far in the distance, though distance was not the right word, and watched as it hurtled across the gray plane towards him, push at him, press against him, and then rush over him.

Again there was an explosion of color and Jake stumbled into the clearing at the mouth of the ravine in the Outland.

There was Meara, waiting for him.

No... She wasn't waiting for him.

The wolves were in the clearing, and Jake had arrived in the midst of some sort of confrontation. The wolves looked startled, surprised at Jake's sudden appearance. Meara took the opportunity to strike at the nearest wolf. She swung a five-foot staff as if taking the ball out of the ballpark. Jake heard bone break and watched the large animal lift off the ground, its limp body flung to the edge of the clearing.

"What's going on?" Jake asked stupidly.

"Welcome back, sir. Good to see you."

The remaining three wolves shifted position to better defend against this new situation. They were very careful to maintain a safe distance from Meara's weapon, and were still trying to evaluate the threat that Jake might pose.

Jake regained composure and quickly swung his pack around and dropped it to the ground, pulling the pistol free from the side pocket. Seeing this, the nearest wolf leapt at him, somehow knowing it was now-or-never. Jake stumbled back, fired once and missed. As he fell to the ground, he fired again, striking the wolf in the neck. Injured but still alive, the wolf was on him, clawing at Jake's belly, swinging its massive head up to his throat. Jake shoved the pistol up to the animal's head and fired again.

The last bullet...

This time the wolf went lifeless, its body lying heavy on top of him. Jake struggled to push it off. As he did, he saw that Meara had moved nearer to him and turned to defend him against the two remaining wolves.

One of them looked an awful lot like the pack leader they had faced days earlier.

Meara thrust the staff toward the lead wolf, keeping it and its companion at bay. The two stayed just beyond the reach of the weapon, continually watching for an opportunity, studying and reevaluating, knowing that sooner or later Meara would make a mistake.

Jake rolled up onto his side and attempted to sit up. He froze then, suddenly, hearing the sound of snapping brush and breaking tree branches.

Something was coming out of the mouth of the ravine.

Oh, great...

The dragon pushed its way between two trees and came roaring into the clearing. With two quick strides it was on the wolves. The lead wolf jumped aside, but the other wasn't fast enough. The dragon dropped its clawed foot down on the animal and held it. The wolf struggled to free itself, digging frantically with its front paws, but it wasn't going anywhere. Ignoring its efforts, the dragon turned its attention to the other wolf.

The leader of the wolves had moved to the far edge of the clearing, where it stopped and now watched and waited. It clearly wanted to get back into the fight, to win whatever prize it had come for, and was displeased at this turn of events.

It knew that it had lost, and didn't like it one bit.

It gave its companion a final glance and looked up into the eyes of the dragon that held it prisoner. Knowing that it could do nothing to save the other wolf, it growled angrily at Meara and Jake, then turned and disappeared into the surrounding woods.

The dragon turned and looked down at Jake, gave him a studied, knowing gaze. Jake nodded, as if to say *yes, I have it...*The dragon then curled its claws around the wolf, gripping it so that the helpless animal couldn't move. The dragon opened out one great wing, stretching it its full length, then stretched out the other wing. It gave two heavy beats of these massive wings, pushed off with its powerful rear legs, and leapt into the sky. It circled high overhead and turned into the darkness of the ravine, carrying the wolf with it.

"Master Jacob!" Meara ran to Jake and dropped to her knees. She grasped his arm and held him up.

"I'm okay," said Jake.

"No, sir," said Meara. She saw that his shirt was torn at his left side, and the fabric was blood-soaked. "I don't think you're okay at all."

She carefully pulled the shirt away from the wound and studied the injury with a trained eye. She gave a *hmmph* sound and stood up, hurried over to her gear and returned with a small cloth bag. Using a damp cloth, she cleaned the wound, then took out a small tin and pulled off the lid.

"What's that?" asked Jake.

Meara sprinkled green powder onto a cloth bandage and carefully applied it to the wound. "A mix of this and that; something my father always kept on hand." She began wrapping the bandage ties around Jake's torso.

"Some sort of family secret?"

"Not really," Meara sat back on her heels and studied her work. "You just have to know where to shop."

"So I keep hearing. I'll have to bring you along come next shopping day."

Meara smiled, but she still had a look of concern on her face.

Jake looked at the dead wolves scattered about the clearing. "I thought you had an agreement."

"As did I. Something's got 'em stirred up."

Jake started to stand, then thought better of it. Sharp burning pain streaked out from his injury in all directions.

"I think we'll be safe enough here," Meara urged. She nodded in the direction of the ravine. "He'll watch over us."

"Maybe you're right," Jake nodded. "It'll be dark soon. May not be all that safe out there at night."

"We can get an early start in the morning," Meara agreed.

"Exactly," said Jake. "A good night's sleep under the watchful eye of our friend would do us both good."

Chapter Ten

The artifact lay in the center of the desktop. Jake sat in the chair, elbows on the desk, chin in his hands, staring at it. He heard Mr. Griffin come into the Command Center, but tried to ignore him. The man had been glowering at him ever since he had returned from the Abandoned City.

Mr. Griffin stepped from the Hall of Statues and strode smoothly across the room. He stood stiffly beside the desk.

"Master Quigley," he said, quite formally.

"Hmmm," said Jake, continuing to stare at the object on the desk.

"You should be resting."

"I am resting," Jake said absently. He finally lifted his head from his hands and pointed at the artifact. "One of these things for each one of those statues."

"Yes, sir. Please, sir."

"I wonder what the other worlds are like."

"You should return to bed," Mr. Griffin stated firmly. "You must give yourself time to recover from your injuries."

"I'm fine."

"I do not believe so, sir." Mr. Griffin put on his most stern look. Jake had returned from the Outland three days earlier, a difficult journey by Meara's accounting, and Mr. Griffin had been trying, without much success, to keep the young man in his room and at rest.

Jake nodded inattentively. He leaned back in the chair, still studying the artifact. "I'll be better prepared the next time," he said, almost to himself.

Mr. Griffin allowed himself a few more moments of proper consternation, then relaxed his severe expression and let his gaze move to the artifact on the desk. While he hadn't been in the least surprised that the rash Master Quigley had returned to the village injured and near death, he had been quite astonished to find that that the young man had returned with artifact in hand.

"You did very well, sir," he said.

"Thank you, Mr. Griffin." He let out a heavy sigh. "Does May 12 or 13 mean anything to you? Nineteen fifty-nine?"

Mr. Griffin thought a moment, shook his head. "Should it, sir?"

"That's when whatever happened to that town, happened."

"But, does their calendar follow ours?"

"I don't know. But there are so many things similar between that world and ours. What if it's our world in a parallel universe? What if most things are the same, and there's just a few things different?"

"Dragons, sir?" Mr. Griffin said doubtfully.

"Ah, but there's a dragon in our world, Mr. Griffin. Probably a bunch of 'em, in that ravine."

"Perhaps they originated in that Other World."

"Or yet another," said Jake, pointing a finger at the elderly gentleman. "We're talking not just dragons, but *talking* dragons. Now, what if there's a planet somewhere where dragon-like creatures have evolved to intelligence? What if Uncle Tobias found this planet? And what if he made friends with them?"

"From what you have said of your encounters with the creatures, they do consider Master Quigley an ally."

"Brothers in Arms against these *Rhetani* that we keep hearing about." Jake looked again at the artifact resting on the desk. "A dragon watching the gateway. Another watching over this artifact."

"You may encounter others."

Jake leaned forward and picked up the artifact. "Those dragons looked like the one in the hall over there. The very statue that held the scroll."

"Coincidence is unlikely," said Mr. Griffin.

"Exactly my thought," said Jake. "So let us pursue our hypothesis, dear sir. Let us see what we find in dragon Number Two."

"Sir?"

Jake stood up. "Let's do it." He took the artifact piece into the supply room and returned with the set of keys. He removed the one he had already used and tossed the set to Mr. Griffin.

"Pick a key, Mr. Griffin. Any key."

"I'm not sure that—"

"Just pick one."

Mr. Griffin cautiously studied the keys, an anxious look on his face. He finally held one key delicately between two fingers.

"An excellent choice," said Jake. He grabbed at the key ring, keeping the selected key separate from the others. "Let's see just what that choice be." He led the way to the Hall of Statues. Turning into the hall, he looked at the polygon shape on the key and slowly walked past each statue. He stopped finally at the lizard-like creature. He warily eyed the monster.

"Aren't you an ugly thing?" He walked around the pedestal, guessing the hidden compartment would be in the same location as the last. He found the likely spot on the base of the pedestal and tried to insert the key into several different shadowed crevices in the surface design. On the third try, the key slipped in. Jake gave a satisfied grunt and turned the key. As before, a solid click sound came from apparatus hidden within the pedestal and a small lid popped open. Jake reached in a pulled out a leather scroll.

Back in the Command Center, Jake unrolled the ancient document and laid it across the desk.

Shaded eyes to setting sun, a pillar leads to seas of sand. Dark and light will take you in, seek then life of green and blue.

"That seems straightforward enough," he said.

"A desert," said Mr. Griffin. "To the west."

"Life of green and blue. An Oasis."

"There is no desert anywhere near here, Master Jacob. To the west or anywhere else."

"Stay with me now, Griff. None of these Other Worlds are going to be near here. Not as the crow flies."

"Right you are, sir," Mr. Griffin said quickly, embarrassed.

"What I'm going to find to the west is a pillar that hides the gateway to this world of *seas of sand*."

"The west is a very big place," said Mr. Griffin.

Jake plopped himself down into the chair. "Take the paths less traveled, I suppose; like the last time."

"That would narrow the search down a bit. The West Outland has several populated locations."

Jake thought about that. The last time anyone had seen Tobias had been at the temple. Had his uncle gone from the temple to this second Other World? Was this where he had disappeared?

He may yet find out what happened to his uncle.

He opened the desk drawer and brought out the handwritten map that he had taken with him on the trip to the Abandoned City gateway. There were numerous scribbles and lines on it, work done while walking the northern trails of the Outland, or sitting on a fallen log, or huddled beside a small campfire. He planned to transfer his notes to a more permanent document later, but for now he wanted to distinguish between the original map and what his observations were.

What if what was left off the map was a clue? Could there be a similar relationship in the West Outland? Mr. Griffin was skeptical, but he was willing to consider the possibility. He was learning that young Jacob Quigley had a bit of Master Tobias Quigley in him. He would do his best not to underestimate him again.

Jake waited another day before making a trip to the marketplace, giving his wounds a little more time to heal and himself time to regain some strength. He went on his own midmorning, wandering casually from booth to booth, purchasing an item now and then, some of which he planned to take on his next journey out, some he would store in the supply room for later trips.

In particular on this trip he sought clothing that would hold up well in a desert climate and fend off the sun and heat. He found a hat and boots that would do him better than what he had, and shirt and pants that would breathe as well.

He also found a water bag with a shoulder strap to supplement his belt canteen. He wondered why Tobias didn't have something like this in the supply room, and then it occurred to him that maybe he had them with him when he went missing.

Yet another indication that he might be on his uncle's trail.

Jake felt a tap on his shoulder and turned to find Meara smiling up at him.

"Good morning, Master Jacob."

"Good morning, Miss Gyles. What brings you to the marketplace?"

"I heard that you were here, and I remembered your suggestion that I join you on your next shopping trip."

Jake held up his packages. "I'm not doing too bad," he said.

Meara glanced at what Jake held in his arms and nodded. "I see."

"A rousing endorsement if ever I heard one."

Meara continued studying Jake's purchases, and from these she thought she had a good idea as to what Master Jacob suspected things might be like on his next trip. He could see in her expression that she was already making plans that included her. She said nothing of this, however. Instead, she looked casually about them and said softly, "I think you should come with me, sir." She started across the square without waiting. Jake had little choice but to follow.

She led him to a narrow passage between two booths set into one corner of the market square. The owners of both booths gave him hard, wary looks as he passed through. Meara didn't seem to notice or care, and held a thin, wooden door open for him. Jake stepped through and down into a short, dead-end alley that ran behind the row of booths.

Shut away from the marketplace, Meara pulled on a rope hanging on one wall and released it. Nothing happened.

"It should be just a moment," she said.

Jake nodded and took the time to look around. The alley was about eight feet wide and ran twenty feet from the steps he had taken to a brick wall at the far end. The walls on either side were made of wood panels of various sizes, shapes and colors. It all looked haphazard.

He was about to ask what they were waiting for when he heard movement and scraping noises coming from behind one of the panels. It shifted suddenly and then noisily slid aside. Jake saw a woman's hand gripping the side of the wood panel and pushing it open.

And then Mrs. Hodges stepped back into view.

"Ah," she said heartily, covering whatever surprise she might have felt. "Young Master Jacob."

Behind her was a windowless room cluttered with low tables and counters, all lit by several flickering gas lamps. The back wall was lined with shelves of ceramic jars. On a narrow side wall were hung cut vines and branches.

"Mrs. H?" Jake looked dumbfounded.

Mrs. Hodges looked over at Meara. "What is it you're bringing the Master here for, girl?"

"He'll be going out again, Ma'am. He'll be needing your sun cream and your special healing salve."

"Mrs. Hodges, what are you doing here?" asked Jacob.

"She's the village herbalist," said Meara. Mrs. Hodges had already turned around and was walking toward the shelves of ceramic jars.

"Her shop is hidden away in a secret alley, Meara."

Mrs. Hodges set the jar down on a round table in the center of the room. "Some of my methods... and ingredients... well, they are not entirely accepted by the more *conventional* of our citizens."

"Are you like a witch doctor or something?"

Mrs. Hodges laughed lightly. "Not exactly, young Master," she said, continuing about her work. "But I guess there are similarities."

"Well, what then?" Jake was having trouble believing that he had never seen this side of her. "Have you always... I mean, when I used to come here in the summer?"

"And my mother before me," she said, nodding sagely.

"I sometimes think she's a witch," Meara said, mocking a conspiratorial tone.

"Fine, fine, missy," Mrs. Hodges sighed. "Oh, I suppose I have more in common with witches than with herbalists."

"But... how come I never... did Uncle Tobias know?"

"Of course the Master knew." Mrs. Hodges had measured a small amount of something yellow into a bowl and was returning the ceramic jar to the shelf.

"Master Quigley often got supplies from Mrs. Hodges," said Meara.

"I am tolerated because I don't offer my services out where people are forced to acknowledge them. Most folks I get along with well enough because most folks don't come face to face with it." She set another jar on the counter. "Most folks convince themselves I'm nothing more than Master Quigley's cook and housekeeper."

Jake watched Mrs. Hodges as she calmly prepared the mixtures, looking much like she did when working in the kitchen back in the mansion. Meara talked with her, asking her normal, everyday questions as if all this was absolutely normal, everyday activity.

But they were in a hidden alleyway, and Mrs. Hodges was some sort of druid-like medicine woman.

Okay, exactly the kind of person Uncle Tobias would associate with...

Mrs. Hodges finished her mixtures and placed them into two fist-sized leather pouches. As Meara stuffed these into her shoulder bag, Mrs. Hodges went to a heavy wooden cabinet, lifted the latch and opened it. She took down a small metal urn and placed it on the table beside the cabinet.

"It's a bad sign, ya' know," said Mrs. Hodges, speaking over her shoulder. She was very carefully spooning a small amount of the contents into an oily pouch.

"Yes, Ma'am" said Meara. "I sensed their fear."

"You mean the wolves?" asked Jake. Being outside the loop made him feel very uncomfortable.

Meara nods in answer.

"What is it about them?"

"The Outland has a good many strange things, young Master," said Mrs. Hodges. She returned the container to the cabinet and brought the pouch to Meara. "I hope you don't have to use this," she said.

"Perhaps having it will be enough," said Meara.

"What is it?" asked Jake.

Meara stuffed the pouch into a side pocket. "Mrs. Hodges and my father came up with the mixture to fend off the wolves many years ago."

"There was little choice. It was the only way to stop them," said Mrs. Hodges.

"It has kept the peace for a long time, Ma'am."

"What is it?" Jake asked again.

"Monkshood," said Meara.

"That is but the catalyst," said Mrs. Hodges. "There are many plants in the Outland that can be used to harm."

"Whatever it is, the wolves hate it," said Meara. "They're terrified of it."

"The potion is death to them," said Mrs. Hodges. "It is quite dreadful."

"It's ugly," Meara grimaced.

"Why does it affect them like that?"

"They're not like us," said Meara.

They came through a gate... thought Jake. *Dragons and wolves and... what next?*

"The Outland is a very strange place, Master Jacob," said Mrs. Hodges.

You don't say...

Chapter Eleven

Jake stood at the edge of the clearing and carefully studied the perimeter, looking into every shadow encircling the grassy circle. Stunted trees and thick brush pushed in from all sides, but the weed-like groundcover blanketing the clearing kept the scrub-forest from engulfing the area.

A stone pillar stood in the center of the clearing.

"You did it, sir," said Meara. Jake nodded, continuing to scan the woods around the clearing. Twelve days earlier, Jake had tried his best to make Meara stay in the village, but in the end had relented. Truth was, he wasn't ready to take on the Outland by himself. Truth was, she was better at surviving out here than he was. And, truth was, she would be better at dealing with the wolf-like creatures than he.

But he would deal with any dragons...

Twelve days; it had taken them twelve days of mapping and surveying and choosing one path over another. They had stretched their rations out by foraging whenever they could, but they were nonetheless short on supplies. They had four or five days of rations left, and as best they could estimate, it was at least three days back to Serpent's Keep by direct route. That meant that he had two days at most to find a way into the gateway, search and discover the next artifact piece in some desert Other World, and return to the clearing.

Meara stepped into the clearing before Jake had a chance to start forward. She walked toward the center of the clearing, toward the pillar, and stopped two steps from the monolithic stone. She turned about slowly, seeking out any possible dangers.

Jake had stepped into the clearing and was walking the boundary, looking closely into the thick brush. There didn't appear to be any other way into the clearing.

One way in, one way out. That was good and that was bad.

"Two hours till dark," said Meara, looking overhead. "I'll gather up wood for a fire."

Jake nodded in silent acknowledgement, already drawn to the pillar. He was mumbling to himself.

Dark and light will let you in... Dark and light will let you in...

Shadows and light? Sun and night? Sun and shadow?

The last gateway needed a dragon to get him through; could this one need a dragon? How could dark and light involve a dragon?

Jake looked up into the sky. The canopy of ugly, twisted trees surrounding the clearing reached in from all sides, leaving a circle of sky above him not more than sixty feet across. Not much in the way of light. Shadows, though...

Dark and light...

How could the author of the scroll, whoever that might be, know what the vegetation would be like now?

He couldn't... so dark and light had to be something that would be around for a while; sun and earth and stone.

And dragons?

Maybe. But, again, what could dragons have to do with dark and light?

"What do you think, sir?" asked Meara. She had already stacked up a considerable supply of firewood.

"Not a clue," said Jake.

"You'll figure it out, sir." She was standing at the site where she intended to create a fire pit.

Jake reached out and rested a palm on the side of the pillar. It was cool and solid and rough to the touch. He ran his hand slowly across the surface, starting randomly and then laying out a methodical search pattern, feeling every crevice and bump.

He lost all track of time, and when he stood and backed away from the stone, having found nothing, he was surprised to notice that the clearing had fallen into heavy gray. It was after dusk and it would be dark soon.

And he was alone. Several stacks of wood lined one side of the clearing, and gourd-sized stones encircled a shallow fire pit. Kindling was prepared in the pit, waiting for spark to ignite it and get the evening dinner-fire going.

But there was no sign of Meara.

How long has she been gone?

The clearing and the surrounding forest was deathly quiet. It felt wrong to break the silence by calling out for her. Besides, he would feel foolish. There was no reason to suppose that anything was amiss.

For the moment, he would wait. He went to his pack and found the matches. He got the kindling going, and then fed the flames with heavier wood. The fire-bed ashed to hot coals. Jake found the small metal pot that they used to heat water, filled it and set it on what Meara called the *hearth stone*, a flat stone placed strategically in the fire pit; near enough to the edge of the pit to provide easy access, far enough in to sufficiently heat the stone and whatever was set onto it.

All the while, Jake continued to feed the fire with larger wood selected from the stacks that Meara had gathered together. He settled in beside the fire, poking at it with a sturdy stick, unable to concentrate on the pillar, unable to think about anything other than where Meara might be, what trouble she might have gotten herself into, and wondering what he should do about it. Call out? Go looking for her? Make a large bonfire to help guide her back?

He heard a noise from somewhere beyond the clearing. Standing, he turned and faced the mouth of the trail that emptied into the clearing.

One way in, one way out.

He subconsciously held the small fire-poker stick in front of him. He could see nothing. It was almost dark out now, and he had been staring into the bright flames of his campfire. *Smart move, Sherlock...*

"Good evening, Master Jacob," said Meara. Jake could just make out her silhouette as she came into the clearing. "Are you making any progress?"

"Where have you been?" he asked sharply; too sharply.

"I'm sorry, sir. I was foraging." Meara held up a line strung with two fish. "And then I found a creek."

"I'm sorry," he said guiltily. "I didn't mean to jump at you. I was afraid something happened. I thought you might be... I didn't know what to think."

"I'm very sorry, sir." Meara hurried to the fire. She let her foraging bag slide off her shoulder and knelt down. "I found some roots, some blackberries, and we can have fish tonight, if that's all right. It should help stretch our supplies."

"That sounds fine."

"I didn't mean to frighten you."

"Not frightened. Really. I was just concerned. It's okay. Just... let me know before you go off like that."

Fresh fish. After two weeks consisting mostly of dried meat and stale trail mix and some indescribable fibrous foodstuff that Meara had said was good for you and lasted weeks in a backpack, fresh fish sounded pretty good.

"Of course." Meara began preparing the fish for the fire. Jake looked back toward the trail. Night was falling fast, and the campfire was creating shadows that flickered across the encroaching forest.

In their twelve days in the Outland this trip, Jake and Meara hadn't come across the wolves, or any wild animals. The only threats they had faced had been losing their way and having to backtrack and make adjustments to the map, and at one point they had come up on an irate monk who was upset at having his 30-day wilderness solitude interrupted.

Dark and light will let you in...

What could that mean?

Dark and light... two separate things. The key to opening the gateway contains two components, one having to do with darkness, one having to do with light.

That sounded plausible.

While Meara put the fish onto the fire, Jake returned to the stone. He sat before it, stared at the flickering of shadows and light the campfire created.

Back to shadows again...

After a few more minutes of staring at the monolith, Jake heard Meara come up beside him and set a plate in his lap. He stared down at it, then up at Meara. She held a fork out to him.

Jake took the fork. "Smells great."

Meara went back to the campfire and served herself, then returned to sit beside Jake.

The shadows and the bright reflections continued to dance across the rough surface of the stone as the flames of the campfire rose and fell, flickered and licked at the air. It was as hypnotic as staring into the flames themselves and Jake found his thoughts and his concentration slowly feathering away.

"That one looks like a dragon's head," said Meara.

Meara's voice startled Jake. "What?"

"Right there." Meara pointed toward the stone, indicating a dark spot in the surface. "It looks like a dragon's head."

"Really?" Jake leaned a little to one side and turned his head slightly. It did look like a dragon's head, if just a little. It was about two inches across, and faintly resembled the profile of a dragon's head, mouth open and teeth bared, horns rolling back from the top of the head. It was a dark fresco, and in the shifting light of the fire, it looked like it was moving.

Dark and light will let you in...

"Do you see any more?" he asked. "Look for another one... a light one."

"There," she said, almost immediately, and pointed at a location up and to the right of the first. This one was about the same size, and of the same design, but due to the color of the stone and the reflections of the fire, this one was much brighter.

"I think you've done it, Meara." Jake stood and walked toward the stone. As he moved forward, he lost sight of the images. He had been looking right at them, but the images disappeared as his perception changed. He stopped, backed up, and caught sight of them again. He moved slowly forward, but again lost sight.

"I'll guide you, sir," said Meara.

Jake nodded and stepped up to the stone. Holding the palm of his left hand against the surface, Meara directed him down until he was holding two fingers against the dark dragon head. He pushed in on the image, but nothing happened.

"Take me to the second image," he said, and held the palm of his right hand against the stone. Again Meara guided his hand until it was over the light dragon head.

Jake pressed in on both images at the same time. He felt the stone beneath his fingers slide in a quarter of an inch.

Meara stood, sensing something different about the stone.

Jake stepped back from the stone as it began to shimmer and fade. The colors slowly disappeared and then returned as the pillar coalesced from a milky white cloud to a new shape—the same primitive stone archway as the last time.

Jake stepped over and picked up his pack, started toward the gateway. "Keep an eye on things, Meara," he said.

A deep, husky voice, definitely not Meara, came from behind him. "What is that?"

Jake stopped and turned sharply toward the voice. Meara was backing away from three ragged-looking men who had come into the clearing. Jake placed the palm of his hand on Meara's back as she neared him and she stopped.

"That twarn't here before, Eddie," said one of the men.

"No kiddin'," said Eddie. He looked warily at Jake. "So, what's goin' on here, buddy?" As he spoke, Eddie's two companions spread out, one in each direction. They stopped four paces from their leader.

"There's nothing going on," said Jake.

"Now that ain't true, mister." Eddie pointed sharply at the archway. "That wasn't there. There was a plain ole' stone there, no more'n this high." Eddie held a hand up shoulder high.

"Are you suggesting that I somehow removed this other stone and replaced it with this?"

"Don't you be gettin' smart with me," Eddie glared at Jake, and then moved his gaze slowly over to Meara. "You folks is in enough trouble as it is."

"That's for sure," said one of Eddie's companions. "They's in a heap a hurt."

Eddie visibly sized up the scene, returned his attention to Meara, and then finally spoke to Jake. "Now, sev'ral things is goin' to happen here. Nothin's gonna' change that. What you can help determine is how difficult each of 'em is gonna' be. Not that I mind partic'arly, but what say you make 'em easy?"

"I'd say that pretty much depends on what you have in mind, Eddie."

"Now ya see? You're already makin' things difficult. Yur givin' me lip."

"Eddie don't like it when ya' give him lip," said one of Eddie's flunkies.

"First up," said Eddie, pointing sharply again at the gateway, "is that yur gonna' tell me what *that* is and how ya got it here."

Jake slid his hand down Meara's back and took her hand. "It's a sculpture," he said. "Just something that I made."

"That don't look like no sculpture, mister."

Jake eased back toward the gateway, bringing Meara back with him. "Thank you," he said. "I tried to make it look like a part of the surroundings."

"It don't look like that, neither." Eddie stepped toward him. "Yur lyin'."

"That is possible, I suppose." Jake could sense that he was one long stride from the gate. He inched nearer. With Eddie moving steadily closer, Jake's backward steps looked defensive rather than a planned move toward the *sculpture*. There was nothing about the stone archway to indicate that it offered any escape.

"Oh, it's more'n possible," Eddie hissed. His mood was darkening. "You start talkin' true, or this gets ugly." Eddie pointed an angry finger at Meara, "And it gets real bad for her."

Alrighty then, time to go... Jake gripped Meara's hand hard and turned sharply toward the gate. *This better work, or we're going to look real foolish...*

Jake ran into the archway with Meara in tow. The world around him disappeared, replaced with a formless universe of gray that surrounded whatever it was that served as his own existence. A tiny point of bright light appeared in the distance. Just as he began struggling with the concept of distance in an indefinable universe without dimension, the pinpoint of light rushed at him and swept over him. Instantly, the universe exploded into white, and then the white turned to gray.

Jake knew that he was holding Meara's hand, and yet neither of them had a body; neither had any physical presence at all. He couldn't actually feel her hand, but knew that the two of them were connected. He knew also that he had to maintain that connection or he would lose her.

Lose her to what, or to where, he did not know.

Another tiny point of bright light appeared at the center of his vision. Again it rushed at him and swept over him and the in-between place they were in turned white. He had an infinitesimal moment to wonder what Meara was thinking about all this, and then there came the explosion of color and he and Meara were thrown into the Other World.

Chapter Twelve

Meara cried out excitedly. She was gripping Jake's hand so hard that he was afraid she might break his fingers. He managed to free himself and turned to face the gateway. Just as in the Other World of the Abandoned City, a stone archway stood silent and alone before them. It looked just like the one that he had just stepped through, just as the gateway to the Abandoned City had looked. And, just as before, this one shimmered and faded, the colors merging into a foggy gray. Within moments, in place of the archway stood a four-sided stone pylon, slate gray and smooth as glass.

"I think we're safe for now," said Jake. If the bandits had followed them into the gate, they hadn't made it. *Where would they be?*

"What happened to the gate!" said Meara in a panic.

"It's okay," said Jake. "Once we find the artifact, we can open it up again."

Meara stepped forward and rested a hand against the smooth pylon. "That was amazing." She was still trying to take it all in. Realization suddenly washed over her face and she looked uncertainly at Jake. "What if we don't find the artifact?"

Jake looked around at their new surroundings. The heat of twin suns beat down on a desert world of rolling sand dunes. The only feature that he could see was the glassy stone pylon standing beside them. "That would put us in a bit of difficulty," he said slowly. "Let's think positive, shall we?"

"Yes, sir." Meara saw the same featureless terrain that Jake saw, felt the same heat from the same twin suns. "Which way, sir?" she asked.

"Well," Jake turned about in a slow circle. There being no other indication, might as well go in the direction the gateway had pointed them. "That way," he said.

Meara looked in the direction he was pointing. It didn't look any different than any other direction. "Master Jacob? What are we looking for?"

"An oasis," said Jake. *Seek then life of green and blue.*

Meara looked at the meager supplies they had managed to bring with them. Jake had his pack; he had the canteen on his belt, but not the larger water bag. Meara hadn't had a chance to grab anything.

"We are short on food and water," she said.

"True enough," said Jake. "The oasis should give us both."

"Of course, sir." Meara squinted and tried to look further into the distance. Scrunching her eyes up didn't help.

May as well get started... Jake calmly started forward. Meara came quickly up beside him.

Walking across the fine sand was difficult. They quickly tired, but knew they had to push, since they had no idea how far they would have to go or how hot the day might get. The larger of the two suns was directly overhead, and its companion was right beside it. For all they knew, a day on this world might last many of their own Earth days, or even weeks.

They crested one dune after another, and at each Jake looked back along the path they were traveling. Two trails of deep footprints reached back to a dark speck on the horizon; the gateway home, should they ever find the artifact.

They had one canteen between them, and they used it sparingly. If they were to reach their goal, they had to drink to maintain their strength, but the thought of traveling this world with no water was terrifying.

What if we're going in the wrong direction? thought Jake. What if they were supposed to go in exactly the opposite direction? What if the oasis had been just over the first dune in the other direction, on the other side of the gateway?

Jake tried not to second-guess himself, but with each passing hour that became more and more difficult. He watched as the smaller of the two suns glided across the sky and eventually set directly ahead of them. The larger sun, the hotter of the two, moved much slower. It took several more hours before it followed the first below the horizon.

When the second sun finally set, they felt the difference almost immediately. The air cooled, making it easier to breathe. The sand beneath their feet began to cool; eventually cool enough that they were able sit comfortably, and when dusk had settled in they decided to take a break before pushing on through the mild evening. The comfortable temperature and the break to relax and have a quick meal of rations gave them a renewed energy. Jake hoped that it would be enough to get them to their goal before the heat of the next day.

With true darkness came an alien night sky and a strange splash of stars. The night grew colder and Jake found himself working to stay warm, exaggerating his movements to keep his blood pumping. Cold or not, however, their forced march was exhausting, and his effort to stay warm only made that worse.

They finally had no choice but to stop, at least to rest and regain some strength. They sat on the lee side of a dune ridgeline, out of the breeze that had been blowing for several hours. They were facing the direction of the pylon, looking back along the path they had taken on their day-long journey. Behind them, somewhere beyond the ridgeline, the oasis they sought was still hidden from them.

They ate more of their ration and washed it down with the last of their water. Unspoken between them was the knowledge that if they didn't find more water before the following midday, they were going to be in serious trouble. Jake tucked the empty canteen back into his belt and gave Meara a weak smile. She smiled back and looked again at the night desert in front of them. This wasn't a desert of dry earth and brush and cactus and scurrying lizards. This was sand. Sand as far as one could travel and as deep as a world; dunes that moved with the wind.

A huge moon began to rise up from the distant horizon. Moonlight streaked toward them, shimmering across the rolling terrain. The footpaths they had left behind shown as a dark band leading from the moon directly to them.

"The wind hasn't wiped our footprints away," said Meara.

"It will," said Jake. That breeze had been growing stronger by the hour.

"There's not much out here in the way of landmarks. Will we be able to find our way back?"

Jake didn't answer. He observed where the moon rose in relation to their tracks. He was about to stand, to suggest that they move on, when he thought he noticed a shifting of shadows several dunes away. "Look there," he said, nodding in the direction of their foot paths.

"I see it," said Meara. She stood and took two steps back, until she was standing at the highest point on the ridge. Jake continued to study the movement from his sitting position.

Meara spoke softly. "He's following our trail."

"Yes he is."

"What should we do?"

Trying to hide was useless. From the speed this newcomer was traveling, he wasn't on foot. Running was useless. A meeting was inevitable.

"Wait for him," said Jake.

"Yes, sir," Meara said softly. She unclipped the strap on the hilt of the knife on her belt. Seeing that, Jake opened a side pocket in his packet and took out the large knife that he had brought with him. He held it clumsily in his hand, finally slipped it into his belt at the small of his back.

The stranger crested the ridge of the near dune and formed a clear silhouette, the large moon serving as a bright backdrop.

"Oh, man," said Jake. *What the heck was that?* The silhouette disappeared as the stranger and his mount started down the slope of the dune.

"What was that?" asked Meara.

Jake was pretty sure the rider was human, but the animal wasn't any kind of horse that he had ever seen. The silhouette was of something low to the ground, legs splayed out to the sides, and a tail jutting straight out behind it.

Jake and Meara watched as rider and mount reached the bottom of the dune and started up the slope toward them, finally coming again into the moonlight. Jake stood and stepped back, so that he was standing directly beside Meara.

The rider was indeed human; a big man with a long bushy beard, brown shirt and trousers, high-top boots, and a large wooden staff comfortably at the ready. He sat in a leather saddle positioned far forward on a lizard-like dragon creature. The animal held its head high, studying the two humans that it was approaching. Its legs were short and powerful, keeping its belly and tail up off the sand, and it easily propelled itself and its rider up the slope.

Rider and dragon veered left as they neared Jake and Meara, reached the top of the ridge and turned and stopped. The human looked down on them, examined them, gaining as much information as he could before speaking.

"Chee han... don la pah," he said, clear and crisp. He waited for a response. The dragon looked to be waiting as well. After Jake's recent experiences with dragons, he had to assume this one had at least some rudimentary intelligence.

"I'm sorry," said Jake. "I don't understand."

"English?" asked the stranger, the word tumbling off his tongue as if seldom used.

"Yes. English," said Jake. "You speak English?"

"Who are you? Why are you here?"

Jake thought before answering. He didn't want to give this man any more information than was necessary to satisfy his questions. "I'm Jake. This is Meara. We are travelers."

"No doubt. That doesn't answer either question."

"As I said, I am—"

"Your names mean nothing to me."

The dragon stretched its head forward and looked closely at Meara, then at Jake. It snorted and grunted. At that, the stranger climbed down from the animal's back and came forward, staff in hand. He stopped within a staff's length of Jake.

"You are blood to Tobias Quigley?" he asked.

Does Tobias know everybody?

"My uncle," said Jake. "I am Jacob Quigley."

The stranger nodded, held the staff firmly at his side. "I am Nehman. I am Guardian."

Guardian? As Tobias was Guardian?

"I'm on a quest left to me by Tobias," said Jake.

"You gather the artifacts," Nehman stated flatly, "to make them again one."

"That's right," said Jake. *Okay... I think that's what I'm doing.*

"There are dangerous times ahead." Nehman looked up at the alien night sky. A disturbed expression swept across his face. "It is true? Tobias is lost to us?"

"I don't know," said Jake. *This man knows things...*

"My heart..." Nehman started, but could not finish. The dragon lowered its head and nudged him, made low grumbling noises. Nehman gave it a pat on the nose. "Yes, my friend. We must prepare for changing times."

"Can you help us?" asked Meara. "We must find the oasis and recover the artifact for this world."

"A three hour journey remains."

"We are traveling in the right direction, then?" asked Jake.

"Yes," Nehman looked at him curiously, as if Jake had asked a foolish question.

"I wasn't given all the information," said Jake. "I have had to be... creative."

"Ah," Nehman smiled. "Tobias' poetry."

Nehman said something to the dragon and it turned about and left, scrambling over the ridge and disappearing down the other side.

"I have sent him ahead," said Nehman. "I will take you to the oasis." He held a leather water bag out to Jake.

"Thank you," said Jake. He took a short swallow, handed the water bag to Meara, then reached down and picked up his pack. "Ready when you are."

Knowing they were only three hours from their goal, Jake and Meara were in better spirits as they set off, following the trail left by Nehman's dragon. Their guide set a steady pace, but one they were able to keep up with. This, coupled with the knowledge and excitement in knowing that they were heading in the right direction and within easy reach of the oasis, gave them the strength and endurance to withstand the increasingly cold night air.

"It doesn't get this cold back where you come from?" asked Nehman, seeing that Jake and Meara weren't dressed for desert nights. His own clothes, while not bulky, kept out the cold and wind. "Serpent's Keep, right?"

"Yeah. Serpent's Keep," said Jake. "We figured we were coming to a desert world; didn't really figure on cold."

"Most deserts are like this. Hot during the day, cold at night. I suppose the extremes might be greater here than some."

"Yeah, well... you know about Serpent's Keep?"

"Sure. Tobias' world. Primary."

"Earth."

"Primary. All gates lead to Primary."

That made some sense to Jake. At least, it fit in with what he knew and the experiences that he had. "And Uncle Tobias was the Guardian at Serpent's Keep?" he asked.

Nehman gave Jake another suspicious side-glance. "And Watcher of the gate that leads to the Rhetani."

"Like I said, I'm a bit in the dark on this. Uncle Tobias was my favorite person in the world, *any world*, and I had no idea that he was involved in anything like this."

"No one did," said Meara. "I've lived in Serpent's Keep all my life. My father was a good friend of Master Quigley."

Nehman nodded slowly, finally grunting out, "Tobias much enjoyed the people of your village."

Jake spoke quietly. "When he went missing, and was declared dead, I was given the estate and this cryptic message that I was to carry on the quest."

They walked in silence for a few moments.

"If he trusted the gathering of the artifacts to you," said Nehman, "then so do I."

"Do you know what happened to him?"

"Only that he was lost to us."

"Any idea what he was doing when he was lost?"

Nehman continued marching steadily forward, his face hard and eyes focused on the horizon ahead. Jake didn't think he was going to answer, and he didn't want to push too hard. Finally, Nehman cleared his throat. "A Rhetani had shown up on several worlds. I do not know how this could be, but it was so. There was much concern that they might find the artifacts and attempt to open the gateway to their world."

"But that's what *I'm* going to do."

"If the Rhetani open the gateway, they will gain a foothold in Primary. From there, they will have access to your world and to all the Other Worlds."

"But if I open the gateway, won't—"

"You will go through the gateway and close it on the other side—permanently."

Jake kept walking. "Oh," he said.

"But sir!" Meara started forward again, coming up quickly and taking Jake's arm.

Jake spoke to Nehman in a dead calm. "And that will keep the Rhetani in their own world."

"That's the idea," said Nehman. "With all the artifact pieces locked into Serpent's Gate, the Other Worlds will be closed to one another."

"Master Jacob, you can't do this," Meara pleaded. "You will be trapped with these... these *Rhetani*."

Jake walked on in silence. So that was it. That was Tobias' mission, his quest, and he had bequeathed it to his nephew.

All the Other Worlds closed to one another...

"What about you?" Jake asked Nehman.

"Do not concern yourself with me."

The moon continued its slow trek across the night sky, until finally Jake found himself directly marching toward it. They trudged their way over one rolling dune after another, following the trail left by Nehman's dragon. They seldom spoke, intent on pushing forward, on reaching the oasis before morning.

Nehman stopped at a high crest and waited, and once Jake and Meara caught up to him, he pointed toward the moon, now just touching the horizon. There, silhouetted against the great white ball, was a grove of trees, half-hidden beyond several more dunes.

They lost sight of the trees when they descended into the sink between each dune, but the grove was all the nearer as they climbed up to the next ridge. At each crest the moon had sunk a little further into the horizon, until finally it was gone altogether, and the night turned black and the silhouette of trees disappeared.

They climbed the last dune in darkness. Nearing the top, Jake could see the tops of tallest of the trees beyond, and as they crested the ridge and started down the other side, he found himself surrounded by trees and bushes. Reaching the floor of the little valley, he felt soil beneath his feet rather than sand. The ground was covered in tufts of grass and hardy groundcover.

In the heart of the oasis was a hill of rock and earth. One side had fallen away, leaving a cliff twenty feet tall that jutted out and formed a high overhang. The overhang created a sheltering cover for a small pool inset at the base of the cliff. Resting beside the pool was Nehman's dragon. Its head lay on a bed of grass, one eye open and watching as Nehman brought the strangers to the pool.

They dropped their gear and Meara knelt down and drank from the pool. Jake looked around for some sign of the artifact, but could see nothing.

Nehman pointed toward the mass of vines growing in a shadowed recess in the cliff. "There's a door behind that growth," he said. "The artifact is in there."

"Will I have any trouble getting it?"

"That I would not know."

"You haven't actually seen it, then? You haven't been in there?"

"I had no reason."

Meara stood up and wiped water from her chin. "And you've been here how long?"

"Since the formation of the gates," said Nehman.

"But that was—"

"I have been here a long time."

Hundreds of years, thought Jake.

Nehman walked slowly over to his dragon. He held his hand out, palm down, and the dragon lifted its head until the man's hand was resting on the dragon's brow. Jake thought he could hear Nehman's voice, but couldn't catch the words. It seemed to be a personal exchange, so he turned away and spoke to Meara.

Jake pointed to a spot near the cliff and under trees where they could set up camp. It was near the water and looked like it would stay in shade most of the day. "I'm too tired to think clearly. We'll try for the artifact after we get some sleep."

"Yes sir," said Meara. She nodded toward Nehman as she picked up their gear. "Do you really think that he, you know..."

"Possible, I guess."

"But, hundreds... maybe thousands..."

The two of them carried their supplies toward the camp site. "People like Nehman and Tobias have sacrificed a lot for the rest of us, and no one will ever hear about it."

"But they could be immortal."

"Immortal or not, they've spent their lives standing watch, waiting for the unthinkable to happen. When it does, they fight, maybe die, in obscurity."

Meara stared at the Guardian of this world, watched as he looked after the strange creature that was his only companion. Such an unbelievable life he must have lived.

Jake made himself as comfortable as he could. It was still very cool, and would likely grow colder yet before the first sun came up. Despite the cold, and the recent experiences churning about in his mind, he fell asleep almost immediately.

He woke to the sounds of Meara preparing a meal. Sitting up, he looked around and judged the time to be midday. It was warm but not overly so. The oasis, the surrounding terrain, and the shaded grove in which they had made camp all combined to keep their immediate environment relatively cool when compared to the surrounding desert.

Meara was working over a pot hanging above a small cooking fire. Seeing Jake up and about, she told him that lunch would be ready in a few minutes. Nehman had brought her the pot and the ingredients for a stew from a cache that he kept at the oasis.

Jake had to wonder where Nehman would find food on a world such as this. But then, there was obviously a food source somewhere, as the man had been surviving here for a very long time.

Lunch was ready by the time Jake had finished cleaning up. Sitting beside Meara, he took the bowl offered to him and used the spoon to investigate the contents. He found meat, potato, and three different vegetables. It smelled good. He filled the spoon with broth and sipped it. A bit spicy, but tasty.

As he ate, he studied his surroundings in the daylight. The oasis was in a deep sink, surrounded on all sides by a high ridge. A layer of sand on the surface hid compact soil beneath. There were several groves of trees; some species that he wasn't familiar with.

They ate in silence for several minutes. The stew really was good. Jake wondered what the meat was. What animal around here served as a food source?

"Where's Nehman," he asked.

"I don't know. He left not long after giving me these supplies."

"He didn't say anything?"

"I don't think he interacts much with people," said Meara. "Talks to his dragon a lot, though."

Jake slid around until he was facing the cliff. An entire section was covered in thick vine, and according to Nehman there was a door somewhere underneath it.

"Don't suppose it's unlocked," he wondered aloud.

"I guess that would depend on what's on the other side, sir."

That wasn't very comforting. There had to be to be some defensive measure in place. Either the hidden door was locked, or there was some other protection inside.

So, do I want it locked or unlocked?

Jake set his empty bowl down beside him and stood up, walked determinedly across the camp and up to the cliff wall. The layer of vines covering the cliff was thick and they were tightly intertwined. It took all he had to pull apart a section of the vegetation, only to find that beneath it was only rock. He stepped to one side and tried again.

He found a dark, heavy door on the fourth search. Once found, he and Meara worked together to pull apart the thick vines and clear away an opening.

Carved in the center of the door was the symbol for this world's artifact. *A good sign,* thought Jake. Also on the door was a simple, heavy metal latch. Jake rested his hand on it and pushed down. It moved easily and Jake pushed in. The door glided inward an inch.

"It isn't locked," said Meara.

"No. It's not."

"Then there might be something in there," said Meara, "protecting the artifact."

"Yes. There might be. You wait here."

"But sir—"

"Do you really think you should go in alone?" asked Nehman, coming up behind them. Jake and Meara both jumped at the sound of his voice.

"Geez—" Jake said sharply.

"Pardon."

Jake took a moment to catch his breath, then turned back to the door. "All right," he said. "Okay... but stay behind me."

"Yes sir," said Meara.

"As you say," said Nehman.

Jake pushed the door open. It was dark inside. He was about to ask Meara to go get the lantern when he noticed a faint light at the far end of a long hall, as if sunlight was somehow filtering through into a subterranean room.

"Interesting," said Nehman, standing close behind Jake.

"If you say so." Jake stepped through the doorway, glad now that he wasn't doing this alone. There was an old, musty animal smell intermingled with the smells of dry earth and moldy vegetation.

"The temperature," said Meara. "It's comfortable in here."

Jake nodded, though it was too dark for anyone to see. He continued moving down the hall, unable to see the floor on which he walked. He could hear Meara and Nehman walking in step directly behind him. Far ahead, the filtered light drew nearer.

Jake thought he saw a shadow in the light and stopped. He watched and waited. After a few seconds, Meara whispered. "What is it?"

"I thought I saw something."

"What?"

"I don't know," said Jake. "Nothing." He started forward again.

The pungent odor grew stronger with each step.

"What's that smell," asked Meara.

"Dragon's nest," said Nehman.

Jake frowned. "I knew you were going to say that."

The tunnel emptied into a large, oval room with sloping walls and a high ceiling that was pockmarked with a dozen small openings through which sunlight streamed in like fuzzy laser beams. There were tunnel openings at three locations in the surrounding walls, each set about four feet above the stone floor.

On the far side of the room was a large bed of matted vegetation. Resting comfortably in the nest was a reptilian dragon, its large head resting on its hands. It grinned as it watched the three humans come into its lair.

"Welcome," it said. The word sounded foreign coming from the creature.

"Hello," said Jake. As he continued into the room. "I am Jacob Quigley. Nephew of Tobias Quigley."

"Blood," said the dragon. It lifted up its head.

"That's right."

"Not Tobias."

"Right again." Jake stopped in the center of the room. He glanced up at the holes in the ceiling, at the dark entrances to several exiting tunnels. Peripherally, he saw Nehman step to his right and Meara move to his left.

"You are most welcome here," said the dragon. "I have been a long time alone."

"I've never seen you on the surface," said Nehman.

"Seldom travel surface. All I need here." The dragon lifted one hand and casually waved it toward the tunnels. "Too hot, surface."

"It can get warm."

"Do you know why I am here?" asked Jake.

"Collect what Tobias left in my care."

"Is that going to be a problem?"

The dragon grinned broadly. "Why you think that, Jacob Quigley, blood of Tobias Quigley?"

"I don't," Jacob replied carefully. "From what I've seen, dragons are friends of Tobias."

"All respect Tobias Quigley, Guardian of the Artifact, Watcher of Serpent's Keep, warrior in battle against Rhetani."

Something is wrong...

Nehman took a step forward, standing now well within Jake's view. "The Guardians stand in defense of the Jahai," he said. Jake had no idea what Nehman was talking about, but it was clear the Guardian didn't like the look of things any more than Jake.

"Yes..." The dragon nodded its head slowly.

"Tobias Quigley has conferred the gathering of the artifacts to Master Jacob," Nehman continued. "Do you contest that?"

"I do not," said the dragon.

"Then will you assist Master Jacob?" asked Meara, stepping forward.

Jake watched the expression of the dragon. There was definitely something not right. The creature was an ally of Tobias Quigley, of the Guardians, of the Jahai, yet there was a devious undercurrent about this dragon. Jake didn't think this was going to end well.

The dragon cocked its head to one side and gave Meara another twisted smile.

"You should answer the lady," Nehman said coolly. He moved further to one side, putting more distance between himself and Jake. Seeing that, Meara did the same. There were three distinct targets rather than one.

The dragon cocked its head the other way, studied the three of them, and then looked directly at Meara.

"I have but one master," he said. He turned back to Nehman.

"How can a dragon serve the Rhetani?" Nehman asked sharply. He reached over his shoulder and pulled his sword from the scabbard strapped to his back. The dragon glanced only casually at the weapon, and appeared unconcerned by the accusation.

"Rhetani not master. I serve my heart, human."

"And yet you've given it over to the Rhetani?" asked Meara.

"Give nothing. We travel same path."

"You, my wayward friend, are a disgrace to the race of dragons," said Nehman. He took several more steps to the side and moved cautiously nearer. As he did, Meara slid the pack off her back and pulled her blade free, tossing the pack behind her. She stepped calmly forward.

"A pleasant diversion," said the dragon, lifting itself up and pulling its head back. Its legs were short and stocky, its chest wide and heavily scaled.

"It doesn't have to be this way," said Jake. He held his own knife loosely at his side, wanting to avoid a fight if possible.

"Your blood... the most sweet," said the dragon.

"What have we done to you?"

"Nothing at all."

Nehman moved so quickly that he was little more than a blur. The dragon saw him coming, however, and just as quickly leapt aside to avoid the sword thrust in under the creature's chin. It roared, swung about and pushed forward at Nehman, brought its head in low and tried to clamp its jaws around the man's legs. Nehman, instead of jumping back as expected, jumped forward and brought his sword down like a spike onto the dragon. He missed the head, instead burying a foot and a half of sword into the creature's neck.

Again the dragon roared and pulled back violently. The sudden wrenching knocked Nehman backward, bloody sword in hand. He staggered back several steps before regaining his footing.

Meara had rushed forward at the same time and plunged her blade into the dragon's shoulder. The beast twisted about and batted her aside; she flew back and struck the wall. The dragon lunged at her as she slid down to the floor, but before it could reach her Jake threw his knife at it, striking its belly as it began to rear up. Again the beast roared and clouds of dust rolled from the walls and the ceiling. It spun about angrily and rushed at him and Jake stumbled backward and fell to the ground as the dragon snapped at the air above him. It turned its head and looked down on him with one yellow eye. Its breath was hot and foul, but didn't have the same intensity of the fire-breathing dragons that Jake had recently come across.

"Blood die now," it said and laid a heavy, clawed hand on Jake's chest. The weight made it hard for Jake to breathe, the claws closed in around him and Jake could feel his bones bending and tendons tearing. He stared up into the eye of the dragon and saw a sparkle of insane glee. The dragon must have been harboring an intense hatred for Tobias for centuries and was now venting that hate on him.

Jake's arm was spread out to his side, pressed against the floor of the chamber by the weight of the dragon. He could feel the handle of his knife, the blade of which was buried in the flesh of the belly. Twisting his wrist, he managed to grasp the hilt and turned the blade, pushing it deeper into the monster.

The creature let out a shattering, blood-curdling scream and swung its head from side to side as it fought against the agony. It raised itself up, away from the source of the pain. Jake held tightly to the knife and it pulled free from the beast. Holding the weapon now in both hands, Jake struck up at the vulnerable belly. As he did, Nehman rushed in and pierced the dragon's neck with his sword. The animal shuddered, let out a hollow gurgling rattle, and dropped down onto Jake as several thousand pounds of dead weight.

He couldn't breathe, couldn't expand his chest and fill his lungs with air. He tried desperately to suck in thin threads of oxygen. Then he heard Nehman scrambling beside him, heard the man call out. "Hang on! Hang on!"

Nehman pressed his back against the body of the dragon and lifted it enough that Jake was finally able to crawl free.

"You hurt?" he asked. Jake sucked in three deep breaths, pressed his hands against his ribs.

Jake shook his head, turned and looked over the back of the dead dragon, over at Meara who was slumped down against the far wall. "Meara," he called, and grimaced at the sudden pain that webbed across his chest. He spoke more softly, "Meara. Are you all right?"

Meara lifted her head and nodded without speaking.

Nehman moved from one tunnel opening to the next and peered inside. He really couldn't see anything, but nonetheless hoped that there would be some indication, some sign, something to tell them which one would lead them to the artifact.

"These tunnels go on a ways," he said. "This may take some time."

"Maybe not," said Jake. In those few seconds when he had looked into the eye of the dragon, Jake had felt a connection, an understanding, and he had a sense of the workings of the tortured mind of the creature.

He nodded in the direction of the nest of the dragon.

Nehman grimaced. A dragon's bed had a rather unique odor to it. "Oh, I'd rather not," he said.

Jake gave a chuckle and suffered the pain for it. It would take a long time for the torn ligaments to heal. "I'll do it," he said, and started toward the nest. "My quest, after all."

"I'll help you, sir," said Meara.

"Oh, very well," Nehman moaned. "If it must be done."

They all moved up to the nest. It consisted of decomposing branches from the trees of the oasis, bits of fabric from old human clothing and bedding, soil from the tunnels, and sand from above. There was also a considerable amount of shed dragon skin and broken scales.

The artifact lay half buried in the heart of the nest, as a delicate egg that would never hatch.

"How did you know, sir?" asked Meara.

It was in his eyes.

"Sir?"

"He would not keep it anywhere else."

Chapter Thirteen

Jake, Meara and Nehman stood beside the closed obelisk, Nehman's mount resting nearby. Jake held the artifact, ready to use it to open the gateway. He turned to Nehman.

"You should come with us," he said, though he knew the man would not.

"I will remain here."

"You said it yourself... all the gates will close. Forever. This one included."

"I have been on this world for a very long time."

Jake and Nehman looked at each other for several very long seconds, during which time something seemed to pass between them, perhaps an understanding. Jake finally held out his hand. Nehman looked at it, and for a moment didn't seem to know what to do. Finally, however, the two shook hands.

Jake turned to the obelisk and inserted the artifact. There was only the faintest flicker, and then nothing.

"Master Jacob?" Meara looked concerned.

"It's all right, Meara." Jake removed the artifact. He looked back at Nehman again and gave a curt nod. Turning back to the gateway, he took hold of Meara's hand. "Whatever you do, do not let go of my hand."

Their passage through the gateway started out the same as previous crossings. Jake saw the familiar point of light in the distance. It came at him, grew to overwhelm his vision and was suddenly all around him, turning his world into white nothing.

And then it was different.

In that peculiar world of white nothing, Jake... *saw something...*

There was something in that nothingness... Faint images, shadows against the white, in the white, a part of the white.

Shadows of people.

Jake saw the faint silhouettes of several people.

The bandits?

And then it was past. The white turned to dull gray and he had the odd sense of falling forward. There was another point of bright light in the center of his vision. It rushed at him and over him and the gray turned to white, and then came the explosion of color and Jake stumbled out into the clearing in the Outland, hand in hand with Meara.

"Sir?" Meara asked anxiously steadying herself.

"You saw them?" asked Jake.

Meara nodded sharply. Jake let go of her hand and nervously rubbed his face with the flats of his palms.

So they had followed after them, before the gate had closed, and they had gotten stuck somehow in that in-between place.

This was bad. Nasty as they were... they were trapped—in that place.

"They followed us in," said Meara.

"They had no way out."

The supplies they had been forced to leave behind when they had stepped through the gateway were still in the clearing. That was good news, anyway. They would have food and equipment for the trip home.

"Come on," he said sharply. He was in no mood to hang around. "Let's get out of here."

They gathered up their supplies and made ready to leave. They could put a good distance between them and this clearing before nightfall.

Jake started to the mouth of the trail, and then slowed. His senses were picking up something. He couldn't think or voice what it was, but he knew that there was something... He stopped, turned his head and looked at Meara.

Meara was looking at the edge of the clearing far to their right. Jake continued turning and looked in the direction of her gaze.

Wolves...

"Not again." He watched as one wolf leapt out into the clearing and slowly stalked the perimeter. Glancing quickly at the way out of the clearing, he saw that another wolf was moving down the path, stopping as it reached the mouth of the trail.

Their way was blocked. They would have to deal with these wolves. Jake let his pack slide down from his shoulder and held it in his hand. Watching the lead wolf for any sign that it was ready to charge, he carefully reached in to pull his weapon free.

"Let me, sir," Meara said softly. She had already dropped her pack and was holding one of the leather pouches that Mrs. Hodges had given her. She held it up to the lead wolf. "Do you know what this is?" she asked the animal.

The wolf eyed the object in Meara's hand suspiciously, keeping to the edge of the clearing but continuing to pace. Meara held the small bag up for the other wolf to see. She turned then and held it toward the opposite side of the clearing. Only then did Jake see two other wolves crouched down in the shadows of the brush.

The lead wolf began to creep inward, moving closer with each traverse, one side of the clearing to the other, always watching Meara, watching her gestures, looking for an indication that she would make good her threat.

"He's not going to back down." Jake slowly raised his knife.

"You won't need that, sir." Meara used her free hand to pull open the leather pouch. At that, the lead wolf stopped cold in his tracks. Jake looked quickly at the others, and then turned back to the leader. All were tensely observing Meara's movements.

"You should leave now," Jake said to the leader. The wolf bared its teeth and silently snarled, didn't advance or retreat.

Meara pleaded with the wolf. "Whatever your reasons for breaking the truce, is it worth your lives? You cannot win this."

The wolf gave a long, low growl, but still did not move.

There was the faintest of sounds behind them, like a whisper of air. Jake froze, but Meara instantly went into action. She held out her arm, leather pouch in hand, and began to spin about. A cloud of deadly dust formed around her, expanding outward, reaching out toward the wolves that were rushing at her.

Meara was knocked backward, thrown off her feet by one of the wolves that found itself leaping through the cloud. Jake dropped to the ground and threw his weapon at it, striking it behind the shoulder just as it hit Meara; it was dead before the two of them hit the ground.

The other wolves had tried to turn away from the poison, but neither made it alive to the edge of the clearing.

Only the lead wolf, which had not charged, survived. Jake had rolled over onto his knees and turned toward it. He couldn't see it at first, but as the dust began to disperse he caught the silhouette of the animal as it moved in the shadows beyond the perimeter.

Meara pushed aside the dead wolf lying on top of her and climbed slowly to her feet. She grabbed the second leather pouch and held it high over her head.

She was letting the wolf know that she was ready for it, was waiting for it, and was willing to kill it should it follow them. Only when she was sure that she had made her point did she lower her arm, then wearily dropped to her knees.

"That's really potent stuff," said Jake.

Meara looked down at the empty pouch, nodded. "Yes, sir."

"What about us?"

"Not harmful to us. Only the wolves."

They are not like us.

Jake saw several birds in the brush, happily hopping from branch to branch.

They're not like any animal from this world.

"This clearing will be death to them for many days," said Meara. "It will settle onto the ground, will be active for weeks. A wolf kicks it up as it passes through, it breathes it in..." Meara stood up and walked over to her pack. She stuffed the now empty pouch into it and pulled the pack up to her shoulder. "I think I'm ready to go home now."

"Meara will be fine," Mrs. Hodges said consolingly. "In her brief life, she has had to face much worse."

Jake watched Mrs. Hodges busily moving about the kitchen preparing food for the midday meal. He was sitting at the kitchen island, a glass of iced tea and a small blueberry muffin in front of him, just as he had so many times as a child. The room, the woman, the atmosphere, all helped to soothe his tattered nerves. That at least was something. It helped. But his bruised bones and torn muscles and ligaments would take time, not ambiance, to heal.

"That's hard to imagine," said Jake. He thought about all that had happened on just this one trip. It was a miracle they had made it home.

"I can't speak to dragons and deserts," said Mrs. Hodges, "but missy has been dealin' with wolves and the Outland all her life."

Jake picked at the muffin, tossed a piece into his mouth. "I can see I missed a lot during my summers here."

Mrs. Hodges gave him a comforting side glance. "Now Master Jacob, why should a young cub like you have had to face such things? You warn't much more'n a baby."

"And an outsider at that."

"Oh, now—"

"I could hear it, even if you didn't say it."

"Young Master... most folks within the village walls have no idea of the goings-on in the Outland. And most that do, they choose not to face it or accept it."

Jake leaned forward and stared at his muffin. He studied it as if he might find something special about it. "What's with the wolves, Mrs. H?"

"I don't know what you mean."

"Sure you do. You have to know something. You came up with the potion to kill them."

"The potion wasn't my doing," Mrs. Hodges turned quickly to her vegetables, picked them up and tossed them into the sink. She turned on the water and started cleaning them. "Mister Gyles brought the recipe to me. I just mix the ingredients together."

"Meara's father was certainly a resourceful guy."

"That he was. Master Quigley himself aside, I doubt he came second to anyone else in Serpent's Keep."

"So... what did the resourceful Mister Gyles have to say about the wolves?"

Mrs. Hodges stopped her work, stared thoughtfully at the vegetables in the sink. "I do remember he once said... he said they were *allied to an evil born of another land*. Them's his words, as best I remember 'em."

"The Rhetani?" Jake asked. *What else could it be?*

"Didn't say. Don't know if he knew." She began cleaning the vegetables again. "He did say they came to the Outland millennia ago, and with 'em came all the malevolence that exists there." She smiled thinly, "Don't know if he meant that for true or was sayin' it for color."

Jake was still sitting at the counter long after Mrs. Hodges had left the kitchen; his iced tea gone, his muffin eaten. He was staring down at the empty glass when Mr. Griffin came into the room, on his way to the pantry.

"Good afternoon, Master Jacob." Mr. Griffin continued on toward the tall, narrow door.

Jake spoke up, still looking down at his glass. "Mr. Griffin. You remember that pistol I found?"

Mr. Griffin stopped and turned to Jake. "Rather an antique, if I recall."

"Do you think you could find some bullets for that thing?" Jake looked up from his glass and directly at Mr. Griffin. "In that *other* market of yours?"

"It is possible, sir."

Jake turned his attention back to his empty glass.
"Let's do that."

Jake couldn't sleep. For the third night in a row he wandered
the mansion and its grounds late into the night, looking through
the books in the library, studying the artifacts and maps in the
command center, standing before the stone dragons in the Hall of
Statues and silently asking each of them for some sign, some
guidance. He still had no idea where his uncle might be, or what
he might have been doing when he disappeared. There were
certainly enough dangers out there, and it would certainly be
reasonable to assume that Tobias had fallen victim to one of
them, but Jake didn't think it was a simple as that.

Yes, the wolves could have turned on him, or the bandits
could have gotten him, or one of the dragons.

He could have fallen off a cliff...

Jake didn't believe that it was any of those things. He
believed that something specific about the quest had gotten him,
had swallowed him up.

The quest...

Tobias hadn't collected any of the artifacts; that had been left
to Jake.

So what had he been doing in those last weeks?

Jake stepped out of the dining room and into the main hall.
Straight ahead was Mr. Griffin's room. He could see a sliver of
light at the bottom of the door. Griff often stayed up late, making
extensive use of the library.

Jake turned to go up the stairs. He decided that he might as
well grab a book himself and settle in for another fitful night.

Instead, he veered left of the staircase and stepped into the
shadow of the narrow hall beside the main stairs and came to the
door beneath the staircase that led down to the basement. He
seldom went down there himself, but he knew the staff stored
extra supplies and equipment there. He had gone through the
shelves and boxes more than once during his recent searches of
the house.

Now, though, light coming from under the door had caught
his attention.

*Oh, Mr. Griffin...*thought Jake. *What are you up to now?* He
opened the door and stepped through, stood at the top of the
landing and looked down the steep, narrow stairwell. He could
see a small square of the basement floor at the foot of the stairs,
but no movement, no shadows gliding across his vision.

He started quietly down the stairs, but not so quietly as to imply that he was trying to sneak up on the old man. Ol' Griff's activities might be completely innocent, and Jake didn't want to storm in on the man looking for a jar of peaches.

On the other hand, skulking about the basement in the middle of the night did seem a bit out of the ordinary.

Except... well, Jake was skulking, had been skulking about the place for three nights running...

The basement was divided into two sections. The first was lined with shelves stacked with large boxes of supplies used to replenish the containers kept in supply rooms upstairs. One shelf on the left held the overflow of Mrs. Hodges' canning.

Jake walked through the first room and into the second room filled with plastic-lined bins. To the left were the kitchen bins, to the right, inside a mesh cage, were the yard and garden bins.

Mr. Griffin was standing at the far wall. He had slid aside one section of shelf that lined the wall and was staring at the wooden panel behind it. The grain of the wood was twisted into great whorls and jagged designs.

"I believe that you will succeed in gathering together the artifacts from the Other Worlds, Master Jacob," said Mr. Griffin, speaking over his shoulder.

"I hope so," Jake said uncertainly.

"And when you do, what then?"

Jake stepped up beside Mr. Griffin, tried to see what the old man saw. "I'll use them to open the gate to the Rhetani."

"Where will you do this? Where is this very special gate to which Master Quigley served as Guardian?"

Jake suddenly shivered. "Here?"

"Would it not make sense that he would keep such a thing close at hand?"

Uncle Tobias built his mansion on top of the gate?

Mr. Griffin continued. "No one can remember when the estate was not here. No one can remember the village without this mansion."

"You think the mansion came first, and the village was built around it?"

"The gate came first."

Jake imagined Tobias Quigley, many hundreds of years ago, standing as Guardian over the gate that led to the world of the Rhetani, just as Nehman stood watch in the Other World of the desert. Only this gate, this obelisk in the heart of the Outland, was special. This Outland, serving as the fulcrum for all the gates, was special.

The conflict with the Rhetani had reached its zenith, and in desperation the gates had been closed, and the guardians had been put into place to watch over them.

Here stood Tobias Quigley, guardian at the center of the wheel, custodian to watch the Rhetani gate.

A keep to hold the Rhetani.

Serpent's Keep.

Mr. Griffin raised a hand and pointed at the wall in front of them, long hidden by the dusty section of shelf. "Do you see it?"

Jake looked closely at the panel. Hidden amidst the wood-grain patterns was a definite and familiar shape.

"It's one of the polygons." It matched the shape on one of the keys, and he knew to which statue the polygon belonged. "But, this can't be the gate."

"I believe there is a passageway behind this wall."

Jake moved his hand across the wood. It was cooler in the center, perhaps three feet across. "I see what you mean. There's air space beyond this wall."

"Perhaps a passage to the gate."

"So do we just tear down the wall?"

"I would guess that Master Quigley had a less invasive way of getting in, sir."

"Don't start getting cute with me, Griff," said Jake. He ran his fingers across the small section of wood formed by the polygon. "This feels different." He tried pushing it in, pulling it, twisting it, scratching it. Nothing he tried made any difference. "I'll bet this is the key, but I don't see how it works."

"May I? Sir?"

Jake stepped back, "Absolutely."

Mr. Griffin ran the tips of his long, bony fingers across the polygon. "I don't believe this is of the same material as the rest of the panel."

"Well, that's what I said. It doesn't feel the same."

"I don't believe it is wood at all."

Jake thought a moment. He gave a sudden, sharp nod. "It isn't the key... It's the lock."

He turned and started away. "I'll be right back." He hurried out of the basement and up to the front hall. He stomped up the main stairs to the second floor, thinking that there were times when this was a very big house.

He glanced quickly at the first statue in the Hall of Statues as he ran through and into the command center. He kept the ring of keys in the supply room. He found the one that he wanted as he quickly stalked back to the statue with the ring of keys held out in front of him.

Within the hidden compartment he found the scroll. He also found a bone dagger and the artifact.

Returning to the basement, he held up the artifact. "I do think I found our way in." He had left the scroll and the dagger upstairs.

Mr. Griffin stepped aside and Jake stood before the wall. He pressed the artifact against the polygon blemish on the panel.

He immediately felt a tingling, as if the artifact and the panel were somehow becoming electrically charged; perhaps a circuit was now completed. Jake heard a faint click and a door in the panel eased open an inch.

"Very good, Master Jacob."

"Thank you, Mr. Griffin." Jake stuffed the artifact into his pocket and pushed the door open. Beyond was a long, narrow hallway, most of which lay in darkness. "We're going to need light."

Mr. Griffin brought a lantern down from a nearby shelf. "Perhaps that would explain this, sir."

With the lantern lit, Jake and Mr. Griffin stepped into the hall. After thirty feet, the hall turned sharply right, and after another thirty feet turned left. Jake noted that there were no doors or other accesses. The hall was a tunnel. It was going to take them directly from the basement to the sole purpose for the access way.

Jake stepped into a room twenty feet on a side, and a ceiling that was at least twelve feet overhead. The walls were smooth and unbroken. There was no furniture; there were no objects of any kind.

But there was something set into the cement floor at the center of the room; a small inset in the shape of a hexagon. Jake knelt down before it and brushed his hand lightly over it.

"Look at this," he said softly, his words echoing in the chamber. There was a pattern inside the recess. The pattern divided the hexagon into six polygons. "This is it. This is how I open the gate to the Rhetani."

Restore the individual artifact pieces, restore the artifact to its original state... open the gate.

Mr. Griffin glanced around the empty room. "There is no obelisk like those you have described."

"Nor is there a dragon. Nonetheless, when the artifact is restored, the gate will make an appearance." Jake stood and studied the chamber. There was no telling how the gate might be hidden. "Maybe the whole room is the gate."

"Then we should use caution."

"I'll do that."

This was an important discovery, and Jake was excited. He was also terrified. This chamber, these bare walls, this cold stark floor, would be the last he ever saw of his world.

Chapter Fourteen

The owner and editor of the village newspaper had a pleasant face and manner, bright, inquisitive eyes, and from their few minutes of conversation Jake could assume a quick, sharp mind, though the man's thoughts seemed to jump from subject to subject at the slightest provocation.

Which might explain the condition of the office. The desk that separated the two of them was cluttered with paper and folders. The shelves that lined the walls were filled with haphazardly stacked books, binders and files.

Through the open door in the back wall, Jake could see a very old printing press dominating the center of the back room. The machine looked well taken care of, but the rest of the room looked to be in as precarious a state as the front room.

Jeb Rainey was very familiar with Tobias Quigley's trips into the Outland, as well as the recent excursions of the new Master Quigley. He agreed with Mr. Griffin's observation that Tobias' trips had been more frequent during his last few months, though he didn't know why. He had asked around a bit about what supplies Mr. Quigley had been taking with him on those trips, but the front-door suppliers revealed nothing extraordinary and his back-door suppliers revealed nothing at all.

"I of course looked into Tobias' disappearance, but in the end I found nothing."

"Did you go into the Outland?"

The editor smiled. "I limit my investigations to within the walls of the keep. I interviewed those in the village who would have been in the best position to know something."

"Such as?"

"Our constable, citizens on Gate Watch at the time, members of the Adventurer's Guild, and members of the Quigley Estate household."

"What's this Adventurer's Guild?"

"Ah, yes." Rainey's smile broadened. "The Guild. A rather odd assortment of self-proclaimed adventurers who purportedly seek out excitement and danger, but who for the most part sit around small tables in the Guild Hall and play Serpent's Ladder all day."

"So these guys don't actually go out into the Outland?"

"Some manage to tear themselves away from the Hall now and then. For a guide, though, you probably won't find anyone in the bunch as good as the one you've found in Meara Gyles. But, there are those among them with unique expertise, should you choose to take the time to meet with them." Mr. Rainey leaned over the paperwork covering his desktop. "Just remember to take all they say with a pound of salt."

The editor leaned back in his chair and gave a sage nod. He then gave Jake detailed directions to the hall, interspersing the instructions with tidbits of information on just about every building between the newspaper office and the guild, before suddenly leaning forward across the desk again and asking Jake what he was up to, if not searching for his uncle.

"That's pretty much it, Mr. Rainey. I'm simply trying to find Uncle Tobias."

The man smiled as if he had captured his quarry in a trap of words. "You don't believe that Tobias has passed on to the next life."

"Really don't know," said Jake. "I have doubts."

"Then where could he be?"

"If I knew that, I would just go there and get him." Jake stood and reached over the desk, shook the man's hand and thanked him. He wanted to get to the Guild hall and see if there was someone there whom he would be willing to have join him on his next trip out. He was serious about leaving Meara safely at home, but had seen the value in not going it alone.

He stood outside the newspaper office and tried to get his bearings. The air was damp and cool, and a thick gray fog lay over the village so that the rooftops were hidden and the streets took on the appearance of brick-lined, cobblestone tunnels.

"Hello, Jake!"

Jake looked in the direction of the voice and saw Sparta Vesper crossing the street and coming toward him. She looked as if she may have just finished up a long day at the café.

"Sparta," Jake put on a friendly smile. "How are you this afternoon?"

"Well enough." She came up beside him and stopped, folded her arms across her chest and took in the scene. "What possesses our newest citizen to stand out in the street on this dreariest of days? Lost?"

Jake indicated the newspaper office behind them. "Visiting."

"You know Jeb?"

"Nice gentleman. Friendly."

"And nosy."

"Tool of the trade, I suppose. How are things at the café?"

"Same. Always. You should drop in more often, Jake."

"I'll do that. Have some of that great coffee. Partake of much more than that, though, and I'll have to answer to Mrs. H. I'm walking a fine line as it is."

"Hodges?" Sparta's gaze took on a studied look. Jake could tell that Sparta was struggling with how much to say regarding the multifaceted Mrs. Hodges. She finally pasted on a careful smile. "She's one who'll be watching out for ya'. On that, you have no fear."

Sparta stepped closer and leaned in conspiratorially. She tried to look casual, but only managed to look more suspicious. "You take heed, though, Jake. There'll be those watching out for ya, and those just watchin'."

"How am I supposed to take that?"

"It means what it means. I may not be on the inside on most things, but I am close to the ground. There's some here that know more about the secrets of the Outland than others, and some what carry about with 'em dangerous secrets of their own."

Jake was growing increasingly irritated. "I don't suppose you'd like to point one or two of them out to me?"

Sparta was looking uncomfortable and anxious to move on. "You just mind what I say."

"How?"

She was already stepping away, backing into the street. "Very little happens in the Village without a reason, Jacob Quigley," she said, before turning and heading quickly away.

Jake stared after her in bewilderment, and after a few moments started more slowly in the same direction. He still wanted to check out the Adventurer's Guild before heading back home.

He took several wrong turns before finally finding the narrow side road that he had been directed to. He found an unmarked door midway down the long brick wall that spanned the length of the road and that the buildings behind it shared. As he prepared to go in, he saw a strange man watching him from the shadow of a recessed doorway on the other side of the street. The man's face looked weathered by time and events, and he stood slightly hunched over, as if standing straight would take too much effort.

Great... he thought. *Now she has me spooked...*

Jake opened the door and went inside. In the small foyer, a man stepped up to a counter beside an open double door, beyond which Jake could see a large room with half a dozen tables, half of them occupied with one or two men each.

"Can I help you?" the man asked.

"I'd like to go in, if that's all right?"

"Are you a member?"

What an asinine question... have you ever seen me before?

"Not at the moment, no."

"A guest, then."

"Yeah. A guest."

"Of whom?"

"Mr. Rainey suggested that I come here." He didn't need this. "Listen, if you're gonna make a big stink about it, I'll just leave."

"And you are?" the man arched one brow.

"Quigley," said Jake, quite ready to leave.

"I see." After a moment's hesitation, during which time the stuffy old turd gave Jacob Quigley a thorough look-over, he stepped over to the double door and waved his arm, bidding entrance. "You are most welcome, Mr. Quigley. Please consider yourself an honorary member of the Guild."

Jake entered the main hall without saying another word. Several of those inside glanced up at him, but most did their best to ignore the newcomer. All had no doubt heard the exchange and knew that there was someone attempting to enter and exactly who that someone was.

They would do their utmost to restrain their enthusiasm.

Jake walked casually over to the nearest occupied table. Two older men were playing a dice game. One of the men gave a gruff grunt and handed the cup and dice to the other. He put a score on a pad, spoke without looking up. "Mister Quigley. Have you ever played Serpent's Ladder?"

"Afraid not."

"You should try it sometime."

The second man spoke up. "But not now and not here."

"Don't be disrespectful, Madsen," the first man said sharply.

Madsen studied the throw of his dice. "We're in the middle of a game, Jeffers. I don't want to start over."

"Not a problem," said Jake. "I don't want to interrupt." Looking around the room, he noticed a man watching him from a corner table. When the man nodded a silent hello, Jake walked over and stood before the table.

"Good evening," said Jake.

"Good evening, Mr. Quigley," said the man. He nodded at the two men playing dice. "Ignore them. They've been unpleasant for forty years. I don't think they would know how to be otherwise."

"I'll try not to let it get to me."

The man leaned forward and held out his hand. "I'm Troy McLaughton." They shook hands, and McLaughton indicated an empty chair. He watched Jake pull out the chair and settle in. He had a friendly face, but there was an air of deviousness about him that Jake couldn't quite point to. "What brings you to the Guild, Mr. Quigley?"

"Curiosity."

McLaughton smiled. "A vital component in the character of the adventurer. That, and greed."

"Is that why you're in it, Mr. McLaughton? Looking to get rich?"

"It pays the bills," McLaughton shrugged, not taking offense. "But curiosity and excitement are just as important to me. At the moment, I'm quite curious as to what you are all about."

"Loyalty, honor, all that pompous, high-brow stuff."

McLaughton gave out a genuine, cheerful laugh. "Excellent," he said, nodding. "I like that."

"And just what is it that you do, Mr. McLaughton, when you're out there adventuring?"

"Tracking mostly. Guiding, some."

"You know your way around the Outland pretty well, then?"

"Are you looking for a guide, Mr. Quigley?"

"Just curious; like I said."

"So you did. I understand that Meara Gyles has been shepherding you around."

"We've made a few trips out."

McLaughton nodded slowly. "She knows her way around, so long as you stick to the more traveled routes."

"I have no complaints," said Jake.

"You lookin' to go beyond the more traveled routes, Mr. Quigley?"

"We've managed a few deviations on our own, and I may have plans for one or two more."

"Perhaps you could use a little more muscle."

"Meara has acquitted herself quite well in that regard, Mr. McLaughton." Jake studied the man carefully. "But, I wouldn't be opposed to bringing along a trustworthy sort, one who is familiar with the Outland and able to respond appropriately, when faced with the unexpected."

"There is little out there I haven't seen, Mr. Quigley, and even less that I can't handle."

"Overconfidence is not a trait that I'm looking for in a travelling companion, Mr. McLaughton."

McLaughton gave a dismissive shrug. "Just stating fact."

"The opinion of someone who mistakenly believes that he has seen it all." Jake stood up. "Pardon my bluntness, but whatever you've seen, whatever you've encountered, you have yet to leave the park. I don't hold that against you. That is to be expected. But I need someone with some imagination."

Jake turned and started away. He had taken three steps when McLaughton sat up straight and called after him.

"All right, Mr. Quigley. You have my attention. How about I buy you a cup of coffee?"

Jake took a few more steps and stopped near the table of the two men playing Serpent's Ladder. When he looked at Jeffers, Jeffers gave him a knowing smile before rolling the dice.

Jake gave Jeffers a wink, turned back to look at McLaughton. "A quick cup, and then I really have to go. Mrs. H. will have my hide if I'm late for dinner."

Jake told McLaughton very little about his experiences other than those of the Outland itself, though he did allude to the fact that there was something more. He dropped hints as to creatures beyond the unique creatures of the Outland. All of this was to gauge the man's reaction and try to draw out specifics on what the man may already have seen.

He found that McLaughton had made quite a number of the trips into the Outland, and had crossed paths with the obelisks, though he saw them as ancient stone markers and did not discern their real purpose or power. And he had faced the wolves on several occasions.

He had also been to the ravine, and had seen the silhouettes of great flying creatures within the abyss. He had wanted to go into the ravine, but hadn't been able to at the time. He planned to return there one day.

He and Jake came to an agreement, a fair flat rate for services for five to seven days. With a deal struck, Jake told him that he sought a stone marker to the east, and from there a Dark Lake.

"I know the marker you're looking for, but there's no lake to the east, dark or otherwise."

"You show me the stone obelisk, Mr. McLaughton, and I'll show you the lake."

"You're the boss, Mr. Quigley."

Tomorrow, then," said Jake, standing. "East gate."

"First light," said McLaughton. He stood and they shook hands again. Jake turned and started across the room.

"Hah! Look at this Quigley!" said old man Jeffers, pointing to the dice on the table. Jake stopped and tried to make since of it. "Dragon's Tail, son. A tough roll to get."

"I see," said Jake.

"It should be worth more; don't you think?"

"I really wouldn't know."

"Sure you would, son," said Jeffers. "Sure you would."

Jake stood at the island counter in the kitchen stuffing supplies into his backpack. Meara stalked out of the room just as Mr. Griffin entered.

Jake spoke up without looking up from this packing.

"You here to give me grief?"

"Absolutely not, Master Jacob."

"I got enough from Meara."

"Mr. McLaughton is adequate, if not always fully aboveboard."

"I don't want Meara to get hurt."

"I understand."

"You don't agree?" Jake stopped his packing and looked curiously up at Mr. Griffin. "You weren't all that keen on my bringing her along before."

"She has served you well; but I fully understand your concern for her safety." Mr. Griffin took a long, cautious breath. "My own concern at the moment is for your safety."

"McLaughton will do."

"I believe it is specifically in regard to Mr. McLaughton that Miss Gyles takes issue."

Jake closed his backpack and lifted it from the counter. "He knows only what he needs to know to get me to the next obelisk."

"Of course." Mr. Griffin stood silent. Jake looked at him warily, sensing there was something else. Mr. Griffin took an awkward step toward the counter as he reached into his jacket pocket.

He brought out four bullets and set them on the counter.

Chapter Fifteen

The sandy soil formed a narrow strip of beach opening out to the dark lake. Jake and Troy McLaughton stood at the water's edge, looking out across the black, glassy surface to a small island out in the heart of the lake.

Dark, heavily shadowed forests encircled the lake. The sky overhead was a sooty grey.

This Other World was a dark, still place. It made Jake feel uneasy.

McLaughton had been good to his word, taking Jake directly to the gate. From the possible description that Jake had provided, McLaughton assumed that it could have been no other clearing in the East Outland.

Accessing the gateway hadn't been quite as straightforward.

Toward the birth of day and the birth of life. Walk the path of reflection and enter there, search then within the hidden world to which those above are blind.

While the *birth of day* reference had brought them east, once the stone was found, Jake continually looked to the second line for the way to access the gateway. He just assumed there was something that he had missed when it came to the rest of the first line, and simply ignored it.

Once he forced himself to look at the *birth of life* reference as the possible key, the solution came, albeit with much difficulty.

He had noticed a concave recess set into the top of the stone, as if something that might be created by thousands of years of water dripping onto the stone and slowly creating a cup-like pocket. He had wondered about it, having not seen anything like it on the other stones that he had come upon. He had even tried pressing the spot, but nothing had happened.

Wasn't water supposed to be birth of life?

Jake took his canteen and poured water into the depression. He stepped back then and waited.

Nothing happened.

He stepped back toward the stone and looked into the depression. The water was gone.

Startled, he took a step back and studied the stone, looking for a sign that it was going to turn into the gateway. After a few moments, he saw something. He almost missed it, as he wasn't looking for it. He was looking for the mysterious change from solid stone to ethereal gateway.

There was a small dark spot on the face of the stone. He was certain it hadn't been there before. Moving nearer, he raised a hand and lightly brushed a finger across the spot.

It was damp.

Jake pushed in. There was a slight give. Jake stepped back and watched as the obelisk became a gateway to an Other World.

Now, as he and McLaughton stood at the shore of the lake, Jake felt drawn to the island beyond, but he wasn't sure how the text of the scroll could mean the island.

Walk the path of reflection could mean that they had to cross the water, perhaps even walk on the water.

"You figure whatever it is you're looking for is out there?" asked McLaughton, pointing to the island.

Jake nodded silently. He hadn't told McLaughton about the artifacts, the gateways or the scrolls. He hadn't even warned the man about the possibility of coming face to face with dragons, beyond telling him to watch out for unexpected obstacles that might stand in their way.

Meara had been very outspoken in her objections to Troy McLaughton, and it had been more than just leaving her behind in favor of the man. She knew McLaughton, mostly through reputation, and didn't like or trust him. He was going to find out about the gateways, about the Other Worlds, and about the artifacts. With such knowledge, he could become a dangerous man and a powerful enemy.

Jake didn't completely trust the man either, but had weighed the pros and cons and believed that he was making the right decision. McLaughton would be told only what was needed in order to help recover the artifact and return to Serpent's Keep.

None of this made Meara feel any better. He might not start out knowing very much, but in the end he would inevitably know way too much.

Staring out across the water, McLaughton stated that if they were going to get out to the island, they were going to need a boat. They split up, McLaughton heading north and Jake going south, agreeing to check back in a few minutes, boat or not.

Jake followed the shore for several hundred yards, having to skirt around thick brush a number of times but always managing to stay within site of the shoreline. He saw nothing, and, more ominously, he heard nothing. It was all deathly quiet.

Still, the air wasn't too hot or cold, wasn't too muggy, and the terrain was easily traveled. Despite some uneasiness that he couldn't quite shake, Jake was beginning to regret not allowing Meara to come with him. Particularly as he held the same misgivings as she did regarding McLaughton and the knowledge that he was going to come away with from this trip. He could cause trouble.

Jake returned to the beach to find McLaughton standing beside a small wooden boat.

"Nice work," said Jake.

"Found it tied to a little dock a couple of hundred yards up," said McLaughton. "I guess that means there's folks here after all."

Citizenry or visitors? Jake wondered. Or it could mean that there was a Guardian around, like Nehman. "We'll need to put it back, once we're done."

"If you say so." McLaughton held the bow of the boat steady and waved a welcoming arm, bidding Jake to climb aboard.

The journey out to the island was an eerily quiet, anxious one. Jake studied the water and the distant island as McLaughton worked the oars. The only sound was that of the wooden shafts of the oars twisting within the metal eyelets and the blades pushing easily into the water.

They appeared to be all alone; just the tree-lined shore, the lake, the island, the oppressive gray sky, and the two of them in a borrowed small, wooden boat.

And yet there were scurrying shadows moving about beneath the black, glassy surface of the water. They may have been nothing more than a trick of the eye as the boat glided through the water and the reflections of the low-hanging sky dancing across the mirror-like surface.

Jake thought it was more than that, but said nothing.

As they approached the island, the blackness behind the trees and heavy brush reached out to them and drew them in. Jake spotted an inlet and a clear stretch of shore inside it and directed McLaughton toward it. The air grew cool and damp and there was a strange heaviness about it.

Once the boat was secured, McLaughton took a moment to study their surroundings. The vegetation grew all the way to the water line on either side of them, and it was only where they had come ashore that there was any open ground at all.

"There," McLaughton said finally, pointing to a location in the tree line. Jake didn't see anything, but followed his guide. Reaching the brush that reached out from the trees, McLaughton pushed the bramble aside and stepped into the shadows.

The path, such as it was, led them inland, meandering in and around twisted trees and large, misshapen bushes. Again and again, McLaughton stopped and knelt down close to the ground to examine signs that would tell him if the nearly invisible trail led one way or another, or if the left fork or the right fork was the most used and hopefully the correct trail.

As they traveled, Jake struggled to hear a sound, any sound, that wasn't of their own making. He tuned out his breathing, his footfalls, and the brush of air against his eardrums as he walked. He tuned out the light footfalls of his guide.

What remained was silence. No animal noises, no rustling of a faint breeze through the canopy overhead. Nothing. It was as if this world wasn't there, that it was but a three-dimensional snapshot of a world from another time or place; it was as if they had stepped into a picture.

McLaughton stopped and waited for Jake to come forward. Without turning to acknowledge his presence, McLaughton nodded toward a large clearing ahead of them. In the heart of the clearing stood a small open temple; stone pillars at the corners supporting a flat stone roof.

"This what you lookin' for, Mr. Quigley?"

"Most likely, Mr. McLaughton." Jake looked around the clearing before stepping into the open. There was no movement, no sign of danger. He left the shadows of the trees and moved out onto the damp green grass that surrounded the little temple. Reaching the stone steps, Jake stopped and looked around again at the surroundings.

It was eerily peaceful. Well... the scroll did say to *walk the path of reflection...* and this would certainly be a quiet place to reflect; reflect on what, he had no idea. He turned and climbed the three steps up into the building.

The walls were open to the elements, with thick stone pillars standing at each corner, holding up a wide, flat roof. At the center of the roof was an opening in the shape of an oval, three feet wide and six feet long. The opening was directly above a large pool of water set into the center of the smooth stone floor of the building. The pool might have been kept filled by rainwater from overhead.

"Okay, you got me," said McLaughton. "I've never seen anything like this place before. Temples, yeah, but this... this is just weird." He walked along one side of the pool, studying the black water and the opening overhead. The pool was twenty feet long by eight feet wide, taking up a major portion of the interior of the temple.

Reflecting pool...

The phrase came unexpectedly into Jake's thoughts. He wasn't really sure what it meant or just what a reflecting pool might be. It was just a phrase that he had heard somewhere.

Walk the path of reflection...

Jake stepped up to the pool and positioned his toes right up to the edge. The length of the pool ran directly away from him. Looking down at the water, it was impossible to see beneath the surface. He could see his reflection and the reflection of the ceiling with its oval opening exposing the gray sky.

He had a thought, then. He stepped out into the pool, one foot, followed quickly by the other. McLaughton turned and started to call out, then snapped his mouth shut.

Jake was standing on the surface of the water. He paused several seconds and then took two short steps and stopped.

"It's only half an inch deep," he said. He stared down at his feet. He saw only himself looking back, and the oval opening in the roof beyond.

Walk the path of reflection...

He took another cautious step, stood now at the center of the pool. He felt something shift beneath his foot and there was a hollow grinding sound.

"Quigley?" McLaughton asked uncertainly.

The thin layer of water began draining away from the pool. Directly in front of him, a section of the floor of the shallow pool slid aside as an access to a narrow stairwell yawned open.

"Not bad, Mr. Quigley," said McLaughton, stepping out onto the empty pool. He gazed down into the black pit of the stairwell. "You figure on you and me going down there?"

"That's the plan."

McLaughton shook his head doubtfully. "Okay," he said. "I'll be right behind you."

"I appreciate that." Jake pulled his pack from his back and dug around for his hand lamp.

With the dull sphere of light pushing its way ahead of him, Jake cautiously worked his way down the steep stairs. The stairwell was just wide enough for him climb down without having to turn sideways, and once he was fully inside, just barely tall enough that he didn't have to hunch over. The stone walls were damp, the air held a stagnate smell, heavy with mildew.

Reaching the bottom, Jake stepped out into the room and found that the ceiling was just as low as the stairwell. His head almost brushed the wet, mossy ceiling.

Search then within the hidden world to which those above are blind.

Okay, Jake thought. *I'm searching...* He held the lamp out in front of him and turned about in a slow circle. The light reached out to only one wall, the others beyond the reach of the lamp. He was going to have to move back to the stairwell and then follow the perimeter. McLaughton grumbled something about following right behind him and Jake started out.

He found an open doorway in the center of the far wall, and after investigating the rest of the room and finding nothing else, returned to it. The hallway beyond was very narrow and in some places the ceiling was so low that he had to crouch down to continue. It twisted and turned and sloped down and then up and then down again. There were no side passages, though occasionally Jake saw small, round openings set high in the wall that he suspected might provide what little air there was.

The passageway began sloping upward again, this time at a fairly steep grade. After eight or nine steps, it turned right, continuing the same steep rate of ascent. Once he made the turn, he was able to see a dull glow up ahead. He slowed and turned off the lamp. Behind him, McLaughton quietly readied his pistol.

Jake stepped out into a round cavern, the centerpiece of which was a large, dark pool. The ceiling overhead was riddled with hundreds of tiny openings, and through them Jake could just make out the gray sky beyond.

"Man, what's that stink?" McLaughton scrunched his face against the onslaught of the smell of dragon's nest.

"Keep a sharp eye out," said Jake.

"For what?" McLaughton walked cautiously to the right of the pool and Jake walked to the left.

"Something resembling a dragon."

"A what?"

"Dragon."

"You're kiddin', right?" McLaughton asked anxiously.

Jake stopped beside a bed of decayed and dried water plants and damp soil set into a recess in the far wall. It looked vaguely similar to the nest that he had found in the desert. "One lives here."

"Yeah? Doubt that." McLaughton pointed up at the ceiling, speaking now in a harsh whisper. "Nothing bigger than a raven is gettin' through there. And as for the way we came, well, if it's coming and going through there, it's gonna be a mighty puny dragon."

Jake indicated the pool. "That's its way in and out," he said. "Amphibian." The statue in the Hall of Statues had in fact looked like it lived in water but could walk on land.

"You mean like a salamander?" McLaughton leaned out over the water and looked in.

"I'm guessing it's a bit larger than your garden variety salamander." Jake indicated the bedding. Turning his attention back to the pool, he thought about the last stretch of passageway they had travelled and the uphill climb. Considering that, and the visible sky in the ceiling, he figured they were back up to ground level. "I bet this connects to the lake," he said. "There's probably an underground waterway leading out to it."

"And this giant salamander of yours spends his days out there, and comes in here to sleep?" McLaughton was not quite convinced as to the whole dragon thing, but was growing slowly more concerned. He could think of more plausible explanations for all of this than dragons, amphibious or otherwise. Still, if any of what this guy was saying was true... "Then how about we find whatever it is you're looking for and get out of here before it comes back?"

"Excellent idea, Mr. McLaughton." Jake climbed up onto the creature's bedding and began digging around with his feet. McLaughton watched, grimacing at the smell emanating from the decomposing mulch that this mysterious animal slept on.

"What am I supposed to be looking for?" he asked.

"Smooth, flat polygon, a few inches across."

"Poly what?"

"A geometric artifact. Flat, about half an inch thick; polygon shaped, you know... rectangle with extra sides."

"What?"

"You'll know it when you see it."

McLaughton glanced around the cavern. There weren't a lot of places to hide one of these *geometric artifacts*. He wandered slowly about, looking into shadows, scratching at the dusty floor with his foot. All the while, he kept an anxious watch on the dark pool, expecting Quigley's mysterious dragon to make an appearance. "Ya' know, a serpent is snake. Dragons have legs."

"What?" Jake glanced up for a moment, returned to digging around the nest.

"Serpents and dragons aren't the same thing."

"I didn't say they were."

"But it's called *Serpent's* Keep, not *Dragon's* Keep."

"Dragons might not be serpents, but serpents are dragons," Jake said impatiently. "Dragons without legs."

"What?"

Jake stopped searching. It wasn't in the nest.

"Do you know all about dragons? Maybe the dragon at Serpent's Keep didn't have legs."

"There's a dragon at Serpent's Keep?"

"I don't know."

"Interesting," said McLaughton. He still thought this Quigley character was a bit bonkers. But... he was Tobias Quigley's nephew, and Tobias Quigley was into some pretty weird stuff. "So, if a serpent is a dragon, and a snake is a serpent, then is a snake a dragon?"

"I didn't say *all* serpents were dragons."

"Sure you did."

"I don't know. I'm not a dragonologist."

"A dragon-what?"

"I didn't name your village."

"I know that, but I thought you said—" McLaughton gave up and shook it off. He put his hands on his hips. "Your poly-whatever isn't here, Mr. Quigley."

Jake stepped down off the nest and took several steps toward the pool. He stopped at the water's edge.

McLaughton studied the man's face, then looked down into the water. A faint panic washed over his face. "Nuh-uh. Not me."

Jake sighed. "If it's not up here, it has to be down there."

"I don't care."

"I'll do it."

"You said it yourself. The dragon is in there."

"I thought you didn't believe in my dragon."

"I believe there's *something*."

Jake pulled off his shoes and sat down, slid his feet into the water. At least it wasn't cold. He wouldn't die of hypothermia before getting eaten by a giant salamander. "Wish me luck," he said, and slipped into the water.

"Well, *duh*. You haven't told me how we're supposed to go back through that gate."

Jake grinned and let himself drop beneath the surface.

The water was dark but clear, and whereas from above he could see nothing, from beneath the surface he could see a fairly good distance. He wasn't able to see all the way across the pool, however, so he concentrated his efforts on the near side first, using his hands to push himself deeper and deeper.

There was no life visible in the water. The wall was rough stone with very few recesses. It was as eerily quiet in the water as it was in the woods of the island above. It made Jake nervous.

After going down twenty or twenty five feet, he returned quickly to the surface to catch his breath. He gave McLaughton a quick *'nothing yet'* and slid back under the surface again, moving to another section of the cavern pool.

On his third trip beneath the surface, Jake found a large tunnel opening in the wall about twelve feet down. Afraid at first that the as yet unseen dragon would rush out at him, he frantically pushed himself back and up, scrambling out of the water as soon as he reached the surface.

"What is it?" McLaughton leapt up and back, certain that something was going to come flying out of the pool at him.

"A tunnel," Jake said between deep breaths. "I found a tunnel."

"Yeah..." McLaughton looked at Jake with a puzzled expression. "Well you said the pool was connected to the lake."

"No. I think that's deeper down. This is different. This goes somewhere else."

"Your dragon has a summer cottage?"

Search then within the hidden world to which those above are blind.

"I'm going to have to go in there," he said.

"You be careful," said McLaughton, as Jake slid back into the water.

"I know," Jake smiled. "I gotta show you the way out of here."

"Exactly."

Jake slipped beneath the surface and vanished from sight, leaving McLaughton staring at his own reflection.

Jake quickly swam down to the tunnel entrance, stopped and stared directly into it, placing one hand on the rim of the opening to steady himself. He saw nothing but black. Realizing that he was either going to have to go into the tunnel immediately or return to the surface, he pushed himself into the darkness.

He propelled himself by pushing himself first off one wall and then the other, noting that the underwater tunnel was large enough to accommodate a dragon, albeit a slim one: long and sleek and amphibious; and capable of reaching out from the darkness and snapping up unwary intruders.

Half a minute into the tunnel, Jake considered turning back. He had no way of knowing how much further he might have to go, but did know how far he would have to go to get back to the surface. If he continued much further, he would have trouble making it out.

Just as the phrase *beyond the point of no return* came to mind, he thought he could see a faint glow in the water far ahead. He rushed forward, almost in a panic, hurtling himself towards the dull light. It grew slowly brighter, which encouraged him to continue pushing onward.

The underground waterway opened abruptly into a pool similar to the one that he had left behind, and he quickly swam up to the surface. After taking several moments to breathe in fresh oxygen, he looked about and glided toward the nearest bank.

He was in a cavern of sorts, though the dome-like roof had large, gaping holes opening to the sky. The interior was exposed enough that there were trees and brush growing in the cavern, and there was a groundcover of grass and weed over much of the floor.

There was no dragon, and no sign that a dragon lived there.

An alter stone stood near one wall. On it was a box similar to the one that Jake had found in the Abandoned City, and in the box was the artifact.

He suspected that if he had searched around enough in the caves of the Desert world oasis, he probably would have found an alter stone there as well, but in that world the dragon had taken the artifact and hidden it in its nest.

Finding an alter with a box containing an artifact in two different worlds was definitely a good sign. This gave Jake a commonality to look for once he was through a gate and had used the scroll to reach the location in the next Other World.

McLaughton was staring down at him as Jake surfaced once again in the main cavern. "You were gone a long time, Mr. Quigley," he said, reaching down to pull Jake out of the water. He sounded very relieved.

"Sorry about that," Jake sat at the edge of the pool and took a moment to catch his breath.

"Did you find what you were looking for?"

Jake pulled the artifact out of his shirt and handed it to McLaughton. He saw no reason to hide it from him. If the man had bad intentions, not showing him what he found wasn't going to stop him.

McLaughton looked unimpressed. "This is it, huh?"

"That's it."

"What's it do?" McLaughton tossed it casually back to Jake.

Jake stood and walked over to his backpack. "It's just one part of a puzzle, Mr. McLaughton," he said, stuffing the artifact safely away.

"Puzzle..." McLaughton said flatly.

"Yep." Jake lifted his pack and slung it over his shoulder. "How about we get out of here?" He wanted to get as far from the cavern as possible, as quickly as possible. While the artifact hadn't been easy to find, at least he hadn't had to do battle for it, and he would just as soon keep it that way.

They took the long, narrow passageway back to the stairwell and eventually climbed out and up to the temple. It was as quiet as when they had last been there, what seemed like days earlier but in fact had only been a few hours. Dark shadows lay over the scene, crawling in from the surrounding woods. Jake found the entire island creepy, and the temple clearing gave him the willies.

The walk back through the forest to the boat was long and overshadowed with the heavy sensation that something was about to happen; something bad... Jake and McLaughton hardly spoke at all throughout the entire return journey, and Jake was certain that his companion was fighting that same ominous sense of impending disaster. When they finally stepped out of the woods and onto the small beach, he had the odd feeling that they had somehow averted some great and horrible confrontation.

They silently pushed the boat into the water and left the island, grateful for their good fortune.

Then, halfway between the island and the shore, just as Jake was beginning to shake off the gloom and doom that he had been wrapped in, there was a surge beneath the boat and the smooth, sleek head of a serpent-like dragon rose up from the water directly beside them. The curve of its long neck undulated as the creature rolled its back slowly forward and backward, rising up and looking down upon the two humans in the tiny, wooden boat. It twisted its head and studied first McLaughton and then Jake.

"Greetings," it said at last, its calm voice as smooth and slippery as its damp, shiny skin.

McLaughton started for his weapon, but Jake held his arm. McLaughton gave a quick, questioning look, and then relented, though he didn't look happy about it.

"Hello," said Jake.

"What brings you uninvited to my water?" The cadence of the sentence curled as the curve of the neck rolled down from head to shoulder. The dragon wore the disquieting façade of a broad, slippery smile. It had observed the response of both humans, and had calculated various possible scenarios.

"We are on a gathering quest for my uncle, Tobias Quigley."

The dragon looked unsurprised and unimpressed. "I smell Quigley blood, human, but I see only you..."

"Tobias Quigley and I are of the same family; the same blood."

"Even if that be true, how does that give you the right to come unbidden into my home?"

McLaughton leaned close to Jake. "Talk isn't how we're going to deal with this, Quigley," he said harshly.

"Your companion is not of a friendly sort, is he, human?"

"My name is Jacob Quigley." *Was this dragon more articulate than the others that he had come across, or just more slippery with words?*

"Jacob Quigley," breathed the dragon. "I take seriously the responsibility given me."

"I understand your responsibility. The same as has been given to others I have met on my quest. They have seen and understood my duty, given to me by my uncle."

"The gathering..." the dragon said silkily.

"Yes."

"No," the dragon said suddenly and sharply, turning its gaze quickly away from the human. He sniffed the air noisily. "You have taken that which belongs to me. I will have it back."

"That's it," said McLaughton, and he pulled out his weapon. Jake struck McLaughton's arm and grasped the man's wrist.

"Stop it, you dolt."

The dragon held its chin high in the air, but turned its gaze askance down at the two humans in the boat. It carefully watched the interaction between them.

When Jake and McLaughton finally returned their attention to the creature, it gave a loud grunt-like *snuffing* sound, and then waited, no longer deigning to look at the intruders.

Jake stood slowly, careful not to tip over the boat. He held his hands out and spoke respectfully. "You have served well as Guardian of the artifact. I stand before you now and humbly ask that you allow me to fulfill my duty. Please, allow me to pass."

The dragon looked down at the human for a long time. Jake could hear the creature's breathing, the only other sound being the placid noise of the water thumping gently against the hull of the boat.

"Blood of Tobias Quigley," the dragon said at last, speaking in a slippery but formal tone, "You... and your unpleasant attendant, may pass."

The dragon slid beneath the surface of the lake so smoothly that there was almost no ensuing wake. Jake waited several moments before carefully returning to his seat.

"We can go now," he said.

"That was something," said McLaughton, putting away his weapon. He took hold of the oars. "I still think we could have taken it."

"It's on our side, Mr. McLaughton."

"Didn't look that way to me."

It was almost dark when Jake and McLaughton stepped through the gate and returned to the Outland, so they decided to make camp near the gate obelisk and start the trip back to the village in the morning. It was only a day's journey, and if all went well they could be home by nightfall the next day.

Once McLaughton had finished his inspection of the perimeter, he returned to Jake and sat down beside his gear. He pulled out his canteen and took a deep swallow, then watched as Jake got the kindling burning. "A cup of coffee sounds good about now," he said.

"We have enough for one more pot." Jake was starting the campfire in the fire pit they had used during their time spent in the clearing earlier; the days during which Jake had searched for a way to open the gateway.

"Okay," McLaughton sighed. "It can wait till morning."

McLaughton looked over at the stone as if reassessing a long-held belief. "I never knew the old girl had such a secret in her, Mr. Quigley. She surprised me."

"Come now, Mr. McLaughton... I wouldn't think that anything in the Outland could surprise you." There was just the slightest edge of sarcasm in his voice.

"Ah, my own words, back at me. Guess I deserve it." He gave Jake a studied look. "The other stones hold similar secrets, then?"

"I don't know about all of them."

McLaughton took a step nearer the stone. "Those things have been staring me in the face my entire life."

It was the middle of the night when Jake was awakened. The clearing was quiet, and was enveloped in a bluish glow. Sitting up, He saw that McLaughton had activated the gate and was standing mesmerized before it. Jake reached anxiously into the pocket of his backpack, was relieved when he found the artifact was still there.

He stood and approached McLaughton. "I wouldn't go in there," he said.

McLaughton spoke without taking his eyes from the glowing magic in front of him. "An amazing piece of work."

Jake stepped beside McLaughton, held the artifact out protectively. "Without this, you'd never get back."

McLaughton coolly watched Jake tuck the artifact into his shirt pocket. "Have you thought about the possibilities, Mr. Quigley? The opportunities that are opened up to you; and you alone know the secret."

"Not me alone."

"Where it counts, Mr. Quigley."

"As may be, Mr. McLaughton. But it's not about opportunity."

"It's always about opportunity." He indicated the artifact in Jake's pocket. "Of course, it doesn't really matter who knows, does it? Even if someone can figure out how to open a gateway, without an artifact, the specific artifact, it doesn't mean much, does it?"

"Depends on what that someone is after."

McLaughton silently agreed, then smiled and nodded in the direction of the open gateway. "How about letting me take a trip through and back?"

"I don't think so, Mr. McLaughton."

"What would it hurt? I'll be gone and back before you know it."

"It's not a toy."

"It's the greatest toy in the universe, Mr. Quigley."

Jake turned away from McLaughton and the gate. From past experience, he knew that if no one went through, the gate would eventually close on its own.

McLaughton reached out and grabbed Jake by the upper arm. "I think I'd like to go through." His tone strongly hinted that he was going to insist that he go through.

"Go right ahead." Jake tried to be just as stern. "I won't stop you."

"I'm going to need that little trinket."

Jake slowly shook his head no.

McLaughton softened his tone, but it came across more menacing. "I'll be right back... Mr. Quigley."

Jake looked down at McLaughton's grip on his arm, as if studying it. He looked up then into the eyes of the man.

"Stop and reflect, Mr. McLaughton. What do you think you're going to get from this one gate?"

"It's a start," said McLaughton, and with that he pulled Jake around and pushed him into the gate, holding onto him as he followed him in. Once inside, as they rushed toward the Other World of the Dark Lake, McLaughton dug into Jake's shirt with his free hand, and the two of them began to wrestle for the artifact.

Jake suddenly realized that McLaughton planned to strand him in the Other World. With the artifact in hand, he could reinitialize the gate and return alone. Once back in Serpent's Keep, without Jake to hinder him, he would no doubt attempt to locate the other artifacts that Jake had already gathered.

Jake absolutely could not let that happen.

He gripped tightly to the artifact; he brought up his right leg and, leaning back, put his foot against McLaughton's chest and pushed.

McLaughton's grip on Jake was broken.

Troy McLaughton just disappeared. He didn't fade away. He didn't slowly drift out of sight. He simply vanished.

Jake had entered the gateway first. He was the directing entity to the other side. So long as McLaughton held onto him, they could pass through together. Without Jake, McLaughton was lost somewhere in the in-between place. Jake didn't know what that meant, only that it had happened before to the marauders that he and Meara had confronted at another gate.

Jake knelt down beside the hexagon pattern in the floor of the Serpent's Gate room and set the latest artifact piece into place. He stood then and looked down at the partially completed artifact.

Mr. Griffin stood near the doorway to the hallway that led back to the mansion basement.

"I trust Mr. McLaughton was helpful?" he asked.

"Very subtle," said Jake. "Yes, he was helpful. No, I shouldn't have taken him."

"I'm very sorry to hear that." Mr. Griffin walked to center of the room and looked down at the pattern in floor. Three pieces were now in place.

When Jake had returned to the village alone, the guard on duty had not been the same person who had let them out a few days earlier, but he had known that Jake had left the village with Troy McLaughton and so asked about him. When hearing that McLaughton would not be returning, the guard had simply nodded and told Jake that he would need to check in with the sheriff.

The sheriff listened calmly and dutifully took down the facts, as Jake had described the incident. He glanced up from his paperwork at the mention of wolves, but chose not to press the matter. He no doubt suspected that McLaughton had attempted to move in on whatever Jake was doing and had paid the price, but for now it seemed that he would remain silent. An attack by wolves would do for now.

"Will he be a problem?" asked Mr. Griffin.

"No." Jake stated flatly and started toward the hall. "Mr. McLaughton won't be a problem."

Mrs. Hodges said little during dinner, but Jake could tell that she knew what had happened. By that time, most of the village must have known. Sheriff Smith had probably only informed those that needed informing, but they had no doubt told a few, and those few had told a few... and then of course there was the guard at the gate. He may not have known the facts, but he knew that Troy McLaughton wasn't coming back.

Jake had insisted on eating in the kitchen rather than the dining room, and regretted it. Mrs. Hodges' silence as she hustled about the room made him uncomfortable. It wasn't that he felt guilty about what had happened, nor did he think that she blamed him for it, but the whole thing had changed him and maybe that change had altered his relationship with Mrs. Hodges.

Later, as he lay awake in bed, unable to sleep, he thought about how this latest trip out might have gone if he had taken Meara instead of McLaughton. Certainly it would have taken longer to find the gateway, and McLaughton had definitely helped as they searched the paths on the island. And he wouldn't have liked for Meara to have had to face the dangers they had faced. He wondered whether he would have acted differently in the confrontations had Meara been beside him instead of Troy McLaughton. Would that have changed the outcome?

He had no idea what he was going to do on his next trip into the Outland.

Chapter Sixteen

Jake could barely make out the figure of the monk. A heavy fog was rolling through the forest and the trail ahead quickly faded into the wet mist. The robed man maintained a brisk pace, faster than Jake wanted to travel, and he had to stop and wait for Jake at each fork in the trail to ensure that Jake didn't get lost.

That was just too bad. Jake was walking as fast as he was willing. If the monk didn't like it, he could leave him behind. Jake had made this trip to the temple before and he could probably find his way again.

And after all, the man had come looking for him, not the other way around. That was surprising in itself, and Mr. Griffin had literally been at a loss for words when the monk had shown up at the mansion asking for Jacob Quigley. He had been even more taken aback when the monk had asked Jake to accompany him to the temple.

The guard at the West Gate had been just as surprised. The temple monks only rarely came to the village, usually for supplies they couldn't produce themselves or acquire elsewhere. They never came looking for residents of the village, and certainly never sought them out in order to escort them back to the temple.

So it must have been important.

So the monk could just slow down. Jake would walk at whatever pace he wanted and would get there whenever he got there.

The open clearing in front of the temple was shrouded in the same shifting mist as the rest of the Outland, and the tall temple spires reached into low, gray clouds that blanketed the world. The monk moved smoothly through the fog and stopped at the foot of the steps. Standing at the top step was another monk, whom Jake recognized once he drew near.

"John," he said. He didn't really know what John's role in the temple was, but he thought of him as Peter's assistant.

"Hello, Master Quigley. It is good of you to come."

"My curiosity got the best of me. Your man here wouldn't tell me anything."

John nodded to Jake's escort, who silently climbed the steps and went into the temple. Once the monk had gone inside, John said softly, "Master Peter is most anxious to speak with you."

"What about?"

"That would be for Master Peter to address." John turned to the door. Jake gave up and climbed the steps. Once inside, John led him through the narrow hallways to the library. He left him there, stating simply that Master Peter would be with him shortly.

The library was much as it had been the last time he had been there. It smelled of ancient paper and old glue, and there was a golden glow emanating from the lamps. Jake went to one of the tables and casually turned the pages of several books that were stacked there. The words were of a language that he was not familiar with, and he closed the books one by one.

"Brother Jacob," said Peter, coming into the room. He closed the door behind him. "Good of you to come."

"So I hear."

"I hope it wasn't too much trouble." Peter moved to one of the larger tables, waving a hand for Jake to follow and sit in one of the high-back chairs.

"Not at all," said Jake.

"Good, good." Peter sat down, placed his arms on the table and clasped his hands together. He wore a genuine smile on his face. "You have been a busy man, Brother Jacob."

Jake shrugged in answer.

"Oh, come now, don't be modest. I have been kept apprised of your journeys into the Outland."

"Oh?"

"And all is going well?"

"Well enough," said Jake. He chose not to speak of the Other Worlds or of the artifacts. If the leader of the monks already knew of the Other Worlds, then he had chosen not to tell Jake of them during his last visit; and if he didn't know of the Other Worlds, then Tobias had chosen not to tell the monks, and there had probably been a reason. "Master Peter, you didn't bring me all the way out here to ask about my walkabouts."

"No, no, of course not." Peter stretched to his left and grasped a very large, very old book that was sitting on the table. He slid it in front of him and placed both hands flat on the leather cover. "This is a collection of narratives put down by the founding members of our order. They were written in an ancient, nearly forgotten dialect that was used, quite frankly, to keep those within the order *in the know,* and those not in the order *in the dark.*"

Jake indicated the shelves around them. "Many others in this... dialect?"

"Some of them very important works." Peter softly patted the ancient book in front of him. "As such, the necessity of learning the language."

"And what did you find this time that you think I need to know?"

"Yes," Peter raised a finger and pointed down at the book. "An interesting passage, considering your quest."

Jake visibly stiffened at the word *quest.* Peter leaned over the book and slowly nodded.

"It refers to a labyrinth. It is quite cryptic, and does not speak to specifics, other than to say that it lay in the path of a great quest."

"You believe that this quest is my quest?"

"I do."

"But how? I mean, if this thing was written hundreds of years ago—"

"Millennia ago, actually."

"Then how could the author know—"

"Brother Jacob... there is much that I do not know, but I can say with absolute certainty that the events of the distant past blazed the trail you now travel. Those who participated in those events knew the events in which you are now involved would occur."

Given all that had happened since his arrival at Serpent's Keep, Jake could no longer completely discount such a thing. And, considering the preparations that had been made at the time the gate to the Rhetani had been closed and the artifacts had been scattered to the Other Worlds, the people back then had indeed anticipated the events surrounding the gathering of them up again.

Okay, I can accept that they knew at least some of what would be faced by the person who would one day gather the artifacts.

"So, this labyrinth... I haven't come across one yet, so it must be something I have to look forward to. Where is it?"

"From what I can infer through my translations, I believe that it is not of this world," said Peter. He studied Jake's face for a reaction, but saw none. "There is also have a phrase that translates to something like *'The labyrinth lay beyond the way and in the path, and must be navigated'*."

Jake frowned, but said nothing.

"You will have to face this. It must be navigated."

"So I gather," said Jake. Somewhere beyond one of the gates, between the obelisk and wherever an Other World artifact was hidden, would be some sort of labyrinth. What made Jake anxious was that the writer of this manuscript had seen fit to document this. Up to now, all he had needed to know had been on the scrolls hidden away in the pedestals of the dragon statues. What made this different?

"And there is this," said Peter. He pulled a sheet of paper from the inside cover of the book and slid it across the table. On the paper, someone had recently drawn a diagram. Jake had only to glance at it to recognize it as one of the artifact symbols. "This image was annotated in the margins beside the text. There was no explanation."

"This will help," said Jake. He would be able to combine the information of the labyrinth with the scroll belonging to the statue that bore this symbol. He looked up from the paper and gave a gracious nod. "I appreciate this, Peter."

Peter slid the heavy book aside. "I have no doubt that we are all dependent upon the success of your undertaking."

"Of that I am increasingly certain."

It was a rare warm afternoon in Serpent's Keep. Jake and Meara sat at a table in the plaza across the way from the estate. An old map was spread out between them. Meara pointed to a location on the map.

"The North Highway is about two hours beyond the Farm. Take that west; it should get you where you need to go." The Farm was known to everyone in the Village. Most of their food was grown there. This highway, though, was new to Jake.

"I like the sound of that," he said.

Meara looked up at Jake. "It is still Outland. There will be dangers. There are some who prey on those traveling the highway."

"I've had to deal with bandits all over the Outland. How will this be different?"

"It won't. And the North Highway will get you there faster."

Jake sensed movement behind him and turned to see a man carrying a long flame-rod. He was moving from pole to pole along the plaza's main walkway, lighting the gas lamps. Only then did Jake notice that dusk had fallen. It would be dark soon.

He turned back to look at the map, then at Meara. "Thank you for your help, Meara."

"You should know that near the end of the North Highway, where you leave the highway, you'll be entering rough lands. That part of the Outland is probably the least hospitable you'll find out there."

Jake studied the map, noting where he had marked his departure from the North Highway. He had the used the hand drawn diagram given him by Peter to locate the next scroll. He had it memorized.

> The winding path leads north and west, through and
> beyond well travelled trails. See the face that is seldom seen,
> find south and east to get you through.

The first line could very well have referred to where Jake would leave the highway, the path through the rough country that Meara referred to. The second line... in the past the second line was usually a clue as to how to open the gateway. But this time? Jake really had no way of knowing.

Once he got through the gateway, somewhere between the obelisk and wherever the artifact was hidden, lay the labyrinth.

"Please, Master Jacob," pleaded Meara. "You need to take me with you."

"We've already been through this." Jake's thoughts continued to pull first in one direction, and then another. He spoke then as if to himself. "There's something odd about this one. Up to now, all that I've needed I've found on the scrolls. This one is different. Why this warning from some ancient temple text?"

"Sir, everything about this trip says that you can't go alone."

"Everything about this trip says that I *have* to go alone."

"Sir—"

"I go alone."

The road from the village to the farm was well-defined from many years of use by wagons loaded with supplies and food. The first part of the trip was familiar to Jake, as he had taken the north route out of the village on his first expedition into the Outland. Early on, however, where on the previous journey he had veered east, this time he continued north.

It was midday before he reached the Farm; a vast expanse of cultivated fields spreading out to his right, the dirt road running along the western edge of the cleared land. It had been cut out of the forests of the Outland, with the road that he walked serving as the boundary between wilderness and agriculture.

The Farm was as much a part of the village as the marketplace; this was where the village got its food, with only very little coming from the *outside world*. The land looked well-tended, though he didn't see anyone out in the fields. There was a cluster of buildings in the heart of the Farm, but they were too far away for Jake to make out anyone.

It was all a bit too quiet, and at first he assumed this was the reason for the uncomfortable feeling that he had about the scene. Then he remembered having the same sensation back when he was on the island in the middle of the Dark Lake; there was no sound, no movement; it was like a picture, like a painting made by someone who didn't really know what a farm was like. Everything was right, and yet something was wrong.

However intently he studied the scene before him, Jake could not figure out what it was about the place that made him ill at ease, but he knew that the next time he sat down to a meal, he was going to look more closely at what was on his fork.

It took a long time to get past the Farm. It was a big place, with a lot of fields growing a lot of different crops. He noted that all the while he had been walking past those fields, there hadn't been so much as a breeze blowing across the wheat, the corn, the tomatoes, the potato plants. The world was still.

About two hours beyond the last field, Jake found the North Highway running east to west. It was sixty feet wide, smooth and straight; a hard, flat surface was covered in a low, yellow-green grass. He suspected that there might be something artificial just underneath the groundcover, but didn't take the time to investigate. He turned west and started down the center of the wide road.

He had been traveling only a few minutes when he saw a shimmering far on the horizon that eventually formed into the silhouette of someone or something coming towards him. It took another quarter of an hour or so before he could make out that it was the figure of a man leading a horse and wagon. As it drew nearer yet, he could see that the wagon was empty.

"Hello," said Jake, when the man was finally close enough that they could speak in a normal voice. He kept moving toward the stranger, and the man continued to lead the horse forward.

"Hello," the man said cautiously. A large rifle was cradled in his arms. He had probably brought it down from the wagon when he had first glimpsed Jake.

When they were twenty feet apart, Jake stopped and waited. The man continued slowly for another few steps and then he too stopped.

"You heading for the Farm?" Jake asked.

The man nodded. "Heading there," he said.

"A nice place. The Farm, I mean."

"I like it."

Jake indicated the road behind the man. "Any problems?"

"Been no problems to now. You should be all right."

"Good to hear," Jake said, nodding. "Ways to travel yet."

The man shifted his weapon and gave the horse a light tug. He started forward again. "Good luck to you," he said, with little emotion.

"Yeah," said Jake as he watched the man pass by. "You too." *Nice talkin' with ya...*

He walked the highway throughout the afternoon. The forests of the Outland pushed up close to the highway most of the way, though there were occasional clearings and small meadows along the roadside. An hour before dusk, he came upon a small group of people that was gathered in one of the clearings. They had made camp and had started a small cooking fire. The two men in the group stood as a wall between Jake and the camp. Behind them, several children ran over to a woman who may have been their mother. Another older woman sat near the fire and ignored the commotion.

"Waddya want?" asked one of the men, cold and firm, but not overly snippy.

"Not a thing," said Jake. First the man with the wagon, and now these guys... Maybe there was real cause to be nervous when traveling the highway. "Just passing by."

"We ain't got enough to share."

"Not asking," said Jake. He started walking. "Be seein' ya."

The men stood unmoving, their eyes fixed on Jake's every move as he passed by.

"Good luck to you," said one of them, with as little emotion as the man with the wagon had spoke hours before.

"Yeah," mumbled Jake, not caring whether they heard him or not. "You too." *Nice talkin' with ya...*

He found the trail that he was looking for just before the sun went down. Wider than most that he had come upon in the Outland, it led away from North Highway just after the highway began to narrow. If what he had seen on the map was correct, the highway itself would end another mile to the west.

Jake followed the trail for a thousand paces before moving off to a small clearing on the left, where he set up camp for the night. He cleared away much of the brush around the perimeter, exposing those shadows that could hide someone or something that might try to creep up on him, then gathered kindling and firewood. He made a small campfire and prepared a light dinner. Afterward, settled into a comfortable spot near a bed of warm coals, he had some quiet time to think on things.

Despite the nervous manner of the folks that he had met that day, his hours on the North Highway had been trouble-free and there had been no sign of danger. Highwaymen may yet jump out of the dark at any moment, but up to that point it had been a peaceful day. Still, he would let the coals die out and let the cool night close in on him. He probably should have eaten a cold dinner, but he hadn't exactly hidden his arrival in the area and his small dinner fire had probably not given anything away that hadn't already been given.

He thought about Meara and regretted, yet again, not bringing her with him. But he believed that leaving her back in the village had been the right thing to do. The dangers yet to come were very real. This, he knew. If his attention was directed to her safety and not to the goals of the quest, and it would be difficult to do otherwise, then he was more likely to make a mistake. And if, despite all his efforts and all her ability, something were to happen to her, he would never forgive himself.

Yes. Leaving her behind had been the right thing to do. Despite her knowledge and expertise, her strength, and the fact that at that moment he felt very alone and very vulnerable, leaving her behind had still been the right thing to do.

And still he wished that he had brought her.

Chapter Seventeen

The journey from the trailhead at the North Highway to the clearing with the obelisk had been as difficult as he had been led to believe. The trails were narrow and twisted and overgrown, when he could follow them at all; the forest was dark and heavily shadowed, the trees misshapen and gnarled and ugly. The sounds that emanated from the dark were chilling and ominous. It all seemed... haunting.

The clearing, when he finally found it, was obvious. A great stone stood in the center of an open area that seemed to push back against the encroaching forest, rather than the forest pushing in on the clearing. The ground was covered in a mulchy layer of dead leaves and twigs and other decomposing vegetation.

As Jake stood before the stone, the great obelisk loomed high over him, its shadow laying over him. He calmly tossed his gear aside and quietly circled the clearing and surveyed the perimeter. He cleared away brush and began preparing his encampment, glancing now and again at the obelisk.

The winding path leads north and west, through and beyond well traveled trails. Seek the face that is seldom seen, find south and east to get you through.

The *winding path* had brought him to the clearing. He wondered now whether the *face seldom seen* was a clue to opening the gateway or to locating the labyrinth. Perhaps the *find south and east to get you through* reference referred to locating the labyrinth.

More likely, the entire second sentence referred to opening the gateway and the labyrinth was not referenced at all in this scroll text.

Once camp was set up, Jake sat before the small fire and studied the pillar. When the coffee was ready, he poured a cup and walked slowly around the stone, cup in hand, studying the ethereal images formed by the changing shadows. The world was as quiet as ever, and he found himself easing peacefully into the oncoming dusk.

He eventually returned to the fire and prepared a small meal using the standard rations. After dinner, once the sun had fully set, he studied the surface of the stone with only the light of a flickering torch to bring out the shifting images. From past experience, Jake had learned that he needed to be patient when seeking the key to these gateways. He now thought nothing about giving it up for the night and settling in to sleep.

Perhaps the answer would show itself in the morning. After all, the scrolls weren't meant to prevent him from accessing the gateway, but rather to aid in overcoming the precautions put into place to prevent anyone from inadvertently opening a gate. It had to be assumed that if someone had recovered the scroll from the Hall of Statues, and had arrived at the correct, corresponding stone pylon, that the individual had some inherent right to access the gateway. Because of this, the scroll needn't be too cryptic.

The morning found Jake staring at the stone.

Face seldom seen...

Find south and east...

The side of the pillar facing southeast? But how is that *seldom seen?*

Jake didn't get up from his place near the fire. He had already checked the southeast side of the stone a number of times and had found nothing.

His thoughts returned to the original assumption that the *face* reference meant the face of a dragon. Somehow, some way, dragons always seemed to be involved.

But he saw no image of a dragon, or a face of a dragon...

If not a dragon, then what was meant by the *face seldom seen?*

The sun's rays spidered through the trees and daggered across the clearing. The stone pillar took on new life as shadows and light danced across its surface. Jake watched in fascination, hoping for some sign, some clue that might lead him to the key.

A quick reflective glint flickered momentarily and was gone. It had appeared at about eye level, and if he hadn't been looking at exactly that spot on the stone, he wouldn't have seen it. He stood, staring at the location, leaning to one side and then another, lowering his head and raising it. A flash of light came and went several times as he changed perspective, and he moved slowly toward the stone, never losing sight of the position on the surface.

There was a spot on the rock's surface, several inches in diameter, that was smooth to sight and touch. He rubbed at it with two fingers and found that the surface almost shone. He wet his fingers and rubbed at it again.

It was almost like glass. Leaning forward, he saw his eye reflecting back at him. He leaned his head back a few inches and saw himself reflected in the small, mirror-like surface.

A face seldom seen...

People seldom saw their own faces, and back in the time the scroll was written, people likely saw themselves much less often than they did now.

Jake pushed in on the blemish. Nothing happened. He frowned, furrowed his brow and stared harshly at the spot. He was certain this was the key.

But there had to be more to it. Over the centuries, someone could easily have spotted this shiny spot in the stone, rubbed its surface, and even pressed on it.

Find south and east to get you through...

Jake took a step back and slowly let his gaze move down the stone and to the right, south and east from the face seldom seen. There were several likely candidates, several circular dark or shiny blemishes in the stone that might serve as the second half to the key.

He held two fingers lightly against the mirror-blemish, reached down with his other hand and placed two fingers over a dark, raised knob of stone. He pushed in on the two locations at the same time.

He heard and felt nothing. He gave it a few moments, and then moved on to a second thumb-sized blemish, again raised to form a slight knob. Again he pressed on the two locations at the same time. Again there was nothing.

On the third try, however, this time a dark spot set into a slight dimple in the stone, Jake felt a slight click and release against his fingertips, felt a slight give in the stone. He stepped back six steps and watched the now familiar transformation from ancient stone pillar to shimmering gateway.

Moments later, Jake stepped out of the gateway and into another clearing. This one was surrounded by an even darker forest than the one he had left behind. A damp, pungent smell pushed in from all around him. Overhead, the sky was a dull gray with low, black clouds that hung unmoving above him. Far in the distance, a castle of menacingly tall walls stood on the crest of a high hill, silhouetted against black sky and blacker clouds. Somewhere between the clearing and the castle, Jake should find the labyrinth. Considering the gloomy atmosphere of this Other World, he wasn't looking forward to it.

Noting there was only one path out of the clearing, Jake steadied himself and started forward. Once he left the clearing, the trees and bushes and shadows of the surrounding woods quickly closed in. The barely discernable trail was little more than a narrow footpath, probably used only rarely by the occasional small animal. The path wound its way through the forest, fading into and out of existence as the underbrush and groundcover reclaimed it for the forest floor.

Jake knew the direction that he had to go, so whenever he lost the trail he trekked through the woods, managing to pick it up again each time before growing too concerned, relying on the trail to eventually point him to the entrance of the labyrinth. If the monks' scroll was correct, bypassing the maze would mean losing the artifact. Going through the castle's front door wouldn't be enough. The labyrinth was the only way into the castle that would get him to the artifact.

As the day crept toward dusk, the shadows stretched further across the forest floor, making it even more difficult to see and follow the trail. He found himself doubling back more and more as he followed false paths that led nowhere. Finally, coming into an open area, surrounded by short, scrubby trees and with a clear sky overhead, he decided to stop for the night. He dropped his pack in the center of the clearing and quickly set about to make the site a camp.

He cleared the perimeter, gathered kindling and wood, and prepared a spot for a campfire. It was dark before Jake had a fire going and he was able to heat his rations and make coffee. He settled back then and ate his meal. He tried not to stare into the flames, knowing that it would blind him to any possible movement in the darkness, but campfires were made to be watched. That's just what people did.

Jake felt very alone. He realized that he was probably further from home than any human he had ever known. Serpent's Keep was out of the way, but this, this was real isolation.

No one knew where he was, and even if they had known, there was no way to reach him if something happened. If anything did happen, he had no way to ask for help.

This would be a very bad place to have something go wrong.

Had Uncle Tobias been somewhere like this? Had he been alone, far away in some distant Other World, unable to reach out for help, when something went wrong?

As the fire began to die down, the cool dampness crept in on him. In defiance of whatever might be watching from the shadows, he added wood to the fire and moved in closer. He stared in at the glowing coals building up at the base of the flames and tried to push away thoughts about where he was and what he had to do, but this world had a way of seeping into his bones and crawling into his thoughts.

A movement overhead caught his attention and he lifted his head in time to see a shadow move across a half-moon that was peeking through the clouds. As he watched, the shadow came back across the moon again, this time much larger.

Whatever it was, it appeared to be getting closer.

Jake stood and stepped around the fire so that it was behind him. He looked not directly at the bright moon but a few degrees to one side. He watched as something flew towards him, casually drifting one way and then another, occasionally passing in front of the moon. It was big.

It was a dragon.

Passing directly over the clearing, its wings blotted out the sky. It had a long, thin neck that supported a large head that it held high. Its tail slid smoothly from side to side as it shifted direction. Jake turned about as it passed over, watched as it turned to the right and gained altitude. It flew full circle and came back for another pass, dropping altitude and coming in just above the treetops. Coming in to one side of the clearing, it turned slowly and studied the scene of the campsite and of the man standing beside his small fire.

It turned away again and glided casually upward. Jake heard and felt the pounding as it began beating its wings in slow powerful strokes. It climbed higher and disappeared finally into the clouds. Jake waited for a full minute for it to return, and when it didn't he eventually sat down again in front of his fire.

Was this dragon a guardian, like others Jake had come across, or did it serve as the eyes of someone else?

Either way, for good or for bad, Jake's presence in this Other World was known.

The massive steel door was set into the side of the hill. Jake estimated that a person twice his height could walk through without having to lower his head.

Or a big dragon...

The trail that he had been following continued on to his left, winding its way around the hillside, and he assumed right up to the front door of the castle another half a mile ahead. If he hadn't been advised otherwise, he would certainly have taken that route. It sure seemed easier, and safer, than trying to get through this ominous door and on into whatever dangers may lurk beyond.

He stepped up and placed his hands on the door. It was smooth and cold to the touch. His right hand slid down to the heavy latch. It didn't appear to be locked, and it looked like it was probably the kind of latch that was accessible from both sides.

I can come and go as I please?

Jake pushed down on the lever.

It didn't budge.

Empowered with an unreasonable sense of confidence coming from he knew not where, Jake lifted himself up and pushed down hard; and then a second time. The mechanism within the door came free and the latch released.

Here goes...

The hinges howled as he pushed the door inward, shattering the silence of the world outside and alerting anyone or anything inside that someone had been foolish enough to enter. He stopped when the door was open enough that he could squeeze through. Poking his head in, he saw that the chamber within was in absolute darkness.

Naturally...

He had already pulled his pack off in order to squeeze through the narrow opening. He scrounged around within it until he found the hand lamp. Holding this in one hand, his backpack in the other, Jake stepped sideways through the open doorway.

There was a hollowness to the sound of his footsteps, but he could sense that the walls on either side were close by. The ceiling was beyond the reach of the sphere of light from his lamp. Beneath his feet, the floor was stone.

The air smelled dank and stale.

Old...

The entire world had an overwhelming impression of age about it, much more so than any other world that he had been to; this was a very, very old place.

He crept slowly forward in the dark. He occasionally sensed, and even rarely could see, side passages. He stopped at each one and listened, but heard nothing. After traveling for some time, the tunnel that he was in emptied into another that ran left to right. Again he stopped and listened. Again there was no sound.

But there was a faint breeze. When he turned his head he could feel it against his cheek. It was very light, but it was definitely there, coming from the left. He turned and followed it. He didn't know whether it would take him where he wanted to go, but at least it was something. It provided a reason to choose one direction over another.

Coming to another fork, he again followed the barely perceptible breeze.

And then again.

He eventually found himself in a large square chamber, only to discover that he had reached a dead end. He searched it thoroughly to make sure there wasn't a hidden door, an object, perhaps the bedding of some animal. He thought that he could smell something animal-like in the chamber, and maybe there had been something there at some time in the past. Now, though, it was an empty room with one way in and one way out.

He retraced his steps and took the first side passage that he came to, and then again. In this way, he came up on several dead ends, some leading to empty rooms, others simply ending. There may have been some secondary access, such as a hidden panel high on a wall, but he could find none.

Several hours into his search, he had yet to find a way through the labyrinth. He grew increasingly anxious and began to pick up the pace.

He almost didn't see the pit in time.

It was little more than a dark shadow on the floor in a passageway filled with dancing shadows that were continually chased by the sphere of light created by his small hand lamp. His right foot hung over the open air above a deep darkness. He sensed more than saw the emptiness beneath him, his muscles tensing and his mind racing to respond to this unexpected situation. His heart beat six times before he could pull back and he dropped to the ground, sitting heavily on the stone floor.

Oh, man...

He let his backpack slip off his back, then scooted around and crawled forward on his hands and knees, keeping the hand lamp in front of him. He reached the lip of the pit and stopped. Moving the lamp from left to right, Jake could see that the passageway had widened and the edges of the pit reached the walls on either side of the tunnel. Holding the lamp up and forward, he couldn't see across to the other side.

Jake stood slowly. He turned his head from side to side.

The breeze he had been following seemed to come from the pit.

Oh, man... he thought again. *And I bet there's something down there...*

He couldn't hear anything; he didn't sense anything.

This was an obstacle that, by design or by circumstance, he would need to overcome in order to reach the castle and the artifact.

He moved to his right along the edge of the pit until he reached the wall of the passageway. Holding the hand lamp out, he sought for some way around the pit. There was nothing. There were no handholds or footholds that he could use to get past the pit.

Moving over to the left wall, he could see a few places that he might be able to grasp onto, a few places to put his feet, but it looked very precarious.

He knelt down and looked again into the pit, this time studying the pit wall for a possible way down.

Maybe...

Jake took a long, shaky breath.

Oh, man...

He stood and returned to his pack, put it on and tightened the straps. Back at the lip of the pit, he mapped out his first few footholds and handholds, then clipped the hand lamp to one of the pack straps, turned, dropped to his knees and slid himself over the edge.

He found the first foothold, and then the second. Pressed tight against the rough rock wall, he carefully slid his left hand down and found the handhold that he knew to be there, then did the same with his right. Secure, he eased himself down and sought out another foothold. He began working his way down into the pit, working mostly in the dark but for the faint light that spilled out to his left from the lamp clipped to the strap near his shoulder.

He slipped only once, and recovered with little more than minor scratches to his palms. It was a long, painfully slow climb down, but eventually his left foot touched bottom. He didn't trust himself at first and carefully tested the ground beneath him before bringing his right foot down and turning around.

The light shone on a tunnel entrance leading away from the bottom of the pit. It was just tall enough that Jake wouldn't have to crouch, and was narrow enough that the light from his lamp would be able to reach both side walls.

Before moving nearer the tunnel, he glanced up. The darkness had swallowed him up; he couldn't see the opening of the pit. Looking again at the mouth of the tunnel, he stepped forward. In all likelihood, this was what he had been looking for, and whatever might lay ahead, he had no intention of going back.

Once in the tunnel, a new smell quickly overwhelmed the constant background odor of dank and damp that he had grown accustomed to. It was a musky smell, and Jake was immediately reminded of the dragon dens that he had been in lately. He wondered if the flying dragon that he had seen earlier lived down here. If it did, it certainly didn't use this tunnel. There would need to be a much larger access.

He continued forward, lamp out in front, its yellow glowing sphere of light pushing its way down the tunnel. The passageway twisted and turned, but there were very few side tunnels and none beckoned him away from the main path. It was a long, winding passage from the pit to... where?

Following a slow arcing curve, Jake stopped and stared at the tunnel ahead, the right wall disappearing beyond the bend. He turned off the lamp and let his eyes adjust.

There was definitely a lessening of the dark; the black was not quite as black. He was certain that he could see the curving wall in the darkness.

Leaving the light off, he crept cautiously forward, holding his free hand out in front of him, keeping the lamp in his other hand with his finger on the power switch, ready to turn it back on in an instant. As he continued around the curve, the darkness continued to grow less so. Beyond the curve, once the tunnel straightened, Jake could clearly distinguish a square grey shadow in the distance, as if the passage was taking him into the light.

As Jake continued ahead, the grey square slowly grew, slowly brightened, until at last he stepped through the grey and into a high-ceilinged chamber; one large section of the roof was open to a late-afternoon sky. Visible through this opening, the great, dark castle rose above a sheer cliff, looming high overhead, silhouetted against purple and black clouds.

In the chamber, the dragon sat on a low ledge at the far wall, its wings folded atop its back, watching the human step slowly into its lair. Its eyes were sharp and clear, and somehow sad.

Jake walked into the center of the hall and stopped. He bowed his head respectfully. "Hello," he said. "My name is Jacob Quigley."

"Human."

"Yes." Jake spotted a small wooden door a dozen feet to the left of the dragon. It probably led up to the castle.

The dragon sniffed the air, leaned its head forward and looked more closely at the human. "I..." he examined Jake. "*know...*"

"Tobias is my uncle," said Jake. "I am blood of Tobias Quigley."

The dragon pulled its head back and settled in again. "I am Guardian."

His uncle must have had a lot of respect for these dragons. He had selected them and they had served as Guardians for a very long time. "Tobias has sent me on a quest to gather together the artifacts." He pointed to the door leading up to the castle. "May I pass?"

The dragon studied Jake a moment. "You see... *Little Ones?*"

"I don't understand."

"Little Ones," it said. "You see?"

"I'm afraid not." *Were these 'little ones' like those that he had come upon in the Abandoned City?*

"Not see them..." said the dragon. "Not heard them... Long time."

What did the dragon mean by long time? Weeks? Months? Years? Hundreds of years?

"I'm sorry," said Jake.

"You find," said the dragon after a long, studied pause.

The labyrinth? I don't want to go back in there...

"I saw nothing in there."

"You find." The dragon showed no sign of aggression, but it sat only a dozen feet from the door to the passage leading up to the castle. "Then you pass."

"But—"

"No pass."

Jake looked at the door, then looked behind him at the tunnel entrance leading back into the labyrinth. If he wasn't going to fight his way past the dragon, then he was going to have to go back in the labyrinth and see if he could find these Little Ones. But if they really weren't in there, or if he just couldn't find them, then what?

"All right," he said. "I find."

"You find."

Jake had tried to keep a map in his head of his journey through the labyrinth, tossing out the misdirected routes he had taken, should he have to return the way he had come. There had been only a few side tunnels between the dragon's chamber and the pit, and he hoped that he would not have to go beyond the pit in his search.

The first side tunnel led Jake into a confusing maze of passageways that continually turned back on each other, bisected one another, occasionally dead-ended, and in its center opened into a large, low-ceilinged chamber. There were some signs of it having been occupied in the distant past, or at least been visited by some creatures, but nothing had been there for many years.

The second side tunnel took him into a maze that looked to be a mirror image of the first, with a similar central chamber. Again there were signs that the *Little Ones* had been there in the past, though Jake doubted they had actually lived there. There was no indication of it being a den.

The third side tunnel started similar to the others, but Jake quickly noted that there were far fewer branching passageways. This sector wasn't nearly the maze of the other two.

He also noted an odor in the air, not as strong as the muskiness of the dragon, similar but more intense than the smell he had picked up near the central chambers of the other sectors. *A den long ago abandoned?* Possibly.

The light from hand lamp revealed the walls curving away from the entrance into the chamber. Stepping cautiously into the room, his footsteps echoed away from him and into the dark. He could tell that the room was big. Glancing up, he saw that the glow of the lamp didn't reach the ceiling.

The air was warm and heavy, which surprised him considering the size of the chamber. He would have thought it would have been fresher. The fact that it was as stale as it was meant that there was no flow, which probably meant the only exit was the way he had come.

The silence was as oppressive as the darkness. If there was something alive in the room, it was very quiet; sleeping or waiting?

If there was something sleeping in the room, he didn't want to surprise it. If there was something waiting for him to pass near, then it already knew that he was in the room.

"Hello?" he called out. The sound of his voice reverberated in the chamber. He listened carefully for a reaction, a scurrying, a scratching on the stone floor, anything. There was nothing.

Quiet as a tomb...

Five paces into the room the lamp shone its light on something laying on the floor. He stepped very cautiously forward, his outstretched arm holding the hand lamp toward the object.

It was a skeleton; reptilian or something very like it. Jake had no doubt that it was one of the little ones. Kneeling down beside it, Jake studied the old bones. The skull had been crushed, and a leg bone had clear markings of trauma, as if struck by a staff or sword. Jake mumbled under his breath. *What happened to you, boy?* He stood and held the lamp out. He could see other piles of bones within reach of the lamp's light. Moving to each, he found that each had signs of trauma.

These creatures had been attacked.

He found the remains of what he took to be their bedding, long since decomposed to dust, lining the curved walls. Near one of these, he found the skeleton of a very different animal.

This one was human. The clothing had long ago gone to dust, the flesh and muscle was gone, leaving only the bones to hint at what had happened so long in the past.

Humans had come into the chamber and attacked the *Little Ones*; provoked or not he had no way of knowing. Perhaps the *Little Ones* had confronted them out in the labyrinth and had been chased back here to their den. Maybe the humans had come into the labyrinth looking for them. But whatever the reason, the creatures had been slaughtered in their lair.

Other than the remains of the one human, his body left behind by his companions, there was nothing else in the chamber to provide any further clues as to what had happened. Jake would have to return to the dragon and explain that the Little Ones it so desperately missed would never again be coming out of the labyrinth; that they were dead, that they had been killed by humans.

Jake saw the pain in the dragons eyes as he told it what he had found. He had considered lying to the great creature, saying that he had found nothing, or telling it that he had found the den and the remains of the Little Ones, but hiding the fact that humans were somehow involved, but in the end he had told the truth as best he knew it, describing the scene exactly as he had found it.

"Thank you, blood of Tobias," said the dragon.

"I am sorry—"

"I afraid that what you find."

Jake wondered if the dragon had already known what had happened, but had needed verification in order to have resolution. Had it been involved in some conflict or confrontation a long time ago? Had a band of humans run into the dragon's lair after having killed the *Little Ones*, only to then be killed by the dragon? The dragon would certainly have made the connection between the appearance of the humans and the subsequent loss of contact with the little creatures.

Jake had been afraid that the dragon would associate him with those other humans and seek revenge, but he had chosen to tell the truth nonetheless. He had felt an obligation to do so.

The dragon had its own sense of honor. It spoke stoically. "You pass."

Jake nodded in acknowledgement, approached the dragon and the heavy wooden door beside it. He pushed down on the thick metal latch and pulled the door open. Glancing a final time at the creature on the ledge, he stepped into yet another passageway.

This passage went straight into the mountain for a hundred paces. Jake stopped at the foot of a staircase of stone steps. It spiraled steeply within a cylindrical shaft that reached up into the castle hundreds of feet above. It took him ten minutes to climb the stairs to the door at the top of the shaft, the yellow glow of the light from the hand lamp pushing up in front of him all the way.

He was afraid that the door would be locked and that he wouldn't be able to go any further, but he found a simple latch and pushed down. The hinges screeched noisily but the door opened easily enough.

The room beyond was oval in shape, with a single narrow window and no other obvious access. In the center of the room was a wooden chair and table. On the table was a box similar in appearance to the others that had held artifact pieces.

Ignoring the box for the moment, Jake went to the window. It was a thick glass pane set into a wooden frame, with no curtain. It looked out over the dark forest, beneath which must lay the underground labyrinth that he had navigated. Pressing his face against the glass and looking directly below him, he could just make out the dragon's lair, but couldn't see any details.

He turned his attention back to the room. A leather map hung on the wall beside the door. On it were the details of the labyrinth; the dragon's lair, the den of the Little Ones, the central chambers of the other sectors, the pit, the maze of the upper labyrinth beyond the pit.

Also detailed were the trails of the dark forest beyond the labyrinth, including a path leading from the castle's front door all the way back to the gateway.

Then there should be a way out of the room and into the castle.

Jake turned quickly at the thought and studied the curved walls that enclosed the room. The wall opposite the door was the only one that could have a room on the other side. This room in the top of the tower could actually be two.

The wall was a mix of stone blocks of different shapes and sizes. At first glance, there was no indication that any one of them would give way and provide him with a way out. Besides, if it had been as simple as that, then someone on the other side could have as easily gotten in, and the whole point had been that the only way in was by way of the dragon.

From past experience with the gates, he knew that these things weren't overly complicated, and weren't meant to keep people out but rather to prevent inadvertent access.

With each, there had been several layers to access. The first layer was the assumption that if someone was there and was seeking access, that person had knowledge of the gate (or door) and knew there was something to be sought after.

Jake knew of the artifact, knew of the gates, and had gained knowledge from another source as to the whereabouts of this gate. He had discovered the gateway, found a way to open it using knowledge from the scroll, and had passed through.

In the second layer of protection, the person attempting access had to have acquired knowledge from another source that would indicate that the person should have access. In this case, Jake had found that he would have to travel the labyrinth to get to this room. He also had to have successfully made his way past the dragon.

Now that he was here, what knowledge would he need to have brought with him that would serve as the key to this hidden door?

Jake stared at the wall, standing as stoic and as silent as he had at every gate that he had faced.

With each gate, the answer had been hidden levers and catches within the stone. Jake gave a mental shrug. Well... it would make sense that the same would be true for a door in a wall; perhaps more so.

He studied the features of the wall. As he noted before, it consisted of an array of differently shaped stones of all sizes. Studying the mortar and grout that held them in place, he saw no obvious sign as to the edges of this hidden door.

What knowledge had he brought with him that justified his entry?

He looked again at the individual stones.

The shape of the artifact?

He knew the shape of the polygon for this Other World, for this artifact.

Jake began systematically examining each stone in the wall. It took him half a minute to find a stone with the same shape. Stepping forward, he pushed it.

Nothing happened.

Of course nothing happened. It had never been so simple at the gates, either. There was usually a pair.

He found the second stone three rows down. He stepped forward again, reached out and pushed them both simultaneously. There were two satisfyingly loud clicks as something fell into place within the wall.

And yet no door appeared. Jake pushed and pulled and nothing happened. He stood back and studied the wall again.

The two stones were definitely hinges of some kind; of that he was certain. So what was it that he had missed?

Hinges in a door...

A doorknob?

Jake scanned to the right of the hinges. Midway up between the hinges, about three feet to the right, just about where a door knob would be, Jake saw a rectangular stone about six inches wide and two inches tall. He took a step forward, reached over and pressed in on the stone.

The stone gave a fraction of an inch and there was another click as the latch within released another lever. Jake stepped back and watched a section of wall silently slide open, revealing an empty room beyond. He stood tensed and ready, should something come through. Not until he felt fairly certain that there was no imminent threat did he relax enough to gather his things together. He went over to the table then and opened the box. The artifact was there. Picking it up, it felt cool and heavy in his hand. He tucked it safely into the side pocket of his backpack, zipped the pocket shut, and looked back at the opening in the wall. Filtered sunlight shone through an unseen window and gave the room beyond a bright gray glow. From where he stood, he could see only the same stone floor and curved walls that looked as though they were continuing on from the room that he was in.

He walked through the opening in the wall. The room he entered had one window, as had the hidden room he had just left. Instead of a door, however, there was a hole in the floor near the far wall, through which Jake could see stone stairs descending into darkness. Looking back at the wall that he had come through, he could see that the hinge stones didn't have the shape of the artifact as they had on the other side of the wall. He pushed the door shut and returned to the stairs, pulling out his hand lamp as he strode across the room.

Starting down, he found himself growing increasingly uncomfortable. The light was reaching beyond the curve of the stairwell and he was afraid it might alert someone to his presence before he knew they were there. He didn't want to trod down the stairs completely in the dark, so he finally compromised and held his free hand in front of the lamp. This lessened the light, if only a little, while continuing to illuminate the steps directly below him.

He had only traveled downward a quarter of the distance that he had traveled coming up through the other staircase when he came to a door. It had a lever-style door handle, and it wasn't locked. He would have been surprised if it had been. Why lock an interior door leading from an empty room with no other obvious access?

Jake stepped out onto a mezzanine. The wide landing looked down onto a grand hall that appeared to serve as a kind of main room for the castle. Jake ignored the doors on the second floor and took the treacherous, narrow stairs down to the first floor. His footsteps echoed in the hollow chamber as he walked across the main hall towards the massive set of doors that had to be the front door to the castle. Tall, narrow windows were set high into the front wall and let in the gray light that seemed to permeate this Other World.

Jake stopped in the middle of the huge room.

Another light, brighter and painting a yellow glow across the floor, was coming from somewhere else, somewhere other than the front windows.

He turned and looked at an open set of doors to his left. From where he stood, he could see chairs and tables of dark wood, an area rug covering the cold stone floor, and drapes hanging on the far wall. Light was streaming through the open doorway and into the front hall.

Jake felt cold creeping up his back, yet his skin burned hot.

Someone is in there...

He stared dumbly in the direction of the other room, watched the narrow section of the room that he could see, knowing there had to be someone in there.

The strange thing was, all Jake could think of was that he was breaking into someone's house and that he was going to get caught... he was going to get in trouble...

Oh, man...

He had to go over and see what was in there. What if he went all the way back to Serpent's Keep and found out later that there was something in that room that he needed? All he had to do was walk over and pick it up.

Oh, I really shouldn't do this...

He took one step toward the open doorway.

A shadow moved across the floor of the other room.

Oh, man...

Jake lowered his backpack to the floor and pulled out the small sword that he had used against the dragon in the Desert world.

He really had to look into upgrading his weaponry...

Stepping up to the open door, he slid to one side and carefully pushed it the rest of the way open. The room beyond looked like a study or a sitting room of some kind. Several oil lamp fixtures hung on walls, each shedding a soft golden light into the room. A small fire burned in a large, stone fireplace. A small, strange looking man sat in a high-backed wing chair near the fireplace, set in such a way so that the man could see both the fire and the door. Shadows danced across his face as the flames of the fire actively flickered above the glowing wood and embers.

"You are *his* blood," said the man. His voice was a soft hiss. The tone was cold and precise. His mouth worked in a peculiar way, as if the act of speaking was an unfamiliar and unsavory activity. "I can smell it on you."

"I am Jacob Quigley."

"Of course you are."

There was a movement behind the man's chair; a shadow reached out across the floor. A moment later the head of a creature appeared, peering around from the back of the chair, looking anxiously at Jake, seemingly frightened at this intruder. The creature was perhaps three feet tall, the head was large and thin, faintly reptilian, thick skin, eyes set wide on the sides of the head. Three fingers slid around the edge of the chair, long thin claws.

Jake eyed the creature cautiously but tried to maintain an air of calm. "Cute pet."

"Not amusing."

Jake shrugged absently. "Nice place ya' got here."

The man said nothing.

"Been here long?"

"A thousand years, give or take." If the man expected a reaction from Jake, he didn't get one. Jake had seen and heard too much to be surprised by much of anything. What he wondered, though, was whether this man knew of the secret room and of the artifact. He would have to watch himself and not give anything away.

"Yeah," said Jake. "Just you and the dog, then?"

Again the man said nothing.

"Must get lonely," Jake continued. "What made you choose such an out-of-the-way location?"

"Out-of-the-way doesn't begin to describe it, young Mr. Quigley."

"So what keeps you here?"

"I didn't have much of a choice in the matter. Circumstances dictated my sanctuary."

"Ah... there's a lot of that going around."

"You, by contrast, have managed to get around quite a bit."

"Not so much."

"Now that's just not true, Mr. Quigley. You have visited a number of... *out-of-the-way* locations as of late."

"Oh... well... if you want to count *those.*"

"And you have acquired a number of souvenirs."

"Mementos," said Jake. There was a faint rustling sound and he saw the creature hiding behind the chair stretch its neck and twist its head to get a better look at Jake.

"They don't belong to you."

"You gonna tell me they belong to you?"

"I shall see that they get into the proper hands."

"Thanks just the same."

The man didn't sound in the least surprised. "What Quigley did was wrong. He had no right to shut down the gates. One man doesn't have the right to isolate entire races to a single universe, or to a single world."

"And you are going to correct that..."

The man nodded sagely. "And prevent you from committing an even more egregious wrong than the evil perpetrated by Tobias Quigley."

"He saved worlds and all of the people in them from the Rhetani. As for me, I fully intend to follow Tobias' wishes. You will find that I am not easily stopped." Jake wasn't quite as confident as he sounded, but he figured that he may as well go down with a little dignity.

"You have no idea who I am."

Jake didn't like the sound of that. Still, he did his best to hide his anxiety. "Would it make a difference?"

The man smiled thinly. He leaned his head back, rested it against the back of the chair. "My name is Marcus," he said. "Your uncle and I arrived in the Outland together."

Human, then. Kinda hard to tell...

"We got swept up in the whole mess between the Jahai and the Rhetani."

"You were friends?" asked Jake.

"Comrades," said Marcus precisely. He lost his smile. His glare was unnerving. "He gave up everything for the Jahai. That wasn't enough. If it had been, at least it would have been something I might expect of Tobias. No. No, martyrdom wasn't enough. He had to drag the rest of us down with him, to pull us into a cause that we did not believe in, one that—well..." He let his commentary fade.

So how did you end up here, Jake wondered. He was afraid to ask. Tobias had probably stranded him here after this guy tried to do something really bad.

"How can defending worlds against the Rhetani be wrong?" he asked, finally.

"The Rhetani will bring only good," Marcus said crisply. "I will not argue this with a simpleton."

"No problem, I'll just be leaving, then."

"I don't think so."

"What you think is not my concern."

"It should be."

The continuing calmness in Marcus' voice and manner was unsettling. The man just sat there, relaxed, the fire in the fireplace sending its flickering shadows across his face.

"I'm leaving," said Jake. "Not you, not your little friend there, can stop me."

"My friend?" Marcus paused, looked at Jake as if for the first time. "You *are* in the dark. Do you know anything at all about what you've gotten yourself into?"

"I manage to pick up what I need to know."

"You stumble blindly and clumsily along, with no knowledge as to the true purpose behind your task or the consequences of your actions."

"I understand that the Jahai believed the Rhetani were a threat," said Jake, defensively. "Tobias believed the Rhetani were dangerous enough that he shut down the gates to stop them. The dragons, at great sacrifice, joined Tobias to serve as Guardians."

"The dragons," Marcus leaned forward and hissed, "*are* the Jahai."

Jake stared dumbly at the man. He was at a loss for words. This was completely unexpected.

Marcus shifted back again in his chair. "A dozen species spread across four habitable planets, not bound as others are bound, not limited to a single, crowded world."

"This somehow gives the Rhetani the right to conquer other worlds? Other races?"

"The Rhetani will free worlds from squalor and childish conflict. They will spread their civilization for the benefit of everyone." Marcus turned his head and fixed a sharp glare at the small creature that peered around the chair and looked side glance at him. "The Jahai shut away what they cannot control, imprison what they fear."

"They sent you here?"

"I came of my own accord," Marcus said dully.

"If you—"

"This is the only world where they will let me live. I remain safe so long as I remain here. I am under threat of death should I leave."

"Wow... you must be a nasty sort."

"My only crime is that I do not share the same beliefs as the Jahai."

Jake nodded silently. So the creature behind the chair must serve as the eyes of the Jahai, ensuring that Marcus remained in his prison. But, even if he hadn't been under watch, how could Marcus leave? Wouldn't he have needed the artifact to open the gate?

Another thought occurred to him. If it was true that Marcus had been here a thousand years, how could he know the things he knew? And wasn't the language of a thousand years ago different than the language spoken now? He sounded very contemporary.

"And you've been here..."

Marcus managed to smile again. "I could not get very far without this little monster raising the alarm, now could I? I could kill it, I suppose, but that would raise as big a stink as leaving."

Jake looked at the creature peering around from behind the chair. "It doesn't appear to have any qualms about my leaving."

Marcus said nothing, did not acknowledge Jake's comment. He calmly watched Jake turn away and start again toward the door. As he reached it, Jake heard a mechanical click. He knew the door had been locked.

"Unlock the door, Marcus," said Jake, not turning from the door.

"Give me the artifact."

"Not gonna happen."

"Then you and I shall keep each other company. I am of a patient disposition."

"I am not." Jake slowly turned away from the door. Dropping his backpack, he held his short sword at the ready.

"You *are* a primitive creature, aren't you?"

"I am whatever I have to be," said Jake.

"You are too ignorant to know what that really means, young Quigley."

Jake moved forward, came within sword's reach of Marcus. "You will let me out of here."

"Or what?" Marcus didn't look as though he was someone being threatened with a sword. This made Jake uncomfortable. Everything about this man made Jake uncomfortable.

"Since starting on this little quest, I've had to do some things I didn't like doing. This would be just one more."

Marcus was unimpressed. "I've waited a thousand years for someone to bring the artifact down from the tower. You're not leaving this room until you take it from your pack and set it here on the table beside me."

Jake looked over at the small table next to the chair. There was nothing on it, as if it were waiting for the artifact to be placed on its smooth surface.

He turned his attention back to Marcus. "Now, you know I'm not going to just hand it over to you. What is it you really want?"

"I want the artifact."

"You can't have it." Jake turned away from the man in the chair, looked carefully around the room. He knew that Marcus knew he wouldn't just run him through with the sword. He knew that Marcus knew that he wasn't going to just hand over the artifact. So what was going on? And what were his options?

"What's your game?" he asked.

"I do not play games, Mr. Quigley."

"Now that's just not true," said Jake, throwing the man's earlier statement back at him. "I may be a primitive creature. I may not know what I've gotten myself into, and I may even be totally in the dark on one or two things. But I know when I'm being played."

Marcus started to say something, but Jake turned suddenly and lifted the sword, dropped it quickly down onto the table. The moment the blade made contact with the image of the table, Jake found himself rushing through an electrified version of a gate passageway. The unexpected rush of light and warped vision made him dizzy and he stumbled forward the moment he came out on the other side.

The room that he found himself in was the same room that he had left, and yet somehow... more real, more substantial. He turned quickly, readied himself against an attack by Marcus.

Marcus remained in his chair, calm, almost serene. "Welcome, young Quigley."

"Okay... I'll bite. What's going on?" Jake took a step away from Marcus, studied the room around him. Everything was the same, even the fire that was burning in the fireplace. The Little One was still hiding behind the chair. The door, leading who knew where, was closed. "Where am I?"

The air smelled different. It was cleaner, fresher.

This was definitely a different world.

Marcus smiled, said nothing.

"The room that I was in," Jake spoke softly, quietly. "It wasn't real. Or rather, what I was seeing wasn't the room I was in. I was seeing a projection of *this* room."

"Close. Think of this as a side door to the gate system that you are familiar with. There are a few of them around. Their capabilities are limited, but they can be useful."

"Where are we?"

"The same universal plane as that of the castle. Different location on this world, and a different time. I suppose you could argue that the room in the castle and this room we are in now share the same space in some multidimensional sense; one being just a touch out of phase with the other."

"And you can go back and forth—" Jake waved his arm at his surroundings.

"Between the castle and this despicably pleasant little prison of a community? No. No, I'm afraid that without the artifact, the functionality of the side door is even more limited."

Jake nodded somberly. He had the artifact in his possession, so once he had placed himself into a specific location within this *side door*, he was brought through.

What do I have to do to get back?

He could see nothing that would indicate a gate, side door or otherwise, but since passing the blade of his sword through the image of the table had brought him here, maybe it would send him back.

Marcus saw Jake surreptitiously eyeing the side table. "You would never make it."

"Pardon?"

"I am much more agile than I look."

"Actually, I think you look quite fit for a thousand."

Marcus rose from his chair as Jake moved slowly to one side. He stood between Jake and the table. "You'll like it here, Mr. Quigley. There are a lot of folks here just like you; primitive, ignorant, blind to the truth of the universe."

Jake was through bantering back and forth with this peacock. He said nothing, took another step to his right, forcing Marcus to move to his left in order to maintain his position between Jake and the table.

As Marcus eased to one side, Jake noticed the Little One inch its way cautiously out from behind the chair. He thought at first that he was going to have to deal with the two of them, but the manner in which the creature moved and the way that it positioned itself out of the line of the sight of Marcus indicated otherwise.

"No more amusing quips, Mr. Quigley?"

Jake slid half a step more to the right. Marcus casually repositioned himself, as if he just happened to be moving in that direction.

"You know," Marcus held a finger to his cheek and put on a mock-thoughtful expression. "I think there's a young lady here in town that you might fancy. Her family is a bit thick on the protocols, but then they are about five hundred years behind what you are accustomed to."

The Little One continued to cautiously move in behind Marcus, ever watchful for any sign that the man was going to turn around. Jake kept his eyes directed to Marcus' face, but watched the shoulders for any indication that he was about to move on him. The Little One was at the edge of his vision. Whatever it was up to, Jake was ready to take his cue from it.

So when it leapt up onto Marcus' back, shoving the man forward and knocking him to his knees, Jake dove forward, arms outstretched, and reached for the table. His hands were disappearing into the surface even before Marcus' knees touched the floor.

When Jake came through to the other side of the gate, he continued his fall forward and landed face down on the floor. He realized with a start that he hadn't come through alone. He rolled over and scrambled backward, his sword in one hand pushed out in front of him.

The dragon creature had somehow managed to jump from Marcus and onto Jake in time to catch a ride through the gate. It sat down and eyed Jake curiously. Jake, seeing that he wasn't in any immediate danger from the creature, looked quickly around the room to ensure that Marcus hadn't come through as well.

He and the Little One were alone in the room.

It was dusty and rundown and not anything like he had thought it to be when he had first entered it earlier. It had somewhat the same dimensions, and had furniture in somewhat the same locations, as the room Marcus had lain in wait for him.

That thought brought Jake quickly to his feet. He wanted to get out of that room.

Jake pulled open the castle's front double-door and stepped out onto the large porch landing. Wide concrete steps led down and away from the main entrance to the castle, spilling out into a clearing at the edge of the dark forest. From the high landing, Jake could just make out the trailhead that emptied into the clearing. He knew from the map he had found that this trail would take him all the back to the distant clearing that held the gateway.

The sky was slathered in wide swaths of purple and black and deep, dark blue. He couldn't tell what time of day it was, and had no idea how long he had been on this Other World. He knew only that he was very tired and that the trail between the clearing at the base of steps below him and the clearing with the gateway was a long, winding one.

He turned at the sound of claws on stone. The small creature came out of the castle and sat now beside him. It looked up at him, an anxious expression on its face.

"Hello there," said Jake. The creature gave a series of low, soft groans that could have been a greeting or a plea. Jake nodded at the castle doors behind them. "Doesn't he still need watching?"

The creature didn't answer. It continued to look up expectantly at the human.

Suppose not, thought Jake. *Not any more...*

He turned his gaze back to the black expanse of forest, above which the heavy sky hung, ever threatening. "Hey, I know someone who's gonna be real glad to see you. You up for a walk in the woods?"

Jake sat before a small campfire in the same forest clearing where he had previously seen the dragon flying overhead. It hadn't taken them nearly as long getting here as the underground route via the labyrinth and the tower, but it was dark before he had managed to set up camp.

Little One lay nearby, curled up near the fire. It was sleeping, and seemed quite at ease with the whole situation.

Jake sensed something then, and looked up at the night sky. A silhouette passed in front of the alien moon. He looked over at the little creature. "We have company."

Little One opened its eyes and looked at the human, but didn't move. It took in a deep breath and let out a contented sigh.

Chapter Eighteen

Mr. Griffin came into the sitting room and stood in the center of the oval area rug. Jake was sitting in one of the chairs, an elbow on the arm of the chair, his cheek resting on the knuckles of his left hand. He was staring at the small fire flickering hypnotically in the fireplace. He was deep in thought, and while his senses registered that Mr. Griffin had come into the room, his brain had not yet acknowledged the fact.

"Master Jacob," Mr. Griffin said at last, and waited then for Jake to respond.

Jake lifted his head from his hand but kept his attention directed on the fireplace. "Hey, Griff," he said.

"Mrs. Hodges insisted that I inquire as to your health, and to your state of mind."

At that comment, Jake turned to look at Mr. Griffin. "What?"

"I have been informed that you ate very little of your dinner, and very little of your lunch. That is not like you." Mr. Griffin pursed his lips and raised his brow. "So I have been informed."

"Nothing to worry about," said Jake. "Kinda tired; not much of an appetite." He had returned home from his trip to the Other World of the Castle on the Hill just that morning. This latest expedition had been a particularly exhausting one, both physically and mentally, and he was going to need some time to rebound.

"I shall relay your assurances to Mrs. Hodges," said Mr. Griffin. "I do not believe that they will be considered acceptable, however."

Jake smiled halfheartedly and set his head back against the high-back chair. "I'll grab a snack later. Perhaps that will ease her mind."

"I doubt it." Mr. Griffin turned and started to leave. As he reached the door, Jake called out to him and asked him to stay. Mr. Griffin turned about and took several steps back into the center of the room. Watching the young man's face, he could see that Jacob was having difficulty either sorting out some issue that he wanted to discuss or was having a hard time broaching a subject.

"So... how's Meara?" asked Jake, clearly avoiding what he really needed to talk about. "She was pretty upset about me leaving her behind."

Mr. Griffin had become increasingly concerned that the young lady had grown far too familiar with Master Jacob of late. "She understands her position," he said coolly.

"I was only thinking about her safety."

Mr. Griffin gave a sharp, abbreviated nod. "Of course."

Jake hardened his voice. "I have one artifact piece left to find; one more Other World to travel to. It's pretty clear now that way too many people know more than I do about what's going on. Some of those people would like for things to turn out differently than Uncle Tobias had in mind."

"Yes, sir."

"Now that we're so close..." Jake looked again at the fire. "It's dangerous, is all."

Mr. Griffin waited, seeing that Jake still wasn't finished. There was the matter of whatever it was that young Mr. Quigley really wanted to talk about.

"I figured something out," Jake said finally. "I don't think that Tobias was a thousand years old."

"Is that so?" Despite evidence that pointed to Tobias Quigley's apparent activities in the distant past, he never seriously believed that the Master was immortal.

"I think that Tobias and Marcus came to the Outland a thousand years ago and discovered the gates. They previously discovered a side door gate on some other world and traveled from the past to the present time, and then returned to this world through a main gate."

"Confusing, but plausible."

"I'm betting Nehman was with them."

"And while Master Quigley may have been born in the past, and fought the Rhetani in the past, he spent much of his life in our time, perhaps preparing for the return of the... *the Rhetani*."

"The dragons, the *Jahai*, joined with Tobias and they stood watch these thousand years as Guardians." Jake looked away from the fire, looked up at Mr. Griffin. He took a long, noisy breath. "And something else..."

"Sir?"

"I don't think the Serpent's Keep gate is a primary gate."

"Sir?"

"I don't think our gate downstairs is a main gate. It doesn't look like a main gate, you don't access it like a main gate, and it just doesn't *feel* like a main gate."

"One of those side door gates?"

"Yeah," Jake said, almost surrendering.

"A side gate to the Rhetani?"

"Yeah..."

"I see. If I understand correctly, these side door gates lead to other locations on the same world, but in a different time."

"That's right."

"Master Jacob, you are saying that the Rhetani come from our world, but from a different time."

"I know. Not from the past, as Tobias did. If they had come from the past, we would have known about them. The Rhetani... are from our future."

Mr. Griffin stared numbly at young Mister Quigley. While Jake had had time to try and at least begin to sort out what this might mean, it was brand new to Mr. Griffin. What was there to say to such an idea?

"Yes, sir."

Jake gave a sympathetic smile to the old man. "Kinda my feelings on it, too."

Mr. Griffin looked for some sign that the conversation was finished, and when he could discern nothing one way or the other, he simply gave a brief, sharp nod and backed away.

When Jake was again alone in the sitting room, he turned his gaze back to the fire. It had died down during his conversation with Mr. Griffin, and if not rekindled soon and provided with more wood, it would quickly become only a gray bed of faintly glowing embers.

He remained in his chair, watching the flames slowly subside.

Whatever the truth about the gates, about the Rhetani, or about Tobias, Jake still had one more world to visit. He had little doubt that he would find the last artifact. Once he recovered the piece and set it into place, he would come face to face with the most frightening part of the quest, and the component that he felt the least certain about.

Exactly what was he to do once he crossed over into the world of the Rhetani, wherever that world might be? How was he to close down the gate for good?

Chapter Nineteen

The stone obelisk stood near the far side of the clearing, near the foot of one of the largest trees that Jake had ever seen. The great tree towered above the clearing, over this entire area of the forest and the river that cut through these West Outland woods. The stone itself was larger than the other pylons that he had seen, but other than that there was really nothing very unique about it, nothing to distinguish it from any large rock in the Outland; yet it drew from Jake the same feeling that all the gateway pylons had. There was something about it that radiated an atmosphere, an invisible aura. This was definitely the next gate to the next Other World.

Meara dropped her small pack onto the ground and walked towards the stone. Despite all his protestations, in the end Jake had relented and allowed her to come with him.

Allowed? His concerns about her safety aside, Meara's presence was an asset that could not be ignored. He probably had a better chance of succeeding with her along.

"I never really thought much about these stones," said Meara. She stood before the pylon, drawn to it. She placed a hand on it.

"Why would you," said Jake. "I mean, rocks, right?"

"Gateways to other worlds."

"Other universes," said Jake. "Alternate planes... other Earths..."

"All of it right here in the Outland, Serpent's Keep at the center of it all."

"Now that doesn't much surprise me."

Meara turned to look at Jake. "I've never known anything but the village, and the Outland."

"Prepare yourself, Meara. Your world is not normal. The village is not normal, the Outland is not normal." Jake pointed at the big stone in front of them. "And *that*, most definitely, is not normal."

Meara gave Jake a gentle smile. "I'm glad you came, sir. To Serpent's Keep, I mean. I'm sorry about Master Quigley, but I'm really glad that you came."

"It has been an experience." Jake let his backpack slide off his shoulder and let it drop. He looked around the clearing as he spoke. "I wouldn't have missed it for the world, so to speak."

"Thank you for letting me come this time."

"Completely selfish, I assure you. Chances for success seem greater with you than without you." said Jake. He glanced up at the sky. "Let's get settled in. It will be dark soon, and we may be here a while."

Jake decided to wait until the next morning before exploring the pylon, but the quiet evening gave him time to reflect on the verse on the scroll.

On the western bank stands nature proud, reaching high and broad.
Within lay the path to kin of its kind, and there the ancient dwells.

He let that rest quietly in his thoughts as he sat before the fire, the obelisk a black shape just within the reach of light of the flames.

It seemed to Jake that in this case the message told him where to look and what he would find when he crossed over, but not how to open the gateway. If that was true, then he was going to have to rely on observation alone. He would have to use his past experience with the other pylons to help him find his way in.

When he woke in the morning, he found Meara standing by the stone, studying its features, brushing her hand over its rough surface.

"So much hidden beneath," she said. "And she's beautiful, in her way. I think that what lives within her brings something out in her."

Meara smiled thoughtfully, walked slowly about the stone. The great tree growing at the edge of the clearing began to cast an early morning shadow across it. "That tree and this stone have been together a thousand years," she said.

"At least," said Jake. He leaned his head back in order to see the full height of the tree. "She probably watched this stone get placed here." Even as he said the words, he began to wonder whether there was more to it than that. Everything about this gateway seemed to point to trees or forests, one way or another, and to ancient trees in particular.

Perhaps the scroll verse had a double meaning.

...reaching high and broad. Within lay the path...

Jake stepped away from the stone, stood with his back to the great tree. He stopped and studied the features; let his mind make what it would of the whorls and faults and peaks and shadows. Meara continued pacing around the rock, passing between it and Jake every half minute or so.

After several minutes had gone by, Jake took another two steps back and again let his mind wander across the face of the rock.

On the western bank stands nature proud, reaching high and broad. Within lay the path to kin of its kind, and there the ancient dwells.

Jake turned about sharply and looked at the tree. It was indeed very, very old. It had been old when the scrolls had been written.

It stood proud. It reached high and broad.

Within lay the path to kin of its kind...

Within the stone, or within the grandmother of every tree in the forest?

In the past, he had specifically ignored everything that grew, could change, or could die.

But in this case...

Jake walked slowly toward the tree, lifting his gaze carefully upward as he did so, taking in the features of the deeply crevassed bark of the trunk from the ground on up, until by the time he reached the base he was looking straight up.

"Master Jacob?" Meara was standing behind him. She had to step aside when he started to walk backward, still studying the gigantic trunk.

"We may have been looking in the wrong place."

"You think the way in is through the tree?"

"I think that this tree was expected to be around for a very, very long time."

Would they take such a chance? Perhaps not if it was growing where he come from... but here, in the Outland?

"There," he said.

Twenty feet up, a patch of bark was twisted into misshapen whorls around a gray patch a foot across. Jake ran forward and leapt up onto the trunk, grasped onto the bark and began climbing. The deep crevasses provided easy handholds and footholds and he quickly reached the spot.

Hidden deep within the bark was stone. It was rough, but flat. Jake reached in and laid his palm flat against it. It was cool. He pushed against it, but nothing happened.

It was never that simple. It almost always required two points.

He asked Meara to step back and study the trunk on either side of him, to search for the second pressure point, the key that would release the gate. But she saw nothing. Frustrated, Jake returned to the ground and stood with her.

It had to be there, and it had to be within arm's length of the first. In the past it had on one occasion required a dragon, but it had never required two people. Jake was counting on that rule applying.

The bark...

What if the bark had grown over the second pressure point? After all, it almost completely covered the first.

Assuming the two locations were side by side, within a few feet of one another, Jake climbed the tree again, this time with the small hand hatchet they used to cut firewood. Giving himself a strong foothold and holding tight with one hand, he used the hatchet to pry within the bark crevasses on either side of the first position.

"Don't hurt it," pleaded Meara.

"I'll do my best, Meara."

It took only a few minutes to find the second stone. He quickly tucked the hatchet into his belt and repositioned himself. It was awkward to place both hands into the bark and push at both stones, but it didn't take as much pressure as he had imagined.

He heard the sound of the gateway opening behind him.

The Other World they stepped into was beyond anything that Jake could have expected, or could ever have imagined. They were enveloped on all sides and from above by oversized vegetation, great broad leaves and branches and trunks many times larger than anything he had seen before.

It took a moment for them to realize that they had come out of the gateway not onto solid ground but onto a branch unbelievably massive and hundreds of feet above the floor of a vast rainforest. Looking behind him, Jake saw that the gateway they had traveled through, closing now and reverting to its quiet state of ancient pylon, was set into the trunk of an alien tree the diameter of a large house.

"Sir," Meara said calmly. Her hand was still in his from their journey through the gate, her grip tightening now.

Jake turned back and saw that there was movement in the leaves beyond that created by the faint breeze that was drifting through the canopy. There were faces in the leaves, and arms and legs. There were people huddled in the vegetation, moving slowly, eyes staring out from the shadows, watching the two strangers that had stepped through the gateway.

A small man climbed down onto the branch eight feet in front of Jake and Meara. He wore a leather poncho that reached midway down his thigh and was tied at the waist. His feet were covered in soft, pliable leather that no doubt helped him to move more easily about in the trees. His skin was light and his brown hair hung loose and long.

He took a step forward, his gaze moving casually from Jake to Meara. After a moment, he turned away, lifting an arm and waving for them to follow him. He walked effortlessly along the branch, looking back only once to see if they were coming.

As soon as they began moving, the others in the surrounding vegetation began climbing out onto the branch and followed after them. Most, men and women, young and old, were dressed similarly to the first, though a few wore only shorts and shoes, and one wore an open vest and calf-length trousers. Most had the same brown hair, though there were variations both lighter and darker, and Jake noticed one that had hair almost the color of straw.

They were led to a planked deck some thirty feet wide and twice as long. The wood was worn smooth from years of constant use. There were no rails; the edges of the deck were abrupt, stopping at living walls of green leaves and twisting branches.

There were openings in the leafy walls, however, and through these accesses rope bridges connected the deck to the decks of distant trees. As they approached one of these rope bridges, Meara slowed and finally stopped.

"I don't think I can do that, sir," she said flatly.

Jake looked from her to the bridge. Wooden planks a foot wide, set end to end, served as the base of the triangular shaped structure, two thick ropes set chest high serving as hand rails.

"You don't want to stay here, Meara," said Jake.

"Can I?"

"That's crazy. I thought you came on this trip to help me."

Meara stared coldly at the bridge. The far end was hundreds of feet away, lost in the shadow of the canopy. It bowed in the center from the sheer weight of rope and wood.

The man leading them stopped six paces out and looked back. He gave an encouraging nod, waved again for them to follow. Jake smiled apologetically and turned to Meara. He tried to reassure her that everything would be all right.

"Do you want me to go first?" Jake asked.

"Yes," Meara said quickly, and then abruptly, "No." She walked around him and onto the bridge. Their guide grinned and turned about and started forward again. Meara ignored him, staring down at her feet and taking it one step at a time.

Jake waited until Meara was well out onto the bridge before following after her. He could feel every step she took reverberate back to him and knew that she must also be able to feel his steps. He was careful to keep his distance and make each footfall as soft as possible. Before long, however, he felt the footfalls of others, and the bridge began to bounce and vibrate.

Looking behind him, Jake saw that a handful of the others had begun to follow. The remainder stood on the deck and watched the strangers slowly and clumsily cross the bridge.

Meara tensed and held tightly to the rope rails, but stoically continued forward, keeping silent her fears.

The deck they came to was much like the one they had left. The exception was that one of the open accesses in the walls of vegetation led to an elevator rather than a bridge. It had a wooden floor six feet on a side with a post at each corner supporting an open framework overhead. Attached to this framework was a set of ropes and pulleys.

A single rope set waist high connected each post and served as a rail. Their guide unhooked the rope and stepped inside, waited for Jake and Meara to climb on. Thankfully, he set the rope back into place before the others could join them. Jake thought that it was crowded enough with the three of them, especially considering the feeble appearance of one thin rope as a rail.

The elevator jerked slightly and started downward. The guide did nothing, which meant that someone somewhere was working the block and tackle and easing them, rather quickly Jake noted, to the ground.

The world grew darker the further they descended, with only narrow shafts of light boring through the canopy and providing what light there was. The air had a dampness to it, and an earthy, musky smell.

Three men were waiting at the bottom when the elevator softly touched the floor of the rainforest. One reached out and unhooked the rope, pulled it aside and waited for the passengers to step off the elevator.

Their guide led the way again, with the new escort following behind. The ground was soft and mulchy, the gigantic trees hundreds of feet apart, each eighty to a hundred feet in diameter. The thick canopy was high overhead, with only the occasional opening allowing in the light.

On their march to wherever it was they were going, Jake saw only one other elevator, but he suspected that all the trees were connected by bridge and silently wondered whether they would have traveled the entire distance in the canopy if their guide hadn't observed how uncomfortable Meara had been with the first bridge crossing.

After more than an hour's march, they came out onto an open expanse of wide, rolling terrain, in the center of which sat a primitive village of dozens of wood and grass huts. The huts surrounded a set of wooden community buildings that encircled the community square. Set in the heart of the square was a large, raised platform. The platform was empty but for a single, overly-large wooden chair.

The man sitting in the chair was dressed as all the others, but he nonetheless had a look about him that declared to anyone who approached that he was in charge around here. He watched in pretentious silence as Jake and Meara were led into the square and up to the edge of the platform.

"Hello," the man said calmly.

"You speak English?" asked Jake.

"What is... *English*?" asked the man.

"The language you speak," said Jake. "It is what we call English."

"I speak what I speak," said the man, bored with the subject. "I am Seshan, leader of this village."

"I am Jacob Quigley. This is Meara Gyles."

"You came through the gate."

"That's right," said Jake. He had hoped that invoking the name of Quigley would have sparked some reaction, but it hadn't. "We are on an important—"

"Few come through the gate," said Seshan, cutting him off.

That's good to hear, thought Jake. "We seek an artifact," he said.

At that moment, a great shadow glided across the platform. Jake looked up in time to see a winged dragon just as it reached the tree line and disappeared from view. After a few moments, it returned and circled above the village.

Jake looked back at Seshan. The leader wasn't looking at the dragon, but at the newcomers. Glancing around at the crowd that had gathered around the platform, he found as many people were watching them as were watching the dragon.

They are used to the dragon. They do not fear the dragon.

"A friend of yours?" asked Jake.

"He is curious about your arrival."

The dragon hovered above the platform, spun slowly in a tight circle and came delicately down beside Seshan. It was long and sleek, with smooth, shiny skin and a long neck. It settled in, wings pulled up and back. It turned its head and stretched it out slightly.

"Quigley, but not Quigley," it said.

"I am Jacob Quigley. I am the same blood as Tobias."

The dragon pulled its head back and straightened. "Yes," it said, having deduced as much and apparently satisfied with that deduction.

"Are you guardian to the artifact on this world?" Jake asked.

"Guardian," it said, then looked questioning at Meara.

"I am Meara. I help."

"My uncle has tasked me to gather together the artifacts," said Jake.

The dragon lowered its head to be closer to Jake. Being on the platform, it was still towering above him. "Not good," it said quietly.

"No. I don't think so."

"You close gate to Rhetani?"

"Yes."

The dragon breathed softly, looked at Meara and then again at Jake. It slowly raised its head, studied the crowded plaza, and then turned to Seshan, who had been quietly listening to the exchange.

"Get artifact," the dragon said to the tribal chief.

Seshan nodded, stood and walked to the edge of the platform. He waited until he was certain that he had the attention everyone. "We go to retrieve the artifact," he said.

"You know where it is?" asked Meara.

The dragon had stepped to one side, giving itself enough room to spread its wings. It leaned forward and pushed itself up and away from the platform. Within moments it was once again circling the village, and then disappeared beyond the trees.

"We know," said Seshan.

◊ ◊ ◊

"We were once one tribe," said Seshan. He was walking beside Jake and Meara, a few paces behind several of Seshan's people. Further ahead, lost in the shadows of the forest floor, others scouted the way, ensuring the safety of their leader and their guests. Seshan used a tall walking staff, and from the way he handled it, Jake suspected that it could as easily be used as a weapon.

"What happened?" asked Meara.

"Long before my time, or that of my father, there was disagreement about our loyalty to the Jahai."

"Some didn't believe in their purpose?"

"The virtue of the obligation had faded with time. But for the presence of the guardian, no one had seen or heard from the Jahai for generations. There was only the dragon and the artifact. On the other side, there was the threat of the Rhetani. The legend of their power and ruthlessness, rather than fading, had grown."

"Strange the way that works," said Jake.

"Contentment breeds complacency, while fear festers," said Seshan. "It is the way of things."

Rather gloomy way of looking at things...

"Some began to question the wisdom of defending the artifact against such strength," Seshan continued. "Some wondered aloud why we were tasked with such a responsibility."

"But isn't the dragon the guardian?" asked Meara.

"Tahan is guardian. We serve Tahan."

Jake wondered what that meant, but chose not to pursue it. It may have been as simple as assisting the dragon in protecting the artifact or as dangerous as a dragon-worshiping cult with ritualistic sacrifices. A good subject to avoid.

"Did these others of your tribe turn against the Jahai, or from the obligation?"

"They await the return of the Rhetani so that they can hand to them the artifact."

"They have the artifact?" asked Meara.

"Tahan said to let them go. This is why we are vigilant in our watch of the gate. So long as we control who enters our world, it is not necessary to possess the artifact. Let them keep it safe until we have need of it."

Makes sense, I guess... thought Jake. Much better than both sides continually fighting to regain and hang onto something that neither side would need for centuries, if ever.

"There is going to be a fight then," stated Jake.

"We will take possession of the artifact."

When Jake stepped out of the trees, there were already dozens of others running across the grassy field, racing towards a similar group that was rushing out of a village much like the one they had just left.

He started forward, but Seshan took hold of his arm and held him back. "My people will take care of this," he said.

Meara, already several paces ahead, stopped and looked back over her shoulder. "We should help."

"This is our task," Seshan said firmly. "Leave us to it."

Meara looked anxiously at the two groups, now only moments from clashing. She turned desperately to Jake.

"Sir?"

Jake reluctantly shook his head.

A shadow swam across the grass then, racing towards the two groups about to do battle. The dragon was suddenly down in their midst. It grasped one of the second group by the shoulders and continued its forward momentum, dragging the small man backward towards the village. His feet left the ground, the dragon beating its great wings and gliding slowly upward. The man was six feet off the ground, kicking his legs frantically and pulling at the claws that gripped his shoulders, when the dragon released him and turned away, rising quickly in a circling arc. The man continued in the direction he had been carried, until finally crashing into the side of one of the village buildings.

In the center of the open plain, the two groups had met and were fighting hand to hand. Angry cries and screams of pain and desperation reached across the expanse to Jake, Meara and Seshan. There was the sharp rattling of metal on metal, the softer pounding thumps and crunches of body blows, of clubbed weapons against flesh and bone.

All the while Seshan stood placidly, hands clasped behind his back, waiting for his people to complete their task so that he might continue with his.

The dragon circled around and dropped in again, knocking two of the enemy to the ground before grasping a third. This time, the man's body was used to club several more to the ground as he was dragged and lifted, before finally being hurled against the side of the building.

The dragon then swung around over the village itself, and Jake watched as it dropped again and again down amongst the buildings. From his vantage point on the other side of the field, he couldn't see what the dragon was doing, but he had his suspicions.

The artifact must be right in the heart of the village.

Seshan spoke matter-of-factly. "Tahan will make certain that it isn't taken away before we can get to it."

The fight lasted only a few minutes. A number of Seshan's people were hurt, some seriously. More of those from the other village were hurt, and some had been killed; many more scattered into the surrounding forest, and a few returned to the village in an attempt to make a final stand and carry on the fight. The dragon targeted those that dared to come near the artifact.

As Seshan approached the village with Jake and Meara, he ordered that those who stayed inside their homes were to be left unharmed. Those who showed themselves were to be dealt with.

Seshan had prepared for this moment his entire life. As they walked through the village, Jake remained a pace behind him, allowing him to lead the way to the central compound and the small temple that held the artifact.

Tahan the dragon was perched atop the structure, a simple building six feet on a side and twelve feet tall. A heavy wooden door filled most of one side, a large crossbeam locking it in place.

Seeing the shape and design of the structure, it became clear to Jake why the dragon hadn't been able to get the artifact without Seshan's help.

There were a dozen or more of Seshan's people in the compound. Others moved through the village in small groups, ordering the villagers to remain in their huts.

One of Seshan's men lifted the crossbeam and another pulled open the door. Seshan stood in the doorway, took one step inside and lifted the box from its stand. Stepping outside again, he held tightly to the box. Above him, the dragon shifted uneasily.

"Our obligation is fulfilled," said Seshan, handing the box to Jake. "My people will return you to the gate, that you can continue the fulfillment of your own."

Jake took the box and nodded somberly. He really wanted to open it up and look inside, but it was clearly not the time. Once the ritual was satisfied and he was on his own...

"We go," Seshan announced to his people.

Jake and Meara were quickly led out of the village and into the forest, a large group moving out ahead of them, a slightly smaller group following up behind. Jake could occasionally see the shadows of figures pacing them on either side.

Those they had taken the artifact from would know that Jake would be heading for the gateway with it. Their escort was obviously aware of that and took extraordinary measures to protect them from ambush. The route back seemed random and very roundabout, but the defensive perimeter surrounding Jake and the artifact was strong and alert.

After several hours march, the rays of sunlight that pierced through the canopy were beginning to gray, angles shifting so that they seldom touched ground. The group approached a tree that dwarfed the other great trees of the forest. A maze of walkways, elevators, small buildings, ropes and guy wires, enveloped the massive trunk, winding their way upward to the forest canopy overhead. Lanterns set in place at stepped locations all the way up the trunk gave a haunted glow to the scene. There was a flurry of activity at the base of the tree, a number of the lead travel party scurrying about preparing for the ascent, others already in elevators or on walkways and on their way up.

"Wow," said Meara.

"The Great Tree," said their guide. "Our Gathering Place."

"It's amazing."

"It is our main access to the canopy."

The guide indicated that they should continue to the tree. They followed a well-traveled path between two roots that gradually closed in on them from either side, each rising up far above Jake's head. An elevator waited for them at the base of the tree. Two of their escort stood beside the elevator, a man and a woman, and the woman held the gate open for them. Once the guide and his guests were inside, the woman followed them in.

The elevator started its steady climb upward toward the canopy. It hung on a rope and pulley system six feet from the trunk, its rough bark with crevices deeper than a person's arm. Jake and Meara, looking outward, couldn't take their eyes off the scene that was spread out below them. Beneath the Great Tree was a vast open area with fire pits, long tables, pole lanterns, raised wooden platforms for musical bands, dancing, speechmaking and ceremonies.

Our Gathering Place...

As they rose higher, the guide indicated some of the defensive stations that were set up throughout the area. Some were on the ground, but most were set in the trees at stepped elevations; some had one person, others with two and even three.

The positions were probably more heavily fortified for occasions such as this. He couldn't imagine maintaining such a high human resource all the time.

The elevator came to a sudden, violent stop.

Their escort and the guide grabbed Jake and Meara by the shoulders and pushed them to the floor of the elevator. Looking through the rails, Jake could see the flickering arches of arrow trails tracing from positions in the neighboring trees toward the canopy above them, others to the ground below.

Above them... The enemy had waited until just the right moment to make their move. If they could force the elevator, with Jake and the artifact inside, to plummet to the ground, those waiting below could grab and run.

But those above had to get to the block and tackle, and those below had to get through the defenders protecting the Great Tree.

The elevator shuddered, dropped several feet and began to rock. After a few moments, it slowly settled into its new position.

"I'm not feeling too well, sir," said Meara.

In all the excitement of getting the artifact and seeing the Great Tree, Jake had forgotten how terrified Meara was of heights.

"I know that feeling," said Jake. "Let's trust our friends here to get us out of this and back home."

Meara stared directly ahead at the trees on the far side of the Gathering Place. "Yes, sir."

The elevator shook and began to fall, this time plummeting downward with no signs of stopping. Jake heard the snapping and whistling of lines suddenly free. He grasped a rail with one hand and Meara's wrist with the other. A moment later, the elevator stopped abruptly and Jake heard wood crack. The floor of the car slammed at his knees and his head jerked down and snapped back up.

Their guide took hold of his arm and pulled him to his feet. "Get ready, please," he said, then turned about and opened the gate facing the trunk of the tree. He easily jumped the six feet to an opening in the trunk. He ran a plank out, and the woman escort took hold of one end and set it into place. She turned to Jake, stepped back out of the way.

"Quickly now," she said.

Jake nodded and moved quickly to the plank. It was six feet from the elevator to the safety of the tree. Their guide, waiting within the tree, was reaching out to him. Behind Jake, the woman now had a firm grip on Meara's arm.

Three short, shuffling steps and Jake was across. Turning about, he could see that Meara wasn't going to make it quite as easily as he. When the elevator had dropped, it had dropped a considerable distance, but looking down, he could see that it was still a long way to the forest floor.

Meara saw that, too.

"You can do it, Meara," said Jake. "Three feet up, or a hundred, the plank's the same width."

"Not nearly wide enough, sir."

"Please," said the woman holding her arm. "We must move quickly."

Meara nodded quickly. She was standing at the very edge of the narrow wooden foot bridge. "I know that."

Jake put one foot out onto the plank and reached out. Meara had only to lean forward and she could just about take hold. "Come on, Meara."

Meara nodded again. She took a deep breath and slid one foot cautiously out. The woman holding her arm moved up directly behind her. She cupped Meara's elbow in the palm of her hand. Meara eased forward, reached out and grasped Jake's outstretched hand. She slid forward again, now midway across the little bridge.

The fighting far above them continued, but the sounds were much fainter now that they had dropped so far. Jake wasn't sure why he glanced up when he did, perhaps an inner sense of impending danger, but he did, and just in time to see a body hurtling down towards them. A victim of the battle that was going on in the canopy, the poor man was now little more than a missile rushing directly at them.

Jake didn't take the time to sort the situation out. He had Meara's hand in his, so he gripped it tight and pulled, leaning forcefully back. Meara cried out in panic, and the woman holding onto her arm froze in surprise.

Jake fell backward and inward, landing on his butt, holding tight to Meara. She was dangling half in the tree, half out.

Jake saw the falling body strike the elevator, shattering it. Its remnants hung precariously by its guy wires, spinning wildly. The makeshift bridge fell, and the woman who had been helping Meara fell with it, lost from Jake's line of sight a moment after the collision.

"Oh, god..." Meara muttered shakily. "Oh, please..."

"I have you," said Jake, and he slid backward, pulling her with him. The man inside the tree immediately rushed forward to help.

Meara quickly turned and looked back out, still sitting.

"What happened?" she asked.

"There was... *debris,*" said Jake.

"What happened to—"

"She didn't make it."

"We need to hurry," said their guide.

There was a shaft within the trunk of the tree beginning at the landing they were on and disappearing in the darkness above them. The chimney was about four feet in diameter, with a ladder running along the wall. The guide led the way, with Meara and Jake following.

After a few moments climb, what light that seeped in from the opening below was blotted out, and the sounds of the conflict faded with it. Jake could see nothing above those climbing directly above him. He found himself in near-absolute darkness, with the only sounds being that of the breathing of his companions and their movement on the wooden rungs of the ladder.

After what seemed an eternity, but was in fact probably no more than a couple of minutes, they stepped up and out onto another landing within the tree. The guide looked out an opening similar to the one they had entered below. He said nothing, instead moved to the chimney shaft and climbed up onto the ladder.

Before following the others, Jake went over to the opening and looked out.

They were probably a hundred to a hundred and twenty feet above the destroyed elevator. Looking up, they had at least that far to go before they reached the canopy.

"Please, sir," the guide called down. Meara had already started up the next section of ladder, leaving only Jake on the landing.

Jake gave a silent *okay* and went to the ladder.

Midway up this next section, Jake began to hear the sounds of the skirmish going on in the canopy. There were angry voices, shouted orders, and the sharp cracking sounds of wood striking wood.

Reaching the top landing, Jake found there were half a dozen people defending the access, though there was no immediate fighting going on there. They stood ready, defensively, while the sounds of one-on-one conflict came at them from all around, from within the leaves and branches that lined the perimeter of the wooden platform that served as a porch-like structure beyond the opening to the shaft.

As soon as Meara and Jake were both on the inner landing, the entire team moved forward, hurrying quickly across the platform and through an opening in the vegetation.

The path through the canopy was well defined from many years of use. Those leading the way moved easily and confidently, as if they had traveled this way a thousand times.

As with their original journey through the canopy, Jake occasionally saw the flittering movement of scouts scuttling through the shadows on either side of the main troop.

It was as he watched one of these flitting shadows that he saw something.

The shadow was there, and then it wasn't. It hadn't disappeared through normal movement, as he had come to expect. This shadow looked like it grew larger for just a moment and then dropped from sight.

"Something's wrong," he said softly.

The guide, now following behind him in the group, spoke just as softly. "Yes... keep moving."

Jake could feel it. There was a growing tension amongst the entire group. They all knew that something was wrong.

The man traveling in front of Meara turned about suddenly and threw himself over her, knocking her to the surface of the large branch on which they were traveling. Seeing this, Jake dropped down to one knee, only to be smacked from behind by the body of the guide, knocking him face down. As he was thrown forward, he heard the singing of arrows as they filled the air around him.

Only after he was face down on the branch, the weight of the small man pressing down on him, did he feel the hot stinging of the arrow in his side. As he lay there, he began to feel a dull ache in his gut, a warmth under his shirt. He felt uncomfortable, and tried to shift position. When he did, though, sharp streaks of fire raced out from the location of that dull ache.

"Hey," he grunted. "You gotta get off me."

The guide gave no indication that he was going to get off Jake.

"No, really. You need to get off me. I've been shot."

"I know," said the man.

The rustling of branches and leaves and the cracking of wood came from all directions. Voices echoed throughout the canopy, unintelligible to Jake but clearly communications between comrades.

Jake's protector rolled to one side, rose to one knee and lifted Jake up by his left arm. Another pair of hands lifted him by his right. Looking ahead, he could see that entire troop was up and moving, with Meara directly ahead of him.

They traveled quickly. Sounds of activity continued to push in from both sides, but it all seemed fuzzy to Jake. The world around him blurred and he moved only because he was being carried along with the group.

At several points along the way they crossed wooden decks and then quickly returned to the pathways along the branches.

They stepped out onto another wooden platform and stopped. The troop gathered together, guards taking stations at the several access points. Jake was led to a bench and he carefully sat down, strong arms guiding him down.

"How are you, sir?" asked Meara, sitting down beside him. A middle-aged woman sat down on the other side and began tending to his wound.

"I'm fine," said Jake. Everything was still a bit fuzzy, but now that he was able to rest, things were beginning to clear. He felt really, really tired.

The woman tending his wound pulled out the arrow without warning. It was like an electric shock and Jake almost passed out.

"Sir?" asked Meara.

"Fine," said Jake, this time more hushed.

Their guide approached and stood directly in front of Jake. "How are you doing?"

"Fine," Jake said firmly.

"That is good."

"How much further?" asked Meara.

"Two platforms, yet," the man answered. He looked again at Jake. "We have a rope bridge to cross. Are you up to it?"

"No problem." Jake held up his arms and let his doctor wrap his torso with a wide cloth bandage.

"Very good," said the guide. "We leave as soon as you are ready." He turned and began giving directions to the others of the team. The doctor finished her work and pulled Jake's shirt back into place. Jake slowly stood up, letting Meara help him and using her for support.

Keeping his balance on the rope bridge required that he use stomach muscles that he hadn't realized he had, and this put pressure on the wound, which in turn made him move clumsily as he worked his way across.

They reached the tree with the gateway set into the trunk. The site was heavily defended, shadows within shadows moving within shadows. Jake brought out the artifact and stepped up to the obelisk. As with all the obelisks, there was a place to insert the artifact and open the gateway.

Jake was studying the stone when the world around him exploded in movement and sound. A visual rush drew in on him as men and women frantically fought to get through the defenders and reach Jake. Several men closed in to protect him. Meara stood directly beside him, torn between helping him search for the recess in which to place the artifact and guarding him against any who would approach.

"The dragon," she said suddenly, almost under her breath. Looking away from the stone, Jake followed Meara's gaze. She was looking down a pathway through the canopy. The dragon, crouching low, its wings folded back tightly along its back, was rushing forward along the top of the heavy branch. It struck aside several attackers before reaching the open clearing.

Jake had to force himself to turn away from the sight of the dragon and continue searching the surface of the obelisk. Behind him, the dragon roared, raising its head as much as it was able in the confined space. It struck at the attackers that had made it into the clearing, several of whom fell from the canopy, disappearing into the darkness below.

Jake found the location on the stone and hurriedly put the artifact into place. The change was immediate. The obelisk blurred and the image of it transformed, becoming vaguely transparent. The area took on a bluish glow.

Behind him, the dragon swung around angrily and swept its claws across a group of attackers. Some of their arrows had struck home, burying themselves beneath the creature's scales, and a web of burning pain was enveloping it. It rolled one eye in Jake's direction and saw the open gateway. It knew that it had accomplished its task. It laid its head back and let out another great roar, this time a proud call to all in its charge.

Jake stuffed the artifact into his pocket and took Meara by the hand. He caught sight of their guide and they gave each other a curt nod.

Jake and Meara stepped into the gateway.

"What are *you* doing here," said Meara. She was looking at a figure standing at the edge of the clearing, leaning against a tree. She obviously knew the man, and didn't much like him. Jake thought he recognized him, as well. He was pretty certain that this was the same man that had been standing outside the Adventurer's Guild; he had the same weathered appearance and hunched over stance. He looked as though the years of a lifetime had beaten against him.

"You know this guy?" Jake asked. He and Meara stood beyond the gate, both cautiously eyeing the man. Jake heard the gate close behind him.

"Karl Brogen," said Meara. "Weasel."

Karl Brogen tilted his head back and stared at Jake from under a heavy brow. He gave a dull, tired smile. "So, boy... you think you're something special, eh?"

"As a matter of fact, I find myself to be less special every day," said Jake.

The man snorted. "Yeah, well, you got that right. You're *nothin'.*"

"I certainly appreciate you coming all this way to confirm that."

Brogen look wearily at Meara. "You're as annoying as your father, missy."

Jake took several slow steps closer to Brogen. Every step was a spear in his side. "What brings you out here, Mr. Brogen?"

"You don't know what you're doing, boy. I don't hold your ignorance against you, but you're on the wrong side. If you had the facts, you'd understand that."

"I trust my uncle's judgment."

"Now *that* I do hold against you. How can you trust someone you don't even know?" Brogen pushed away from the tree and stepped toward Jake. He relied heavily on a tall staff. "Up to a few weeks ago, d'ya have any suspicion at all that he had been involved in any of this?"

"I don't feel the need to justify my actions to you."

"Yeah? What do you know of the Rhetani? D'ya know when it came face to face, the Jahai crawled back to their worlds and left the likes of Tobias Quigley to do their dirty work for 'em?"

"How about we get back to *my* question, Mr. Brogen." Jake wasn't going to let Brogen's ranting get to him. "What are you doing here?"

And just what is your part in all this?

Brogen grinned. The man wore Meara's opinion of him well. There was something very unpleasant behind that face. "I've been watching you, Quigley," he said. He tapped a crooked finger against his temple. "I am the eyes of the Rhetani."

Jake felt cold, but did his best to hide any emotion. "And what is it that your masters have you watching for?"

"Not my masters, boy. I side with the Rhetani because they are in the right." He brought back just a hint of the smile. "And because they will win."

This guy sounds an awful lot like Marcus. They must have gone to the same school...

"Sorry, but I'm just not seeing it," said Jake.

"Blind as well as ignorant."

"If you're involved, there's money in it somewhere," said Meara.

"Oh my, yes... Nothing wrong with being well paid for services rendered."

"My uncle needed no reward to do what was right," said Jake. "Neither do I."

"Tobias was a pompous fool. There was never any reasoning with him."

Definitely in Marcus' class, thought Jake. *How many of these old guys are there?*

"I doubt you'll find me any more accommodating than my uncle."

"I don't find you much of anything at all," Brogen growled. "Now give me the artifact."

"Really... just like that..."

"It wouldn't do you any good," said Meara. "Not all by itself."

"Do you think I don't know where the Rhetani gate is? This is the last artifact. It is all that I need."

"Not gonna happen," said Jake. He had barely finished the statement before Brogen lifted and swung his staff. It came in at a level arc, blisteringly fast, and struck Jake across the shoulder. The force knocked him off his feet and to the ground; the sharp, burning pain was mind-numbing, radiating out from his shoulder through his entire body. Brogen moved in quickly before Jake could clear his head enough to react, stood over him and brought the end of the staff down hard onto his chest.

Meara leapt into the air and struck Brogen with a body blow before he could raise the staff and bring it down for a final strike. Both sprawled face down onto the ground and rolled. Jake scrambled aside and frantically dug into his pack, came out with the pistol. He brought it up in both hands, turned and aimed it in Brogen's direction.

Meara was crawling to one side, but Brogen was already on his feet and swinging his staff. It struck Jake across the wrists and knocked the pistol across the clearing. Brogen started to swing again, but this time Jake managed to grab hold of the staff before there was much force behind it. He pulled it around and he and Brogen found themselves struggling in each other's grasp, the staff between them. The exertion tore through the wound in his side. It felt hot and wet beneath the bindings.

Jake was surprised at how strong the man was. His appearance was very deceiving. Beneath the ragged clothes and disheveled look was a tough, aggressive, brawny fighter. He was beginning to think that he might lose the fight when he heard the shot. He felt Brogen tense, and at first thought that the man had been shot.

"Stop," Meara called out sharply. "Right now. I won't say it again."

Jake pushed himself away from Brogen, letting him have the staff for the moment. He turned his head and looked toward

Meara. She was standing three long strides away, pistol raised and pointed toward Brogen.

"Drop the staff, Brogen," said Jake. "I don't want Meara to have to shoot anyone. Not even you."

Brogen was looking angrily at Meara. He gave a side glance to Jake, shoved the staff away from him and stood. Meara took a cautious step back. Jake stood and walked to Meara, careful to stay out of her line of sight to Brogen. He held out his hand for the pistol. When she ignored him, he spoke softly to her. "Rope in my pack."

She handed him the gun and went over to their gear.

Brogen grinned thinly. "You think you can get me back to the village, boy?"

Jake took one step toward Brogen, slowly shook his head.

It took Brogen a few moments to realize what Jake was thinking. When he did, his expression hardened. "You can't leave me here, Quigley."

Jake didn't respond. He was too weak. Brogen must have sensed that, too. He could see Meara out of the corner of his eye. She was kneeling beside the backpack.

Brogen hurled himself at Jake. Jake just managed to lift his weapon before Brogen was on him and the two of them flew backward. Brogen wrapped himself around Jake. When they struck the ground the weapon fired. Jake felt a burning at his belly and thought that he had been gut shot. He quickly realized that it was the flash from the exploding gunpowder. He twisted his hand and pulled the trigger. From Brogen's reaction, Jake was certain that he had been hit. Brogen fought desperately to get at the pistol. Jake fired again.

Mr. Griffin opened the front door and hurried down the steps. Meara was half-carrying, half-dragging Jake up the front walk from the gate. He could hear Jake mumbling under his breath.

"I'm all right, I'm fine... okay, okay..."

Once inside, as they started toward the stairs, Meara made to drop the backpack before beginning the climb.

"No... no," Jake mumbled. *The artifact...*

"Get Mrs. Hodges," said Mr. Griffin.

Meara looked torn. She didn't want to leave him, not after all she had done to get him this far.

"I will get him upstairs," said Mr. Griffin. "Get Mrs. Hodges."

Meara stepped away and Mr. Griffin started up the stairs with Jake.

Jake wasn't about to be parted from the artifact. He forced Mr. Griffin to stop and held his hand out for the backpack. Mr. Griffin let out an impatient sigh and nodded to Meara.

Meara followed Mr. Griffin and Master Jacob up the stairs. "I dressed the wounds as best I could," she said.

"I'm sure you did just fine, Meara. Once we get upstairs... Mrs. Hodges."

"Yes, sir."

Chapter Twenty

Jake opened his eyes. The ceiling above him seemed strangely unfamiliar and yet somehow he understood that he should know it.

He laid his head to one side.

I'm in my room...

He heard the words in his head and the thought made him feel safe and warm. It took a few moments for the realization to catch up: Not his room back home in the real world...

Serpent's Keep... I'm home...

He heard a very faint rumbling noise and rolled his head to the left. Mrs. Hodges was asleep in the chair beside him, a book lying open in her lap. She was snoring softly. Looking around the room Jake saw his backpack sitting on top of the dresser. His situation came rushing back at him.

He had the last artifact. With it, he would be able to open the Serpent's Keep gate. *The Rhetani gate...*

Jake was certain the gate was a side door, and it would take him to this very same world, but in a different time, just as the gate inside the castle had taken him to Marcus. The Rhetani were in Jake's world in another time, though he had no idea how or why. What he did know for sure was that it would soon be his home, for once he permanently closed the gate, there would be no way for him to return.

He couldn't clear his mind enough to bring any of these thoughts into focus, but they wouldn't go away, either. They swam in a blurry sea of words and images until he finally fell back into a restless sleep.

When Jake woke the second time, Mr. Griffin was sitting in the chair, book in hand, oil lamp turned down low and illuminating the pages.

"Hey, Griff." Jake's voice crackled as he spoke. He tried to clear his throat, realized that his throat was dry as old paper. Mr. Griffin lowered his book, reached over and picked up a glass sitting on the side table. He half-filled it from a metal pitcher and handed it to Jake.

"How are you feeling, Master Jacob?"

Jake took a cautious sip from the glass, then took a longer, deeper drink and let it slide soothingly down his throat.

"I think I'll live." He handed the glass back to Mr. Griffin. "How's Meara?"

"Quite well. Concerned as to your health."

"And how is my health? Technically speaking."

"Your ribs are bruised, but not broken. Burns from the gunpowder flashes should heal with only minor scarring. The arrow did some damage, and you lost some considerable amount of blood."

"Sounds scary."

"Mrs. Hodges has significant experience in this area."

"Good ol' Mrs. H."

"Yes," said Mr. Griffin. "As to your follow-up care, you are being treated with medicinal herbs, both topically and internally."

"Cool," said Jake. He laid his head back.

"You will recover, Master Jacob."

"Cool," he said again. His strength was fading, but he felt that he was being drawn back into sleep not so much because he was weak but rather because his mind wasn't yet ready to face both the past and the future. He returned his attention to the ceiling. After half a minute, he closed his eyes. Tiny explosions of light flickered against his eyelids, as if a strobe was flashing above him.

Jake wandered along the high-walled fence that bordered the back perimeter of the estate. Trees and shrubs were strategically positioned around the grounds, giving the property the look of an enclosed private park. The walls that surrounded most of the estate prevented him from seeing the village beyond from ground level, but the sound of the villagers bustling about their midday activities reached into the estate and was as warm as the rays of the noon sun that pushed against his face. He turned his face up to the clear, bright sky, closed his eyes and let his skin turn hot, let the healing warmth work its way deep into the flesh and bone and muscle.

Turning from the sun, he continued his walk along the wall. The heat that had gathered within the stone throughout the morning now pulsated outward. He wore a loose baggy shirt that hid the bandages beneath, the slight breeze helping to cool him. The wooden cane that he used bore much of his weight and eased much of the pressure.

Jake's thoughts were continually drawn to the last remaining action that he had yet to perform in the quest given him by his uncle. He had the last artifact. All he had to do was put it into place and the Serpent's Keep gate would open. That would be it. Whatever had happened up to this point in the quest, whatever he had done, whatever he hadn't done, once he opened the gate, there would be no more choices to make, no more decisions to wrestle over. He would step through the gate and do whatever had to be done to close it forever.

A major, life-changing event if he ever knew one. There would be no returning to life as normal. If he survived, all that he had known—people, places, maybe even the warmth of the sun, all would be gone.

The words from the final scroll came unbidden into his mind.

The heart of the serpent cannot be seen, yet its powerful beat sends life to head and tail. To close its eyes, the aim must be true.

Jake hadn't liked the sound of that. The thought that he might have to kill something as the final act in a moral quest turned his stomach. Yet, the words had the ring of killing in them.

And there had been the dagger that he had found in the hidden compartment with the scroll; a dagger with a blade made of bone.

There was no real reason to think so, but he believed the bone had come from a dragon. A Jahai bone?

Meara came up beside him and moved into step as he continued walking.

"Master Jacob? Mrs. Hodges would like you to come in now. She has soup ready."

Jake had worked his way around the side of the house. He stopped and leaned heavily on his cane. From here, he could see the front gate.

"Sir?" Meara urged.

Meara stood silently beside Jake, waiting for him to head inside, ready to follow him. Watching him, looking at his face, at the way he stood, she realized that he had changed since first arriving in Serpent's Keep. He had aged far beyond his time here, and more than that, his experiences had worn him down. They also seemed to have changed the way he responded to the world around him. She could see it in his eyes. They weren't just sad, they were... mournful; but also careful.

"I think I'll go for a walk," he said suddenly.

"But... sir... Mrs. Hodges..."

"I'll be back later." He started around toward the front of the mansion, in the direction of the gate.

"But... but Mrs. Hodges... she has soup."

Jake stood across the street from the café. He watched the people passing in front him, going about their business. A few looked curiously in his direction; a few nodded to him in silent greeting. A few spoke, offering him *good afternoon*. With each, he smiled and offered a *good afternoon* in return.

The café looked fairly busy. That was good. He started across the cobblestone thoroughfare, reaching the door at the same time as the banker. He remembered Mr. Dante from another visit he had made to the café.

"Ah, Mr. Quigley. Here, let me get this for you." The man opened the door to the restaurant and stood to one side.

"How's business, Mr. Dante?" Jake stepped through the open door.

"Never so busy as to keep me from lunch, yet well enough that I can afford it." Mr. Dante followed him in.

Once inside, the short, chubby man moved around Jake and hurried through the half-filled room to his own personal table, which waited for him against the far wall.

"Good afternoon, Mr. Quigley," said Sparta. She approached Jake, coffee carafe in one hand, cup in the other. She indicated an empty table. "Glad to see you up and about."

"Thank you, Miss Vesper." Jake took the two steps and sat down. He leaned back in the chair. "I think I'd like to start with some of that great coffee, if you please."

Chapter Twenty One

Jake stared down at the collection of artifacts already set into the concrete lattice design in the floor. All the pieces but one were there. The empty space that remained had exactly the same shape as the artifact he held in his hand. It was smooth and hard, cool to the touch. It was heavier than he would have expected had he not had experience with the other artifact pieces.

Jake could feel his heart pounding against his ribs. He was short of breath, dizzy; the air in the room around him was hot and didn't seem to have enough oxygen.

Get it over with...

He stepped forward, knelt down and set the artifact into position. As he stood and stepped back, the grinding sound of stone rubbing against stone filled the room, the hollow reverberations echoing in the chamber until it was a physical pressure pushing against him, vibrating deep into his bones.

The floor beneath the reconstituted artifact emblem began to rise; from below rose the gate, a set of slender stone-like pillars capped by the completed artifact.

Once it had risen waist-high, energy started to crackle within the gate and fire-like threads danced from pillar to pillar. As the gate continued its slow ascent, the energy within it grew brighter and hotter and more intense.

Mr. Griffin came out of the long tunnel and into the chamber, keeping his distance from both Jake and the rising gate.

"Hey, Griff," said Jake. He tried to smile. "I guess I'll be seein' ya."

"It has been a pleasure, Master Quigley."

Jake nodded a silent thank you, turned back to the gate just as the grinding noise stopped. The only sound now was the crackling of electrical energy, which grew suddenly louder. The heart of the gate began to glow, growing brighter and brighter.

All sound stopped suddenly with a dull thud. Set in the heart of the gate, within the pillars and four feet above the ground, was a shimmering blue sphere two feet in diameter. As he watched, the sphere began to expand, slow and steady.

"Perhaps you should move back into the tunnel, Mr. Griffin," said Jake, not taking his eyes off the growing sphere.

Mr. Griffin backed silently into the tunnel. A moment later he turned at the sound of someone running down the long, narrow hallway, held out his arms in time to catch Meara.

"Master Jacob!" Meara cried out, struggling against Mr. Griffin's grip.

"It'll be all right, Meara. This is what I was brought here to do."

He turned his attention back to the gate. The sphere had grown large enough that it had swallowed up the pillars. Images began to form in the swirling, ethereal mist within the sphere. He couldn't tell what the images were at first, but as the sphere continued to expand, the shapes within it continued to take form, to solidify.

The outer perimeter of the sphere crept outward until it was just inches from Jake. The top vanished into the ceiling, the bottom into the floor.

In place of the gate, with its pillars and cap and base, furniture materialized within the chamber: chairs, tables, lamps. From his experience with the *side door* in the castle, Jake knew that he was seeing a room and objects not in the chamber beneath the mansion, but from some other place, some other time.

If this side door of the gate system was like the other, then crossing over should be a simple task. The other gate had required that he have the artifact in his possession and that he move to a certain location within the room. He had done that by reaching for the table beside the chair that Marcus had been sitting in: the first time with the sword, and the second time by dropping his hand through it.

In this case, the center of the chamber itself was the artifact, hidden now, held above the unseen pillars of the gate. Would stepping into the center of the room be enough?

The outer edges of the sphere quietly swallowed him up. He was fully inside the room, though he knew that he was still in the underground chamber beneath the mansion.

Mr. Griffin and Meara were still visible, though from his perspective, Jake saw them standing not at the entrance to the tunnel, but in an open doorway leading to another room. They took another step back, beyond the doorway, safely outside the influence of the chamber. As they did, Jake lost sight of them.

He looked systematically about the room.

The heart of the serpent cannot be seen, yet its powerful beat sends life to head and tail. To close its eyes, the aim must be true.

The walls were covered in light-colored paneling; the hardwood floor was covered in a scattering of area rugs, one large, a handful of smaller. There were several electric lamps sitting on side tables beside stuffed chairs.

A single window looked out over the rooftops of a small, quiet mountain village containing a cluster of buildings with steeply sloping roofs.

None of what Jake saw gave any indication that the scene came to him from a dark, distant future.

The only other door into the room opened and two humans came in, one man and one woman. They were of average height and weight, looked to be in their late thirties or early forties. Their hair styles were rather normal, nothing *futuristic* or otherworldly bizarre. They were dressed in pants and shirts, cotton in appearance, again rather normal.

Jake wondered if he had somehow misinterpreted what he had learned over the course of the quest.

"You must be Jacob," said the man. He spoke English with no discernable accent; at least none that Jake could hear.

"And who are you?"

"We do appreciate what you've done, Mr. Quigley," said the woman.

"Yeah? Who is *we*?" Jake was growing increasingly uneasy with the situation. He had found himself in a number of similar conversations since starting this quest, and not one had turned out good. He began studying objects in the room. One would cross him over.

"We are not the enemy, as some have made us out to be."

Jake turned his attention full to the woman. "You work for the Rhetani?"

The woman gave a patronizing smirk; the man gave a hearty laugh.

"Oh, dear," said the woman. "How you have survived up to now must be an absolutely marvelous tale. Should we have the time, perhaps we can explore it together."

"Sure. No problem." Jake again eyed the furniture, the objects on the furniture, the window, the world beyond. He suspected the small, round table in the center of the room, which was also in the center of the chamber, to be the key to crossing over. He wasn't quite ready to test that theory, though. Once he was on the other side, they would be able to get to him, so before he made the attempt, he wanted to know exactly what he would have to do in order to permanently close the side door.

After that, they could do with him what they wanted. He didn't think it would be pleasant, but at least the sacrifice would have been worth it.

If he crossed over and then failed to close the gate, the connection will have been established; and since the artifact was now a permanent fixture of the gate, they would be free to cross over into his time.

Be very, very careful...

"I apologize, Mr. Quigley," said the man. "But your question was... unexpected."

The heart of the serpent cannot be seen...

"Jacob," the woman held her arms outstretched. "We are all Rhetani."

sends life to head and tail...

What? Jake couldn't help but be startled, and it showed. *What did she mean by that?*

"Just what were you expecting, if I might ask?" asked the man.

"I know that you are in our future. I know that you want to use the side door to access the gates."

"Yes, we are in your future," said the woman. "As such, we can see what you cannot."

"And you want to use the gates to control the universe."

"Look at us, Jacob. Do we look like monsters?"

"Maybe a little," Jake mumbled, continued to search.

The heart of the serpent cannot be seen...

"Oh, come now..."

Jake turned his attention back to the woman. "The Rhetani are human?"

"Of course we are." She wore a soft, gentle, albeit patronizing smile. "Centuries from where you are now, a great leader will unify humanity. The Rhetani were born from that magnificent unification."

I don't like the sound of that...

"And you would spread that unification?"

The woman's face was aglow. "Across time and space and universal plane."

The heart of the serpent cannot be seen, yet its powerful beat sends life to head and tail. To close its eyes, the aim must be true.

"Apparently not everyone wants to be unified," said Jake.

"We're not some religious cult, Quigley," said the man. "The Rhetani aren't about forcing beliefs on anyone."

Just obedience, thought Jake. He had almost said it aloud, but stopped himself in time. He didn't want to get into philosophical or political discourse with these two. And he didn't really think they were carrying on the discussion in some righteous attempt to convert him to their way of thinking.

They were trying to ease him into lowering his guard enough so that they could control the situation when he crossed over.

Jake, on the other hand, wanted only to ensure the situation didn't get any more complicated before he could figure out what needed to be done the moment he crossed over.

The Rhetani are human? Jake wished that he hadn't heard that. It only distracted him from the issue at hand.

At some point in the future of Earth, *his* Earth, humanity will be unified by, dominated by, some government body referred to as the Rhetani. What form of government will this Rhetani take? From where will it come? Political organizations could start from most anything.

Jake tried to shake all such thoughts from his mind. If he accomplished his task, and if he survived, he would have all the time in the world to discover the answers.

To close its eyes, the aim must be true.

Did he have to strike at something?

He again looked quickly about the room, half involuntarily. The man and woman watched him quietly. They had to know what he was doing, but they didn't seem concerned. Did they know that he had faced this situation before, with Marcus?

How could they know? Marcus would have no connection with this gate.

But then, they had known who Jake was. How did they know that? They were from the future... Certainly some information had to have made it across the centuries.

His mind began to swim in a sea of questions. Again he forced himself to push aside such thoughts for later.

The heart of the serpent cannot be seen, yet its powerful beat sends life to head and tail. To close its eyes, the aim must be true.

Did he have to strike at something that could not be seen?

...its powerful beat sends life to head and tail.

The connection would be established once he crossed over. The gate, the side door, would be in both locations; that included the completed artifact, which was directly overhead, directly above the center of the gate, directly above where the woman now stood, beside the small, round table.

The chamber under the mansion that Jake stood in had a low ceiling, easily reachable by simply raising his arm.

The room that he was looking into appeared to have a higher ceiling, but Jake had a hunch that was illusion, or at the very least, the artifact was hovering at the same height in both locations.

He turned his head and looked in the direction of the now unseen Mr. Griffin and Meara. He raised a hand in farewell, at the same time reaching for the bone dagger that he had tucked in his belt in the small of this back. He turned about and stepped into the world of the Rhetani.

Jake moved immediately to the small table and swept the bone dagger through the shiny surface. As was the case with the other side door, Jake found himself hurtling through an electrified version of a gate passageway. Despite the fact that he knew what to expect, the rush of vertigo and lightheadedness sent him reeling. He fought to hold himself steady so that he wouldn't stumble when he crossed over.

And then he was there. Jake quickly turned the dagger about in his hand, held it firmly in the grasp of both hands, and thrust it upward directly over his head.

He felt it strike home, bone dagger against the unseen artifact latticework; the blade struck against solid surface at first, then slipped in as if guided, pushing through a thick, dense, yet yielding barrier.

And the world that he had just stepped into appeared to explode in a sudden blast of light, everything vanishing in a wash of pure, bright white.

And then it all returned.

Nothing moved. The world was motionless, as if caught between one second and the next. The Rhetani couple, the clouds in the sky outside the window, an insect in mid-flight several feet in front of him, all were absolutely still.

And Tobias Quigley was standing in the far corner of the room.

"Hello, Jake." There was a cloudy gloominess to the words.

"Uncle Tobias?"

Tobias took the three steps across the room. He had a smile on his face, but it was a sad smile. When Jake moved forward to give his uncle a hug, Tobias held up a hand for him to stop.

Jake stopped short. He looked around him more carefully. "What's going on?"

He noticed then that the artifact was now visible, hovering above them, seemingly with nothing holding it in place. There was no sign of the gate that had risen from the chamber floor and upon which the artifact lattice rested. The dagger was gone, and the individual artifact pieces had merged together to form a single object with a design on the face depicting the pieces from which it was born.

"You did good, Jake." Tobias walked around Jake and had a close look at the couple standing unmoving in the room.

Jake nodded at them. "You wouldn't know they were evil by looking at them."

"They see only what they have painted," Tobias sighed. "The reality of their words is unknown to them, and is quite unknowable."

"Where are we, Tobias? I know we're not in their world, and I know we're no longer in ours. Mine."

"True, and true."

"And this doesn't look like the in-between place between gates."

"True again." Tobias put on a genuine smile. "The gates allow us to travel to alternate universal planes. To do so, we travel through what you call the 'in-between' place. It has no location in any physical sense."

"But these side doors," Jake urged. "They don't take us from one plane to another. They take us to another time on the same plane."

"Exactly so. And while they are a part of the gate system, you don't cross that in-between place when using one of these side doors."

"So, we're in... like, the door jamb?"

"In order to get from one time to another time, we must step *out of time*, through the... door jamb."

Jake's head was spinning. Very little of what he was hearing made any sense, but he understood enough of it to believe what he was hearing. He tried to push it to the back of his mind, to let it sort itself out on its own. "Okay, so... how did *you* get here?"

Tobias drifted from the Rhetani couple to the open window and studied the scene. The motionless clouds looked as though they were being pushed by a strong breeze in real time. He held a hand out, palm to the world, and closed his eyes.

"I can almost feel the wind." Tobias said. He let out a cheerless sigh. "Each plane has several of these side doors. None cross to other planes, but they are connected to others on the same plane."

Jake had understood that, on some level, from his experience with Marcus. It was only one more step to understanding what Tobias was saying. "You're in some other door."

Tobias turned about then and stepped back into the center of the room. He came face to face with the woman. He moved to within inches, looked directly into the bright blue eyes.

"She's heartless, you know," he said. "She doesn't realize it, but she is. Her obsession made her that way."

Jake had seen a lot of that as of late. He said nothing.

"There is a very fine line between obsession and fanaticism." Tobias was moving in and out of a number of different lines of thought. "Mania, manic, maniac..."

Jake wondered how long Tobias had been lost in this place, alone, with only those thoughts to keep him company. "Are you all right?"

The man turned away from the woman then, let out yet another heavy sigh and looked directly at Jake. "Two of my comrades, Marcus and Janice, turned against the Jahai. Until recently, both had been safely isolated, each on different planes and in different times. Janice managed to get free. We are not totally without means, and Janice was probably the smartest of us all."

"In spite of her misguided loyalties?"

"If our adversaries were stupid, there wouldn't be much of a problem, would there?"

"Would sure make things easier."

Tobias had already moved his mind onward. "Because of a stir of activity, I had begun preparations to collect the artifacts. When I heard that Janice was on the loose, I knew that I first had to stop her. I was afraid that she might use the side doors to reach the Rhetani."

"An alternate time in our world?"

Tobias nodded. "Our world has three side doors: my time, your time, and the time of the Rhetani. The only gates to the Other Worlds lay in the time of Serpent's Keep. Your time."

"You were afraid that she would find a way to bypass Serpent's Keep and go directly to the Rhetani?"

"Janice and I struggled—that side door is forever closed."

"You couldn't make it back out?"

"There was no other way. Closing that door was a simple matter."

"But how did you get there? Marcus couldn't travel the gates. He couldn't get through the side door."

"The gateways, the artifacts... they are not magic, Jake. It is technology. Technology that can be known. That is the reason for the guardians. Discovery was inevitable."

"But—"

"I had pulled apart the gateway system, scattered the components to the Other Worlds, but I had to maintain some method of monitoring what was going on."

"You have a way into the in-between place, but you can't go to other side..."

"I kept a back door into the non-plane, what you call the *in-between* place, but even I can't cross over without an artifact. Without the technology underlying the artifacts, no one can cross over from one world to another."

"Janice found your back door?"

"She created one of her own, or something like it. She was able to enter the non-plane, and control her travel within it. If she ever managed to find the side door of the past, the one that we had originally come through, and then had found a way to use that door to reach the Rhetani, then sooner or later they would have found a way to reopen and exploit the gateways."

And so Tobias had been waiting for her. Jake was curious about what had happened, but it didn't really matter, and it sounded as though Tobias had told him as much as he was going to.

Whether Janice was alive or dead, whether she was trapped in the past or in some non-place, the fact was that Tobias didn't believe she was a threat. Not any longer.

And besides, now that Jake had permanently closed off the only access to the Rhetani, none of it mattered. Tobias had given Jake the time that he had needed, and now the task was done.

And that thought brought to the forefront what had been rumbling around in the back of Jake's mind from the moment that he had thrust the bone dagger into the reconstituted gateway machine.

"Uncle Tobias?"

Tobias was looking once again at the humans-turned-mannequins. "I didn't know what was going to happen to me once you closed the gates. I don't exist in the physical sense. Now, neither do you."

Tobias indicated the scene around them. "It wasn't until you used the key, the bone dagger, to lock the gateway system, that I had any reality. Until that moment, I had no sense of smell or sight. Or rather... I suppose my senses were there, but there was nothing to see, nothing to hear."

"What happens now? What's going happen to everyone?"

"Everyone else is fine, Jake." Tobias nodded in the direction of the Rhetani couple beside him. "By now, they've realized what has happened, that all is lost, and they've gone to tell their superiors."

"But, they haven't gone anywhere. They're right here, frozen in time."

"Jake, you know what has happened and yet you don't comprehend. You know that you can't trust your eyes, and yet you let them draw your conclusions for you."

Tobias held a hand in front of him, studied it closely, distracted for a moment by some other thought process going on in his mind. He rubbed his fingertips together, studying the sensation, continued to speak.

"There is your time, and there is the time of Rhetani. Both exist, both are real. The place we are in now, this *non-plane*, has no time, has no reality. It doesn't exist. In spite of that, up until a few moments ago, a misnomer in itself, it continued to flow along with those realities.

"But when you entered the key and shut down the gateway system, we were... left behind. What you see is that instant of time, of their time, that moment when you thrust the dagger up above your head."

"Oh, man..." Jake mumbled, barely audible.

"I'm so sorry, my boy."

"Oh, man." Jake had been certain that he would cross over to their world, to their time, and would live or die in some future land.

This isn't living or dying.

Tobias turned to face the Rhetani couple. "Our sight is a snapshot of a moment already past. Sound is only that of our own voices. Touch..." Tobias moved his hand toward the chest of the motionless man. It disappeared beneath the man's shirt. He pulled it back. He turned to Jake, held his hand palm out. Jake cautiously lifted a hand. Their palms touched, their hands pressed together.

"I guess that makes sense," said Tobias. "I can hear you, I can see you. I can smell coffee on your breath."

"But... if we don't exist..."

"Where we are doesn't exist, and therefore, to be here, in this non-plane, we cannot exist. The paradox is that we don't exist, and yet we... *are*."

Jake swallowed hard, realized that he had swallowed hard and immediately tried to comprehend the fact that he didn't really exist and hadn't actually swallowed at all.

"Do you have a way out of here?"

Jake could see that his uncle wanted desperately to tell him yes, that he did indeed have a way out. After a few painful moments, in a non-place in which moments didn't really exist, Tobias shook his head.

"Not that I can think of at the moment."

"Oh, man."

Chapter Twenty Two

Mr. Griffin stepped into the empty chamber, the sounds of his footfalls resonating off the concrete walls. He knelt down before the octagon-shaped design set into the floor. He rubbed his hand lightly across the smooth surface.

The individual artifacts were gone. Now, inset within the cold, smooth concrete floor, was an emblem, a pattern composed of what the artifacts once were.

"The gate, that room." Meara stepped out of the tunnel. She had a slightly dazed look on her face. "I don't think I much liked those people."

Mr. Griffin rose to his feet. He felt as though his age might finally be starting to catch up with him. "I don't believe you are going to have to concern yourself about them, Miss Gyles."

"Then you think that—"

"I believe that young Master Quigley has completed his quest."

Meara tried to feel happy about that, but couldn't. She had liked Jacob Quigley, and he had certainly brought some excitement back into this old mansion.

"I hope he's all right," she said.

"The boy has always proven most resourceful." Mr. Griffin offered a consoling smile. "I am certain that whatever predicament he finds himself in, he will undoubtedly find his way out again."

Mr. Griffin stood beside Meara and took her gently by the arm. He turned her toward the tunnel entrance and the two of them left the chamber that for millennia had held Serpent's Gate.

~ end ~